The Squire's Daughter

Also by Terri Kennedy

The Captain's Lady

THE SQUIRE'S DAUGHTER

Terri Kennedy

Parker River Press

Print Edition ISBN: 978-0-9975032-3-4
Digital Edition ISBN: 978-0-9975032-2-7

Parker River Press
PO Box 242
South Yarmouth, MA 02664

www.TerriKennedy.com/ParkerRiverPress

Cover design by Dar Albert www.wickedsmartdesigns.com

To Grace

my amazing daughter who always believed her mother could do anything—even write and publish a book.

So, of course I had to prove you right. How else could I convince you that you could do anything you set your mind to—like running a marathon or getting a doctorate?

Or maybe it's the other way around—you inspire me to achieve my dreams—and push me to put in the hard work that's required.

Acknowledgments

I want to thank Gail Eastwood for reading the rough draft and showing me how to improve it. Thanks also to Janet Jones Bann, editor extraordinaire, who not only fixed all my grammatical mistakes, but also pointed out flaws in the content with suggestions on how to correct them. To Rhode Island Romance Writers, thanks for all the advice, workshops, and craft discussions over the years. I would not have been able to whip this manuscript into shape without you. To the Karate Ladies—Melanie, Ginny, and Rosemarie—thanks for your unwavering support and belief in me. And of course, thank you to my husband for giving me the time and space I need to write and to my daughter for always encouraging me to pursue my dreams.

Prologue

Hapshom on Green, Dorset
1805

"Come along, Shelby. Don't make me late for my own wedding."

Thirteen-year-old Shelby Endicott shuffled behind her mother as they made their way through the churchyard. Stopping at her father's grave, she brushed lichen off the stone with her glove.

"Stop that. You'll get your glove dirty. Can't you stay clean long enough for me to say my vows?"

"What's the hurry? Papa's only been dead for a year."

Mother paused and stared at the gravestone, blinking back the moisture that glistened in her eyes.

"And what a horrible year it's been. Running the farm by myself, making decisions for the two of us. If not for Mr. Granger's help, I'm not sure we'd have survived. He's a good man. He'll make me a good husband. And a good father to you."

"I don't need a father. I had one. He's gone. No one can replace him."

"I loved your father, too. But life goes on. We do what

we must. We need Mr. Granger."

"We don't. We can run the farm ourselves. Uncle Phillip will help us. Please, Mama, don't do this."

"*I* need Mr. Granger," Mother said. "No, I *want* to marry him. I want a husband. It's lonely without your father. You'll understand when you get older. Now, come along. I don't want to keep him waiting."

The church was empty except for the vicar and his wife. And Mr. Granger. He turned when they entered. Smiling, he strode down the aisle to greet them.

"Helen," He took her mother's hand in his and squeezed it. "I was afraid you weren't coming. That you'd changed your mind."

Mother returned his smile.

"Nonsense," she said. "Shelby would not be hurried this morning."

"I'll soon have Shelby well in hand. Shall we?" He motioned toward the altar.

The ceremony was short. When asked for a reason why they should not wed, Shelby wanted to shout that her father was barely dead. This interloper was not worthy to take his wife and his farm. But she held her tongue. If her mother didn't listen to her, no one else would.

They returned to the farm to enjoy the feast Cook had prepared. Fried eggs, rashers of bacon, puddings, mushrooms, sweetbreads and buns. Shelby escaped to her room as soon as she could. Throwing off her good dress, she donned her serviceable skirt and shirt and headed out to the barn to see the latest litter of kittens. But no peace was to be found there because Mr. Granger stood in the middle of the floor surveying what he now owned.

She turned to retreat, but he called to her to wait. She stopped just inside the door ready to bolt. Mr. Granger came to her.

When she was within arm's reach, he swung her around

to face him. Grabbing her cheeks, he squeezed them in a painful vise.

"You can act as sullen as you please, young lady, but it won't change a thing. You are my responsibility now. I own you, I own your mother, and I own this farm. I suggest you try to get along."

He released her, and she ran.

❧

"Why are you planting here?" Shelby asked Josh, one of the local lads who helped with the spring planting.

"Mr. Granger said so," he said.

"You must be mistaken. This field's to remain fallow this year."

"I told him, Miss, but he said he'd get someone else to do it if I wouldn't."

Fury threatened to erupt. Once again, Mr. Granger refused to listen. She'd told him last fall, shortly after the wedding, that they needed to thresh the hay field to put it up for winter, but he let it rot, forcing them to purchase grain for the horses and cows. No, cow. He'd sold their best milker to cover the cost of the feed. He'd threatened to sell her horse, Pegasus, but none of their neighbors would buy him.

Mr. Granger would lead them all to ruin with her mother happily trotting along behind him.

She had no choice but to try to talk to him again, though she'd taken to avoiding him as much as possible. In the early days of their marriage, her mother had encouraged her to go out in the fields with him and help him in the barn. But he ignored all her suggestions, and the way he looked at her made her uncomfortable.

It wasn't just his looks, either. Whenever they were alone, he'd let his hand brush her breast when he showed her something. And the things he said made her squirm.

"You have wonderful breasts," he said. "You look more

like seventeen than thirteen. So young and ripe. I grow hard just looking at you."

She tried to tell her mother, but she insisted Shelby must have misunderstood.

She hadn't misunderstood anything. She'd grown up on a farm. She knew how animals mated. Mr. Granger had the look of a bull in heat—his nostrils flared when she entered a room, and his eyes tracked her with a predatory gleam.

Finding him down near the river that ran through the property, she looked at the overgrown banks with disgust as he sat idly sipping from a bucket of ale.

"Father used to trim the weeds, so we had easy access to the water. He never would have let it get this way."

"I'm not your father," he said, grabbing her hand. He pulled her down on the grass beside him and put her hand on his crotch. "See what you do to me?"

She tried to pull away, but he held her fast.

With his other hand he freed himself from his pants so she could see him thick and hard. He placed her hand on his bared flesh and jerked it up and down.

She struggled, but his hand covered hers. He kept moving it up and down along his engorged shaft until he cried out and white, warm, sticky liquid squirted all over her.

"Your father wouldn't do that, now would he?" He pulled her to him, grabbed hold of her hair to angle her head, and kissed her hard, forcing her mouth open so he could invade it with his tongue. She tasted the ale he'd been drinking, smelled the foul stench of his sweat-soaked body. When he finished, he gentled his arms and held her for a moment in an embrace.

"Go wash your hands in the river," he said softly, almost tenderly.

Shaken, she obeyed.

"I don't want to hear any more about what your father would have done," he said on the way back to the house.

She never spoke of her father again.

❧

She didn't tell her mother about the incident by the river because she was embarrassed and ashamed. But she stopped going about the farm for fear of encountering Mr. Granger. She stayed at home and tried to learn what her mother had to teach her. She spent endless hours in the parlor doing needlepoint, something she could never quite master. Her only refuge was her music. Her father had insisted that she learn to play the pianoforte; she practiced now for hours every day.

"Shelby, cease that incessant playing and go outside," Helen said one afternoon a few weeks after the day by the river.

"I'd rather stay here. I can do something else if you'd like. Do you need me to help in the kitchen?"

Mother sat down next to her on the piano bench.

"You hate helping in the kitchen. You love being out of doors. The weather is fine."

Shelby looked longingly out the window but couldn't take the risk of being caught alone by Mr. Granger.

"I don't want to."

"Why must you be so stubborn? Why don't you want to go outside?"

"Mr. Granger," she admitted. There. She'd said it.

"Oh, Shelby, I had so hoped you would come to accept him. He cares for you very much."

"He cares for me too much," she said. "He touches me and says things to me that I don't like. I'm afraid of him."

"Has he ever raised his hand to you? Hit you?"

"Not exactly," she said. "But he makes me uncomfortable. The way he looks at me. He…" She could not get out the words. Could not tell her mother what had transpired. Her throat choked on the words. "He frightens me."

She held her breath, hoping her mother would understand. That she'd put her arms around her and comfort her. That she'd send the awful man away.

But her mother stood.

"I won't have you talking badly about Mr. Granger," her mother said. "He's my husband now and your stepfather. You need to show him respect. Now, go outdoors. Some fresh air will do you good."

❧

That night he came to her room. He stretched out on her bed beside her and pulled her into his arms.

"I don't want you to be afraid of me," he said.

Her heart squeezed and tears stung her eyes. Her mother had told him. She had no confidant, no one she could talk to. Anything she said to her mother would get back to him. A whimper escaped her lips.

"Shh," he said, stroking her head, her cheek, her arm. "It's alright. It isn't wrong. It's no sin. I'm not your father, so it's not incest. The only way anyone could be hurt is if your mother finds out, so we mustn't tell her. She wouldn't understand. A man like I am has needs that a wife can't fulfill. Perhaps if you weren't so beautiful, so sensual, I could resist your charms, but no man could. You taunt me with your defiance."

"I'll be good," she said. "I won't taunt you anymore."

He chuckled.

"It's your defiance that excites me. Your passion. You are Eve, and like Adam, I am fallen."

He kissed her, possessing her mouth, biting her lower lip until she opened to him and he plunged his tongue into her mouth. She knew what to expect now, when he took her hand and guided it to him. She rubbed up and down the way he'd taught her, hoping that if she did it quickly it would be over soon, and he would leave. He erupted all over her hand and the bed linens.

"Be sure to wash your sheets tomorrow," he said as he cleaned the remnants of his spillage. She didn't dare disobey.

When her mother asked her the next morning why she was washing her bedding herself when it wasn't laundry day, she didn't answer.

❧

He came to her room at night after the household was asleep. At first, having her use her hand on him was enough. She became quite adept at it, even initiating the event as soon as he lay down beside her, so it would be quickly done, and he would leave. Then he started pulling down her nightgown and suckling at her breasts while she rubbed him with her hand. Soon, that wasn't enough for him either. One night, he made her take him in her mouth. She gagged and thought she would choke, but he held her head down and wouldn't let her up.

"You bite me, and you're dead," he threatened. She believed him. She wasn't sure how he'd do it, somehow so her mother would never suspect he was the cause, but she did not doubt that he would kill her.

With her life in danger, she tried again to get her mother to help.

She waited until he left the house the next morning. Waited until the maid had left the breakfast room. Still, she kept her voice pitched low. Who knew what spies he might have in the household?

"Mr. Granger visits my room at night," she said.

"He checks on you before he comes to bed," Helen said. "As part of securing the house."

"No, this is during the night. He lies with me. Touches me. Makes me touch him."

Helen stilled, then rested her fork and knife on her still

laden plate.

"You are mistaken," she said. "You must be dreaming it. Mr. Granger does not leave my side."

Shelby wanted to cry. She'd never felt so utterly alone, not even right after her father died.

She, too, rested her utensils on her plate and rose, leaving her breakfast uneaten. She went to the music room and played for the rest of the day.

⁂

She became listless and withdrawn. She barely ate. She didn't go visiting her friends. She stayed at home all day and played the pianoforte. She dreaded the night.

On her fourteenth birthday, Mr. Granger took her virginity.

"You're old enough now," he said, "for us to have relations. Some girls get married at fourteen." Like that made it right, somehow.

He crawled into bed with her and lifted her nightgown. He poked her with his fingers. He'd done that before, but this time he dug deeper, and it hurt. When she protested, he covered her mouth with his. Still kissing her, he forced her legs apart and inserted himself into her. She cried out in pain when he breached her maidenhead. It didn't take him long to spill his seed into her.

When he was done, he got a wet cloth from the washbasin and cleaned her up. He put her nightgown back down and tucked her in, giving her a gentle kiss goodnight on her forehead.

She ran away the next day.

She went to her Uncle Phillip's estate. Her aunt and uncle were in London, but her cousin Phoebe was there. For two blissful weeks, Shelby recuperated. She ate everything in sight, and she slept soundly every night. She wrote to her mother asking for permission to stay. Her mother wrote back saying she needed Shelby at home to help with the new sister or brother that was on the way. She gave Shelby permission to stay for a month but then expected her to return home.

Shelby begged Uncle Phillip to let her stay on after the month was up. He wrote to her mother, saying, "The girl is thriving here, and she's a wonderful companion for Phoebe." Mr. Granger wrote back. "We really need Shelby at home. Helen isn't feeling well in her confinement and needs her daughter with her."

She was sent back home.

☙

Her mother was unwell and stayed abed most of the day. Mr. Granger became more and more bold. He came in while she was playing the pianoforte, locking the parlor door behind him. He bent her over the bench and took her from behind, right there in the parlor in the middle of the day.

"Don't try to run away from me again," he said when he was done. He patted her bare bottom that was still sticking up in the air. "I don't want to have to get rough with you." Then he slapped her hard on her backside, leaving a welt the size of a fist.

She stopped playing the pianoforte.

☙

"Your breasts are getting bigger," he observed happily one night when he joined her in her bed. His hand skated over her stomach, and he felt the hard roundness of her belly. "Well, well, well," he said. "This is a problem. We're going to have to marry you off soon." And he left without forcing himself on her.

The next morning, she rode Pegasus hard, recklessly flying over fields and carelessly jumping over hedges, hoping, though she'd never admit it, to fall and break her neck or at least hurt herself enough to rid herself of the parasite growing within her. Only when she saw that she was hurting her horse, who was her best friend, did she slow down. With tears streaming down her face, she returned home in defeat.

She brushed down Pegasus herself. It was a task she never left to anyone else. Her father had insisted on it when he gave her the gelding on her tenth birthday. The same day he'd given her the locket she wore around her neck and never took off.

Shelby fingered the locket, missing her father more than ever.

Her mother was waiting for her when she entered the house.

"Mr. Granger suspects you are with child," Mother said when she saw Shelby.

"Did he tell you whose child it is?" She kept her head down, unable to look her mother in the eye.

"Probably some village boy's, he said." Her mother cried. "It's my fault. I've been so ill I haven't been able to keep an eye on you. Mr. Granger and I have decided to keep you at home. We can hide your condition. We'll pass the baby off as an orphan we adopted."

Shelby looked at her mother incredulously.

"Mr. Granger is the father of this baby just the same as he is the father of the child you are carrying."

Mother slapped her hard across her face.

"How dare you accuse him of something so base when it's you who are at fault, going off with some village boy into the fields, rutting like an animal. Mr. Granger is willing to raise your bastard as his own. You should get down on your hands and knees and thank the man."

"I have been on my hands and knees for him," Shelby retorted. But her mother stared at her blankly, like she had no idea what Shelby was really saying.

"You've brought shame on this family, Shelby," Mother said, then gave her the final blow. "Your father would be so disappointed in you."

She had to get away. She couldn't have Mr. Granger's baby and continue living in his house and continue having him visit her night after night while her mother lived in complete denial.

She snuck away in the night. She didn't really care what happened to her. If she got murdered on the road, so be it.

She couldn't go the Uncle Phillip, because he would send her back home again.

She stood on the side of the road as the mail coach approached. She'd packed lightly, a few day dresses and her toiletries. She wore her warm coat with the fur trim that Father had given her on his last Christmas. Could it only be two years that he'd been gone? How could everything change so quickly?

She had wanted to take Pegasus, to get on his back and just ride off into the night, but it wouldn't be fair to the gelding who'd been her best friend since she was ten. She had no way to care for him, and he ate his weight in hay every day.

She'd said her goodbyes to him that afternoon. They'd taken one last ride together.

She didn't want to leave. This was her home. The old farmhouse used to be filled with love and laughter.

The mail coach was big, pulled by four powerful horses. It was going so fast, she feared the driver would not see her in time and would go flying past without stopping. But he slowed as he approached her.

"Please, sir," she called up to him. "May I ride with you to London?"

"It's against the rules to take passengers," he answered.

"I have a shilling to pay you." She held up the coin, the

only one she had been able to procure. She hoped it was enough.

The coachman looked at her thoughtfully.

"Well, climb aboard," he said finally, reaching a hand down to her and hoisting her up on the seat beside him. "Don't have all day to sit here chattering about it. You can pay me one way or t'other."

The seat was high. She felt like she could see all the way to London. The horses went fast, putting miles between her and her home in no time at all.

They stopped at noontime for the coachman to eat and rest and water the horses. It was a small posting house. No one else was around. The coachman shared his meal with her, for which she was grateful.

"Time to pay up now," he said when he was done eating. Shelby fished out her coin and held it out to him.

"Aw, you keep that. You'll be needin' it, I 'spect," he said. "I'll take your fare out in trade."

She didn't know what he meant but went with him willingly enough when he led her to a secluded spot away from the posting house.

Lying with the coachman wasn't much different from lying with Mr. Granger. At least the coachman didn't belittle her and threaten her. He just took his pleasure and was done quick enough.

And she still had her coin.

"What will you be doin' with yourself in London?" he asked when they were once again underway.

"I hope to find a position," she answered.

"I know of a position for you," he said. "A friend of mine is always looking for good help. I'll take you right to her."

Innocent as she was, she accepted the coachman's help. He stopped at his friend's house before going to the mail stop.

"I can't get caught hauling passengers," he said, "so I'm dropping you off here."

Shelby saw the woman give him a ten-pound note before she turned to her and smiled.

"Welcome to your new home. What's your name, love?"

"Sh—" Shelby hesitated. If she told this woman her name, would she contact her mother and Mr. Granger? Would she send her back home?

"Oh, never mind," the woman said. "What a lovely color green your coat is. Almost the exact shade as that French liqueur. Chartreuse, that's what we'll call you. Chartreuse LaRue."

Chapter 1

Hampshire
1811

The coach rumbled down the country lane, jouncing with every rut and pit in the road. It was not well-sprung, nor particularly new. Its leather seats were cracked and worn. Chartreuse bounced uncomfortably upon the backward-facing seat. The shades had been drawn against the late afternoon sun so she could no longer enjoy the scenery. In the dim light of the carriage, her two travelling companions dozed on the bench across from her, Nell's snoring a discordant counterpoint to Bramly's wheeze.

At least Nell was quiet for the moment. Her irritability had increased with every mile that took them farther outside of London. She regretted her hasty decision to join this expedition and took her displeasure out on Chartreuse, as if *she* had any say in the matter. She had done her best to discourage Nell from coming, assuring her that she could handle the business end of things herself, hoping against hope that Nell would let her go alone. But Nell, well in her cups, insisted that it would be a lark. Having never been outside the city, when the offer was made, she accepted.

And had not stopped grumbling since she'd sobered enough to realize her mistake.

The coach hit a deep hole that had Chartreuse flying off the seat. She grabbed for the leather grip to keep from falling to the floor. Nell snorted and woke.

"How much farther?" she asked for what seemed like the thousandth time since they last stopped at the posting inn in Aldershot

"The entrance to the Park is just up the road a piece. Rosemont Cottage, the house you'll be sharing, is a short distance beyond that," Bramly, having roused from his slumbers, responded. He was middle-aged and heavyset with an air of dissolution about him that couldn't quite conceal the fact that he was gently born and raised. His hands were smooth and pasty and had never seen a day's labor. "You're sure you can pull this off?"

"Quite certain, my good sir," Chartreuse answered in the dulcet tones of the nobility. Neither by voice nor appearance would anyone suspect that she was not the gently bred lady she purported to be.

"Well, you'd better," he threatened. "My whole future's riding on this scheme."

She had no intention of failing. Her whole future was riding on this scheme, as well.

The scheme for which he'd hired her was designed to disinherit his nephew of a fortune. She was to be paid handsomely. Enough to start a new life, which was the only reason she had agreed to the preposterous plan when Nell and The Honorable Mr. Bramly approached her with it.

Her part in it was simple. Posing as a young lady of quality, she was to seduce Bramly's nephew and entice him into an offer of marriage. If he didn't offer on his own, her "aunt" Nell would catch them *in flagrante delicto* and demand that he marry her to make things right.

Once the banns were read and the marriage contract prepared, Bramly would swoop in with the magistrate and haul his nephew off for a competency hearing. Surely, the man must be mad to contemplate marrying a known prostitute whose "aunt" was the most notorious Madame in London.

"Are you sure your scheme will work?" she asked, knowing that her payment depended on its success.

"Ian, Lord Chester is known as the Monster Earl. Half the countryside believes him to be mad. He sees no one, only goes out at night, hasn't been off his estate in two years. The fire that burned his body damaged his mind as well, there's no doubt about that. I'm just trying to get control of things before he runs them to ruin. It's for his own good."

She didn't believe that for an instant. She knew Bramly well enough to know that self-interest was the only interest he served. She had catered to his bizarre sexual tastes enough times to see the evil that lurked beneath the affable surface he presented to the world. Whatever he had planned for his nephew, it was certainly not for anyone's good but Bramly's.

Not that it mattered to her what the nobility did to each other. If she could profit by it, she would. It had been her way of life for the past five years, since she had been delivered to Nell's doorstep a frightened, abused child. She wasn't a child any longer.

"With the proximity of the cottage to the Park, you should have ample opportunity to make Chester's acquaintance," Bramly said. "Just be quick about it. The rent is dear, and I don't want to spend a fortune on you."

"Spend a fortune to gain a fortune," Nell said then laughed at her own joke. While Nell looked like someone's lovable grandmother, appearances were deceptive. Nothing could be further from the truth.

Chartreuse had been in Nell's employ long enough to have risen to a position of trust. While she wouldn't consider herself Nell's friend, she had at least thus far avoided becoming her enemy. Nell's enemies sometimes ended up dead.

The carriage slowed and pulled to a stop in front of a neat cottage that fronted on the country lane.

The cottage was lovely. It was small and simply furnished but felt immediately like home. To Chartreuse, at least. Nell started complaining the moment she walked through the front door.

"What a bloody garbage heap," Nell said as they stood in the front foyer. "I expected more from Mr. High and Mighty. My bedroom at home is bigger than this entire place. The rent is dear, indeed. I probably take in more in one night than the cost of this place for an entire year. Bill and Pike had better be keeping an eye on things while I'm gone traipsing about the countryside. The girls'll rob me blind."

Though Nell was a wealthy woman, her impoverished childhood prevented her from really enjoying her wealth. She was always afraid of being poor again, and no amount of money or possessions would ever be enough to make her feel secure.

The front door opened to a small foyer, with stairs immediately in front going to the second floor and a short hallway running to the left beside the stairs. The door to the parlor opened off the hallway to the left and the kitchen was at the end of the hall at the back of the house.

"What's that sound?" Nell asked.

"I don't hear anything."

"I know! It's too bloody quiet. Makes my skin crawl. Like there's not another living soul left on earth. Light the candles. It's too dark in here."

Chartreuse found candles and tinderbox in the parlor. Lighting two candles, she handed one to Nell and kept one for herself. She wandered down the hall to the kitchen and looked out the back door, which led to a small kitchen garden with a semi-detached privy room next to a potter's shed. In the fading October light, she could see that the garden had been harvested and put to rest for the winter, though a few late tomatoes ripened still on their stalks and some squashes littered the ground.

"There'd better be a chamber pot," Nell said, coming up beside her. "I'm not about to go out there at night. Who knows what wild things lurk about waiting to attack some unsuspecting being?"

"Nothing worse than the rats that scurry around the alley behind your house," she said. In the alley and in the rafters and walls. It had taken years for Chartreuse to grow accustomed to the sound of them running behind her headboard and to get over the fear of having a rat chew on her toes while she slept.

"Rats are nothing. What if there are wolves out there?"

"There aren't any wolves."

The house reminded Chartreuse, in its layout and décor, of the cottages in the village where she grew up. As a child, she'd dreamt of marrying and settling in one of those cottages, staying close to home and the parents she loved. But circumstances changed. That dream died a bitter death.

She put the memory away and drew on the cloak of numbness she had developed over the years. The past was past. This was her chance to take control of her future.

"You take the back room," Nell said when they'd toured the two bedrooms above stairs, one in front and the other in back. "I want to be able to see the road, not that there's anything out there to see. Haven't seen nor heard another carriage since Bramly left us here. What if he doesn't come back?"

"He'll come back," Chartreuse soothed.

"I can't believe I let you talk me into this."

She didn't bother to reply.

"So, when do we begin?" Nell asked, coming up behind her as she looked out her bedroom window to the hill that rose above the garden wall. "Shall we go call on his lord-ship?"

"No," Chartreuse answered, "there's no point. He won't see us. Bramly said he receives no one and only goes out riding at night. So I shall be out walking and hope to intercept him when he rides by. A chance meeting is so much more romantic, don't you think?"

"But how will you know where to be? There's a hell of a lot of nothing out there."

Chartreuse laughed. Nell viewed the countryside as foreign territory. She was only comfortable in the crowded streets, alleys, and warrens of London town.

"I'm a country girl, remember? I'll find him. Now, I think I'll get some rest. I have a lot of walking to do this evening."

Ian saddled Demon for their nightly ride. He'd started riding as therapy when he could barely sit comfortably in the saddle. He rode at night so no one could see him seated so awkwardly astride his horse. He, who had been a horseman all his life. Foolish pride, he supposed, not wanting to add one more humiliation on all those that had preceded it, the months of recuperation when his every need had to be taken care of by others, even his most personal, intimate needs. Riding at night now was habit, a habit he enjoyed.

He knew he should be more careful of Demon. A horse could so easily lose his footing at night, but the risks seemed worth it for the sheer exhilaration, the freedom of flying across the fields with no one to bother them.

His servants meant well, he knew. They had become like family through his long ordeal. They worried that while his body had healed, his spirit had not.

They were right. He still couldn't face the life he had known before that tragic night. He still couldn't bring himself to go to London and rejoin the society that had once meant so much to him.

Like a wounded animal, he'd drawn back to his lair to heal and lick his wounds.

Even his family he kept at bay. His sister, Daphne, had hovered about the sick room wringing her hands and gasping with every glimpse she caught of him until he convinced her husband, Derek, to keep her away. She needed to grieve the loss of her parents and didn't need to be confronted daily with the prospect of losing her brother as well. His uncle, Bramly, was more interested in taking control of his finances than he was in visiting his recuperating nephew. Fortunately, his father's solicitors managed to keep his uncle's hands out of the family coffers.

He didn't know who he was anymore. He was no longer Viscount Morely, the sophisticated, handsome rake who was the darling of the ton. The title had been honorary, with no land or seat in Parliament to go with it. Yet, as heir to an earldom, he received all the privilege and respect that went with a title with none of the attendant responsibilities.

He was the Earl of Chester now, but he felt like an interloper. Even after two years he still hadn't come to terms with his parents' deaths. He went over and over the events of that night in his mind until guilt consumed him. He should have saved them. There must have been something he could have done.

But at night, riding on Demon, he could outrun the guilt for a little while.

He tapped Demon's flanks with his boot heels, and the horse lurched forward, as ready as Ian was for their nightly ride.

❦

The night was cool and clear with an almost-full moon providing illumination. Chartreuse had been walking for over an hour. She'd trudged up the hill behind their kitchen garden and through a set of cow pastures below that, clambering over the low stone walls that separated the fields, stepping in cow patties on her way. She was disheveled, dirty, and smelled strongly of manure, but she was having a wonderful time. She felt young and free and joyful just to be out in the autumn night, to be breathing the smells of mud and cow and fall instead of cloying perfume and cigar smoke and the thick, stale odor of sex that usually surrounded her in the evenings.

She was quite lost, but she didn't mind a bit. She didn't even care if His Lordship never made an appearance, though that was the objective of this night's outing. No, she'd just curl up next to a wall and draw her cloak around her and sleep soundly if she needed to, lulled by the night sounds that were everywhere just underneath the overwhelming quiet.

She carried a lantern to make herself visible, but she didn't really need it to find her way. She was in a large field now that seemed to go on for quite a bit before ending in distant shadows that might be trees.

She heard him before she saw him, the thundering sound of a horse galloping through the field. She started swinging the lantern up and down to draw attention to herself—she didn't want to be accidentally trampled.

The beast flew over a hedge she hadn't realized was there and landed only about twenty yards in front of her. Its rider brought the animal to a halt a short distance from her. Both man and animal were breathing heavily.

"Who are you, and what the devil are you doing here?" he asked abruptly as soon as he had his breathing under control. He hadn't even bothered to dismount.

"I'm Chartreuse LaRue, newly arrived in the neighborhood. I went out walking and seem to have gotten myself horribly lost. Are you my White Knight come to rescue me?"

"Most people, Madame, go out walking during the day."
She laughed.

"I quite agree, sir, that would have been the wiser course to choose, but we only just arrived from London late today, and I'm afraid I just couldn't restrain myself. It's been so long since I've been in the country. But I seem to have completely lost my bearings and fear I shall not find my way back to Rosemont Cottage until daylight unless you help me."

He dismounted.

"The road is just beyond that hedge there. Come along, set a good pace. I don't want Demon cooling down too quickly."

He started walking his horse back toward the way they had come even as he was speaking. She ran a few steps to catch up to him.

He wore a wide-brimmed hat that shadowed his face, so she hadn't gotten a good look at him, even when they were in the circle of lamplight.

"And do you have a name, sir?" she asked, feigning to be incensed by his rudeness, though from what Bramly had told her, she expected no less.

"As there is no one to introduce me to you," he said pointedly, a clear reprimand for her lack of propriety. If only he knew how improper she could be. He'd find out soon enough she hoped. "I suppose I shall be forced to introduce myself. I am Ian, Lord Chester."

She pretended surprise and shock, allowing a gasp to escape.

"You've heard of me?" he asked, his voice edged with cynicism.

"My aunt mentioned that we would be neighbors," she replied.

"And what else did your aunt tell you about me?" he said quietly.

She didn't answer right away, choosing her words carefully. This was a critical moment towards getting him to trust her.

"She mentioned only that you had suffered a great tragedy, but she didn't know any of the details."

"She didn't mention that I am known as the Monster Earl hereabouts, who set fire to his father's house in order to murder his parents so he could gain his inheritance a little more quickly? That he was so incompetent that he got caught in the fire himself and is now a scarred, ugly monster who has gone mad with guilt and remorse?"

"No." Bramly hadn't bothered to mention any of those juicy details. "Is he?" she asked.

"Is he what?" Lord Chester answered her question with his own.

"Is the Earl really mad?"

"He's quite incensed with you right now, young lady," he replied.

She laughed, and the tension between them was gone. She relaxed. She knew men, and she knew that if he had even a glimmer of a sense of humor, as he had already demonstrated, that she had him. Her future was all but secured.

They walked in silence down the quiet lane. She knew she should be flirting or getting him to talk about himself. Men loved talking about themselves. But she couldn't bring herself to disturb the comfortable stillness of the night.

They reached the cottage gate. She had to say something; Nell would be furious with her if she let this opportunity go by.

"May my aunt and I have permission to call on you tomorrow, my lord? I should love to see your estate." Inwardly, she groaned. That was so inappropriate. How could she have forgotten her manners so? A lady never invited herself to a gentleman's home.

"I would be happy to have my steward escort you on a

tour of the grounds, Miss LaRue. Acton Park is lovely, though the gardens are past their summer blooms."

He'd adeptly glossed over her faux pas with practical courtesy. She sighed.

"In truth, my lord, it's not the estate I'm really interested in seeing, but you. You've intrigued me, you see. You've been nothing but kindness and propriety, displaying nothing of the madness for which you are so reputed."

"I don't entertain callers," he said.

"Well, then, perhaps we will meet again by moonlight."

"Miss LaRue, do not make a habit of wandering about my property at night. I may mistake you for a poacher and have you shot."

With that, he mounted Demon and rode off.

Chartreuse stared after him from where he'd left her standing at the gate.

"Damnation," she muttered to herself. That hadn't gone well at all. Where had all her charm gone? Surely she wasn't experiencing any pangs of conscience.

Of one thing she was certain. There was nothing wrong with Lord Chester's mind. He was sharp as a tack and was going to see right through Bramly's little plan.

Still, she'd make the best of it. Even if the plan failed and she made nothing from it, she would at least enjoy a few days in the country.

Chapter 2

Chartreuse wanted to take the tour of Acton Park alone. While she knew it would not be proper for her to present herself at the house without a chaperone if she had any hope of passing herself off as a respectable young woman, the chance to spend a few hours of daylight out of doors all by herself tempted her like a golden nugget.

Nell had other ideas and insisted on accompanying her.

"Don't even think about running off and leaving me here in this God forsaken place without you," Nell said.

"There are cottages all along the lane. The village can't be too far."

"Too far for me," Nell panted, winded already and they'd only turned onto the drive from the lane. "Where's the bloody house?"

"Probably just beyond these trees." The drive was lined by beautiful old maples decked in gold leaves. "Aren't they lovely?"

Nell merely snorted. She paused to dig a stone out of her shoe.

"I should have stayed in bloody London," she said. "The girls are probably robbing me blind."

"Bill and Pike will make sure everything runs smoothly while you're gone. Enjoy your holiday, Nell."

Nell narrowed her eyes.

"This is no bloody holiday. It's business, and the sooner it's done the better. Let's get the bugger into bed and get him to offer for you. And don't get any ideas of some romantic fairy tale where you get to be his wife. Bramly will make sure that doesn't happen."

If Nell had slapped her, she couldn't have jerked her back to reality any faster.

"Don't worry, Nell. I know what I am and what I'm here for." Though after meeting Lord Chester, she didn't think they'd succeed in Bramly's scheme; she had to put in her best effort, or it would go badly for her.

Nell had made her fortune pandering to the tastes of those willing to pay for it, whatever those tastes may be, women, men, boys, or girls. She was not above stealing children off the street to satisfy her clients' never-ending need for fresh meat to fulfill their deviant sexual desires. She'd even been suspected of murder a time or two, though it had never been proved.

Chartreuse knew better than to cross Nell.

Her spirits deflated as she discarded her plan to enjoy a few days in the country. She'd do the job she was brought here to do and make sure no blame could be attributed to her when the whole bloody scheme failed.

They rounded a bend, and the house rose up in front of them, a beautiful yellow stone edifice surrounded by lush lawns still green even this late in the year. A fountain gurgled in a circle of grass as the drive curved to the front portico. Gardens with stone-covered paths and sculpted hedges decorated the grounds in front of the two wings that graced each side of the main house. Her breath caught as a feeling of familiarity assailed her. She'd never seen this house before, but she'd known one similar a long time ago.

She blinked back the tears that threatened to leak from her eyes. That would be all she'd need, for Nell to see how affected she was by coming here. Nell would see it as weakness. Weakness wasn't tolerated in Nell's house.

Taking a deep breath, she strengthened her resolve. Seduce the earl, get back to where she belonged. This sham of respectability could not end soon enough to suit her.

"Come on, Nell, let's see if his lordship is at home." She marched up to the front door and slammed down the knocker.

Of course, Lord Chester was not at home, the butler informed them as soon as he opened the door and looked down his nose at them. He directed them to the steward's office tucked away through an arch in a tall hedge to their right.

The steward, Mr. Avery, was pleasant, at least. He was more than happy to show them around the property.

They'd toured the gardens along the east side of the house and were about to take the path that led to the back of the manor when Nell spotted a stone bench that had a delightful view of the front fountain and plopped herself down.

"I cannot go any farther," she said, waving her hand in front of her face. The day had turned warm, and Nell's cheeks were flushed a dangerous shade of red.

Chartreuse sat next to Nell while Mr. Avery hovered nearby.

"We can rest a bit then return to the cottage," she said. "Thank you for your time, Mr. Avery."

"Nonsense," Nell said. "You go on ahead to tour the back. I'll wait here. I should be quite recovered enough for the walk back by the time you return."

Mr. Avery looked uncertain. He'd probably been warned not to leave them unattended. Chartreuse stood and laid her gloved hand on his arm. She couldn't return to the cottage yet. Not without making some progress. Maybe she'd spot Lord Chester in the back garden. She batted her eyelashes and looked imploringly at him.

"I would love to see the back gardens," she said, pitching her voice low and throaty, her bedroom voice. It worked every time. He wavered.

"I promise not wander about," Nell said.

That was all the assurance Mr. Avery required. He acquiesced. Extending his elbow to her, he led Chartreuse to a wooded trail that would take them to the back of the house. From the corner of her eye, she saw Nell make a beeline for an open French door at the side of the house.

She allowed Mr. Avery to escort her all the way to the back patio and well out of sight of the now-empty bench before she stopped.

"I'm sorry, but I don't feel right about leaving my aunt alone. Please forgive me. I'm sure we've taken up enough of your valuable time. I'll take the path back and keep her company until she's ready to return to the cottage."

"Of course," he said, turning to escort her back.

"I'm sure I can find my way on my own," she said. "You must have duties to attend to."

He hesitated, warring between conflicting duties. A gardener waved to him from below, beckoning for his attention, and Mr. Avery acceded to her suggestion.

"I will check on you in a moment," he said.

With any luck, by the time he checked on them, she'd have retrieved Nell and they'd both be back on the bench. All this debacle needed was a charge of housebreaking on their head.

❧

Ian entered his library to find that it had been invaded by a portly woman with reddish-gray hair wearing an abominably low-cut satin gown totally inappropriate for the morning.

The woman gasped when she saw him.

"Look your fill," he said as she stood there gaping. She seemed to finally come back to her senses.

"I'm so sorry, my lord. I didn't mean to invade your privacy." She made him a quick curtsey.

"Didn't you?" he said.

"I was just looking to see if I could find a glass of water. It's so warm out today, and I'm a bit parched."

"And you are, madame?" he said in his iciest tone. Of course he knew who she was. He'd been informed that the ladies of Rosemont Cottage had come for the tour he'd offered them in a moment of weakness last night. Had it been so long since he'd been in the company of a woman that he'd forgotten how to avoid being manipulated by one?

"I'm Mrs. Ryan. Miss LaRue is my niece. Your steward's been showing us around. Lovely place you've got here."

Just then the afore-mentioned niece burst upon the scene.

"Nell, what are you doing here?"

Nell Ryan. The name tickled a memory, but he couldn't retrieve it. It was familiar somehow, but he was quite sure they'd never previously met.

"I was feeling a bit peaked and came in search of a glass of water," Mrs. Ryan said.

Chartreuse turned to him. He had to give her his due. She didn't wince or gasp or show any other outward emotion upon her first good look at him. Most people, like her aunt, could not hide that first expression of horror that crossed their face. Some never lost it. Even some of his own servants could not bring themselves to look at him. They kept their heads down, eyes averted. Not Chartreuse. She acted as if she didn't even notice that his face looked like melted wax, his mouth a grotesque caricature of what it should be, one eye welded shut.

"Please, my lord, if it wouldn't be too much trouble. My aunt has been ill, which is why we came to the country, to see if the fresh air would help her to recover. I'm afraid we overdid it today," she said.

He rang for a servant. He didn't believe for one minute that Mrs. Ryan was truly ill. The woman appeared to be in the best of health, if perhaps a bit overheated from the sun. Still, he'd been raised to adhere to a certain code of proper etiquette, and he could not refuse to offer his hospitality when it had been so directly requested. Even by an unwanted guest.

"Please escort these ladies to the drawing room and bring them a tea cart, Mr. Griggs," he instructed his butler when he appeared. Mr. Griggs raised an eyebrow in surprise, but ever the consummate professional, he caught himself.

"Ladies…" Ian waved his hand to indicate that they should follow Griggs.

Chartreuse stopped in the doorway.

"Won't you join us, my lord?"

"Please forgive me, but I have some correspondence I must attend to," he said, deflecting her.

"Ah, how unfortunate. I would dearly enjoy the opportunity to learn more about your estate, my lord."

"Was Mr. Avery not informative? He usually waxes poetic about the estate. If you have any further questions, you should ask him. Now, if you'll excuse me." He nodded toward the door. She turned her back to him and left. Griggs gave him a pointed look before he closed the door securely behind them. No doubt, Griggs would have something to say about this later.

Going to the open French door, he took a deep breath of warm, fall air before closing it and securing the lock.

Damn! This isn't going to be easy. How am I going to seduce the man if I can't manage to stay in the same room with him?

Chartreuse dutifully followed the servant to the drawing room as instructed. As soon as they were left alone, Nell turned on her.

"What do you think you're doing? Get back there and work on him."

"I have to play the part of a lady if Bramly's scheme is going to work. A lady would not intrude on a man's privacy."

"Well, you'd better intrude on his privates, if you get my meaning, or we're out a pretty sum. We've only got a few days."

"I'll think of something," Chartreuse assured Nell, though she didn't feel at all confident herself. Seduction took time; it took finesse. But she had neither. They were going to have to rely on entrapment.

Raising her voice to a theatrical volume, she proceeded to set the stage for her plan.

"Nell, I'm sorry you are feeling so unwell. I hope you don't have a fit of the vapors when it's time for us to make our way back to the cottage. The long walk home might be more than you can manage right now in your delicate condition. I knew we should have put off our tour of the estate until you were feeling better."

Nell picked up her lead. "I am feeling a relapse coming on."

Ian sat at his desk to tackle the pile of correspondence that awaited him there, but his mind kept mulling the ladies of Rosemont Cottage. While Miss LaRue could pass for a gentlewoman of restricted means, her aunt's manner, dress, and speech betrayed her as not only common, but coarse.

And then there was her name. He knew it somehow, but he could not grasp it. Another lapse in memory since the fire. He snapped his pen in frustration.

It would come if he didn't force it. Reaching for another pen, he tried to focus on the task at hand.

He had finally finished addressing a letter to his solicitor that had taken far longer than should have been necessary when Griggs came in.

"The ladies have had their tea, my lord, and are ready to take their leave."

"It's about time," he muttered, getting up from his desk. He would see them on their way and hope they never darkened his doorway again, though he knew such a hope was probably unrealistic. They seemed intent on invading his peace.

"I trust you are feeling better," he said to Mrs. Ryan when he entered the drawing room. By the looks of the tea cart, the woman's illness hadn't hurt her appetite any. There wasn't a scone or cake left in sight.

"Much better, my lord. Thank you so much for your hospitality. We'll be on our way now." She rose gracefully from her chair then swayed gently. She put a hand to her cheek and uttered a surprised "Oh my!" before sinking ever so slowly to the floor, landing in a heap of wrinkled satin. It was an act worthy of Drury Lane, he thought. Perhaps that's where he had heard of her. Mayhap she trod the boards.

"Nell!" Chartreuse exclaimed and ran over to her. Kneeling next to her unmoving aunt, she lifted Nell's head and placed it in her lap, stroking her cheek in an effort to revive her. "She's fainted," she said, stating the obvious like a player in a melodrama.

Mrs. Ryan gradually came awake.

"Oh, dear," she said, sitting up from her prone position on the floor. "I don't feel at all well."

Her niece gave him a desperate look. "Please, my lord, I hate to impose on you any further, but I don't see how my aunt can make it back to the cottage tonight. Could you find it in your mercy to allow her to rest here until morning?"

He was tempted to let her rest right where she was, on his drawing room floor. This was such an obvious ruse to procure an overnight invitation, he had half a mind to have Griggs throw them out. He would have, too, except for that niggling thought that he couldn't quite bring into focus. Something about Nell Ryan was familiar to him and he had to find out what it was. He didn't believe she was danger-ous, but he knew she was devious. Neither she nor her niece was what they were pretending to be. What better way to solve the riddle than to have the ladies in question spend the night under his roof? He would surely be able to get to the bottom of this puzzle by morning.

"Mr. Griggs, please have Mrs. Hodges prepare rooms for our guests."

Griggs impressed Ian with his ability to mask his sur-prise; though his eyebrow raised slightly, he gave no other indication that the order was at all unusual. It was, though. There had been no overnight guests at Acton Park since the early days of his recuperation. Once he realized that there would be no further healing, that he would be left the mon-ster he was now, Ian discouraged friends and family from calling. As a rule, he saw no one but his most trusted retain-ers.

Somehow, he had allowed these women to manipulate him into being a gracious host.

He did not like being manipulated.

If they were mere gawkers, he would give them some-thing to gawk at. If they were here for more sinister pur-poses, he would make them sorry they had ever set foot upon his property.

"Once you have seen to your aunt's comfort, Miss

LaRue, would you please join me for dinner?"

❧

Chartreuse was unsure what to do. Would it be proper for a lady to dine alone with a gentleman while her chaperone rested upstairs? She hated to decline his invitation and miss the opportunity to be alone with him. Maybe dinner would be the chance she needed to get him in a compromising position. The picture flashed through her mind of sprawling naked on the dining room table with Lord Chester on top of her, pounding away.

Dinner definitely. And she planned to be dessert.

"I'd be delighted, my lord." She curtsied and followed the butler, Griggs, out the door.

The room he showed her to was large and airy. Overlooking the front lawns, it was decorated simply in soft greens and lavenders. And immediately evoked a memory, long buried, of her uncle's country house that she used to visit as a child. For a moment the ache of familiarity was so strong, she felt tears welling in her eyes.

But she had no time for sentimentality. She had a job to do. She'd never visit her uncle's house again. There was no point in dwelling on it. But she could enjoy this one night of living in the lap of luxury.

It was certainly a far cry from her room at Nell's, with its cheap furnishings and gaudy colors. Nell thought red was the most sensual color, and all the girls' rooms were decorated in shades of red, from the paint on the walls to the drapes and bed hangings. Red and gold. Everywhere was red and gold.

Blood and money. That's what it represented. Blood and money.

She dreaded returning to Nell's, but if this scheme worked, she would only be going back for a short time. Combined with the money she had already accumulated, which she had safely tucked away under a floorboard in her room, the take from Bramly's scheme would see her on her way.

Now she just had to decide where she wanted to go. She'd heard that in America one could make a new life for oneself, that it didn't matter so much what you had done in the past. She'd serviced men who were leaving for America. They were full of hopes and dreams.

Her dreams had died a long time ago, but she was struggling to get them back.

Five years in a brothel was long enough. Too long. She wouldn't last five more.

She examined herself in the mirror on the vanity, which was equipped with a silver handled hairbrush. She'd turned nineteen on her last birthday. She looked thirty, if not more. Her eyes were old. She'd seen too much.

There was no such thing as an old whore at Nell's. When the men stopped requesting you, you were thrown out. Even though she was in Nell's good graces now, she had no illusions about what the future held.

She wasn't going to wait for Nell to throw her out. She was going to leave on her own.

The funny thing was, Nell's had seemed like such a safe haven when she first arrived. Nell was warm and motherly and convinced her that she should take control of her life. Why should she let men take what others would pay for?

Nell made the oldest profession sound honorable. For a while, Chartreuse had believed it was, too. She felt empowered by her power over men. She could make them weak; she could control them. She could make them pay.

But there had been so many men over the years. She didn't feel powerful anymore. She felt soiled. And tired of it all.

She liked the way the servants here treated her. She liked being thought a lady. Maybe she hadn't quite convinced Ian,

Lord Chester, that she was his social equal, but he at least hadn't had them forcibly removed from the premises.

She could play the part of a lady, and tonight she was going to embrace the role. At least until the opportune moment when she would throw herself at the good Earl and control him the way she knew best.

He was ugly, though. She hadn't quite expected him to look so disfigured. Bramly had told her about the fire he'd endured and that he was scarred. But he was more than just scarred. He was deformed.

The entire left side of his face looked like raw meat. His left eye was fused shut. His mouth was malformed.

She was not looking forward to seeing what the rest of his body looked like.

But she would do it. She would do what she must. She would make him feel like he was the most handsome man in the world. She would make love to him.

And she wouldn't feel a thing. Not passion. Not desire. Not disgust.

For it didn't really matter what he looked like. He was just a man. A man like any other. They were all ugly.

❧

"Forgive me for being unable to dress properly for dinner, my lord," Miss LaRue said when she entered the dining room.

The room was massive. The table could easily seat twenty. The dining room boasted high ceilings and frescoes on the walls depicting cupids chasing after maidens.

Ian rarely used the large formal dining room, preferring to take his meals in his private apartment. But tonight, he decided formality was in order. With her aunt safely tucked away upstairs, with a footman standing guard outside her room to make sure she didn't make off with the family silver, Ian intended to interrogate Miss LaRue to find out exactly what the two were up to.

"I trust your rooms are acceptable?"

"Perfectly, my lord."

He decided to turn on the charm, though it was admittedly rusty from lack of use. He hadn't felt charming since the fire. At first, he had just felt lucky to be alive. But as the months of his recovery went on and he lived in excruciating pain, he wished only for the pain to stop. When he'd finally healed enough so that he could move without agony, he didn't care how he looked. He only cared that it didn't hurt anymore.

But as time went on and he realized that there would be no improvement, that the scars were not going away, this was how he would be for the rest of his life, he started hating himself.

It wouldn't have mattered if he had been able to save his parents from the fire. His scars would have been worth it. But he'd failed them. They had died, and he had not.

Every day was a painful reminder of his failure.

"Forgive me for my earlier rudeness. I don't choose to entertain visitors for obvious reasons." He gestured toward his burned and scarred face. "However, for such a charming guest as you, I shall make an exception."

Chapter 3

He seated her in the chair on his right while he took the seat at the head of the table, giving her a good view of his right profile. It was undamaged, a fact that most people hardly even noted when they saw him from the front, the obscene disfigurement drawing the eye like a rat drawn to poison—knowing the danger but unable to stay away. Seeing him from this angle, she would realize how truly handsome he had been. His skin was smooth and unblemished on that side, pale yet slightly darkened by the shadow of his beard. His profile would show her a prominent cheekbone and aristocratic features, a long, finely shaped nose and strong chin.

While he wore his dark hair unfashionably long and used it to hide the left side of his face, he pushed the right side back behind his ear so she could see its almost delicate shape and note his perfectly formed jawline.

He had been extraordinary. At least, that's what people used to say. He had never thought much about his looks.

Before the fire.

Now, he looked like a monster. He frightened little children. He hid himself away.

She stared at his right hand when he picked up his fork. It, too, was unmarred. He had long, slender fingers and well-kept nails. His left hand was mottled with blotches of red and brown, his thumb misshapen, its nail missing. The contrast was startling. Even after two years, he still hadn't grown accustomed to it.

He held his fork loosely in his right hand and turned his head to look at her so she could see his full face and have no misapprehension that the perfect profile she'd been unabashedly staring at was anything but an illusion. This was the whole man, the monster.

She quickly averted her eyes, looked down at her plate, picked up her fork and began eating.

He took a bit of his food and savored the taste.

The meal was wonderful. Normally his cook did a creditable job, but this meal was exquisite. No doubt showing off for their guest.

"You have a wonderful chef," Miss LaRue commented.

"Yes," he concurred. If only he'd known how excellent. He would give the man a raise if he prepared meals like this every night.

An awkward silence briefly fell until she filled it with innocuous, polite conversation.

"You have such a lovely home. The grounds and gardens are truly delightful. You must enjoy living here very much."

"It's home," he said noncommittally. In truth, it had been home only for the past eighteen months. The fire destroyed the family seat at Chester on Avon. Ian had spent the first six months of his recovery in the Dower House on the property. But as soon as he could safely travel without suffering too much pain, he had removed himself permanently to Acton Park.

Acton Park was actually one of the Earldom's lesser estates and had fallen into neglectful disrepair under his father's tutelage. Ian chose to rehabilitate Acton Park and make it his residence rather than trying to rebuild Chester Hall.

As far as he was concerned, Chester Hall could rot.

Acton Park suited his needs admirably. He liked its proximity to London, less than a day's ride on a fast horse. Though he had not yet taken his seat in Lords and didn't intend to, he was able to keep up with the political climate from Acton Park.

"Where do you call home, Miss LaRue?"

"Most recently, London," she replied. "But I grew up in the country. In Dorset. My father was a Squire there. We had a small farm."

"I know some people in Dorset, though I don't recall any Squire LaRue. Where exactly was your father's farm?"

He could practically see the wheels turning behind her eyes as she sought a way to deflect his question. Gorgeous eyes. Sky blue, like a cloudless summer's day. Right now they showed an inordinate interest in the landscape painting hanging on the far wall.

"I'm sure you wouldn't know it. It was quite small. Are you planning to go to London for the Season this year?"

Deflection and parry. She'd turned the conversation back on him.

"I haven't been to London in two years," he answered. "Not since the fire."

"Can you tell me about the fire?"

Most people avoided the subject. They spoke in veiled references to "the tragedy." Except at the inquest, no one had asked him directly to talk about it. It just wasn't done.

But for some reason, tonight he wanted to talk about it. Perhaps because he found himself attracted to her even though he knew she was at best a curiosity seeker, at worst a fortune hunter. He needed to remind himself, and make it clear to her, his attractions would get her nowhere. The fire had made sure of that.

"There's not much to tell, actually. I'd gone to Chester Hall to inform my parents about my engagement to Lady Hillary Cross. They were quite well pleased with the match.

"We ate early since my parents kept country hours. They retired at their usual time, around ten o'clock. I was accustomed to Town hours, when I rarely went out before ten in the evening. I was certainly not ready to take myself off to my bed, so I indulged in several glasses of brandy in the library.

"Anyway, I fell asleep in my chair by the fire. I wondered later if I had started the fire myself by knocking over a candle or dislodging a log from the fireplace, but the inquest showed that the fire had started upstairs in the hall outside my parents' bedroom.

"I woke up coughing. The room was filled with smoke. My first thought was escape and I threw a chair through one of the windows and crawled through. There was chaos on the grounds – servants running everywhere. No one had seen my parents. I could see flames through their bedroom windows.

"With some misguided sense of heroism, I went back inside to try to rescue them. I made it to their room but found their bed hangings completely engulfed in flames. I tore down the bed hangings with my bare hand." He held up his left hand, showing her the fire-damaged palm. His hand was surprisingly smooth, no lines marked it, as if they'd been erased. "It was too late. They were already dead."

He imagined their charred bodies lying there so peacefully, side by side as they'd always slept, never having awoken. The image brought him some comfort, at least, that they hadn't suffered.

"As I was making my way back outside again, a burning tapestry swung down from the wall. My clothes caught on fire. I emerged from the doorway looking like a lighted torch, the servants said. They doused me, but I'd been badly burned."

He finished his recitation. She sat still for a moment, looking at him.

"Forgive me," he said. "This does not make very good dinner conversation."

"Does it hurt?" she asked, waving her fork to indicate the burned left side of his face.

"Not anymore."

❧

They ate in silence for a while. Chartreuse had been moved by his story and by the matter of fact way he told it. She'd heard a lot of stories in her line of work. Men crying because of their gambling losses or because their wives were unfaithful to them or their mistress had found a new protector. Having to listen to aristocratic men complaining about their petty problems was enough to make her want to scream.

The women she worked with at Nell's had real problems. The ones like her, who came to Nell's to escape abuse at home. Or those like Katie, who sent all her earnings home to her widowed mother. Or Marge, who had a child fostered with a washer woman. None of the women at Nell's were there by choice. All of them would be somewhere else if they could.

Yet all of them listened patiently while their customers complained about the minor inconveniences they had to endure in their privileged lives.

But not Lord Chester. He had real problems. His made her problems seem petty in comparison. But he didn't complain. He didn't whine. He just stated the truth.

She respected him for it. And she felt the tiniest tingling of guilt at what she was about to do to him. She quickly stamped it down.

She didn't have time for guilt.

Yes, Chester had lost a lot. He'd lost his parents. He'd lost his looks. He'd suffered horribly. But he still had position and power. And wealth. She had none of those.

She'd lost a lot, too. She'd lost her home and her family. She'd lost her reputation and her social standing.

Seducing Chester was her chance to get some of that back. When Bramly paid her for her part in his scheme, she'd have enough money to buy passage to America where she could start a new life. Where no one would need to know what she'd done to earn her passage.

"And what happened to Lady Hillary Cross?" she asked finally.

"She cried off. The engagement was unofficial. I was in mourning and recovering from my injuries, in no position to marry. I understood. She married another."

"Did all your friends abandon you, then?"

He gave her a look of utter disgust.

"No one abandoned me. Look at me. I abandoned them. I am not the man I once was."

She did look at him, fully and thoughtfully.

"No, I suppose you're not."

"Enough about me. Tell me about you."

"There's not much to tell, really. My father died when I was twelve. My mother remarried, and I didn't get along with my new stepfather, so I went to live with my Aunt Nell. Nell was married to my mother's brother, who had died. She was all alone and in need of companionship."

"So, Ryan is your mother's family name?" he asked.

"N…No," she stammered. "She had remarried after my uncle died, a Mr. Ryan. I never met him. He also died, so she's twice a widow."

"LaRue sounds French. Was your father French?" She regretted venturing so near the truth of her own life. Of course, there was no Squire LaRue. Chartreuse LaRue was the name she'd taken when she arrived at Nell's. Even Nell didn't know who she really was.

Why was he asking all these questions? Why couldn't he just take her on face value and allow her to seduce him with her beauty? But of course, the peerage only wants to socialize with its own. She'd have to convince him that she was worthy of his notice before he'd allow her in his bed.

"Norman, actually. Our line goes back to the Norman invasion. My ancestor was a knight under William the Conqueror." There was some truth to that, actually. She was part of a very old, aristocratic family.

"I have a book in my library that lists all the members of William the Conqueror's army. We'll have to look to see if we can find your ancestor."

Chartreuse nearly choked on the sip of wine she'd just taken. She felt herself getting deeper and deeper into the mud of her lies.

"I'd like that," she pretended. "Perhaps in the morning…" By morning it wouldn't matter who her people were or if they could find any knight named LaRue in his bloody book. By morning she'd have him exactly where she wanted him.

A servant came and cleared their dishes away.

"Can you find your way back to your room?" he asked, clearly dismissing her. "I'm sure you must want to check on your aunt."

"She was sleeping soundly when I left her," she lied. Actually, Nell was pacing like a caged tiger, anxious for them to get on with the business at hand. "I'd be more than happy to stay in your company awhile longer." She hoped that wasn't too forward, but she wasn't ready to let him go yet. She needed more time to get him interested in her, though in truth he'd shown absolutely none. She was used to men looking at her with lust. Lord Chester merely looked at her with disdain.

"I'm afraid you'll have to excuse me. It is my custom to go for a ride after dinner."

"May I join you?"

"Do you ride?"

I'd like to ride you.

"Yes, though it's been a few years since I've had the opportunity," she said.

❧

Ian had never met anyone so audaciously determined to insinuate herself on his company. He should send her to her bed in no uncertain terms. The woman was forward beyond all the bounds of propriety, she had no sense of decorum, and she was willing to put herself in an absolutely scandalous position. Going riding at night alone with a man she was not related to. It just wasn't done.

But she didn't seem to care.

And she was quite lovely. Despite himself, he found himself enamored of her. It had been far too long since a beautiful woman had looked at him with, if he was not mistaken, desire in her eyes.

What exactly was it that she desired? Surely not him. He had no illusions about that. There wasn't a woman alive who could feel any attraction for him as he was now.

But she may be attracted to his title. That had to be it. This whole charade was merely an attempt to catch a husband. Miss LaRue and her aunt did not appear to have the resources necessary to finance a Season in London. So, rather than putting herself on the marriage mart, this enterprising young woman decided to go hunting for a husband in the country. Bearding the lion in his den.

Only, what she found was a monster. Would she be willing to go through with it, he wondered, if he were to offer for her? Would she sacrifice herself in marriage to him?

If only she knew that she was wasting her time. Marriage

was not in his future. For he was incapable, since the fire, of performing his marital duties.

He would not be proposing to Miss LaRue, but he was not averse to spending some time with her if she was willing. He hadn't realized how lonely he was for female companionship. For any companionship, really. He had isolated himself to avoid the shocked stares and horrified looks of friends and neighbors. Even his sister could not look at him without tears welling in her eyes.

Being around people had become almost as painful as healing from the fire. Mirrored in their eyes, he could not escape seeing what he was. A monster. Less than a man.

Miss LaRue was the first person who looked directly at him without flinching. She seemed to accept him as he was. It could all be an act and, if so, she was a very gifted actress. But act or not, it fed his soul. He enjoyed having someone flirt with him and treat him as if he were whole.

So, even though he didn't trust her motives an inch, he decided to take her up on her offer to join him on his evening ride. Shadowed by night, perhaps he, too, could pretend he was not marred and imperfect. He could act, too.

"Very, well, Miss LaRue. I believe I have a mare that would be gentle enough for you. We'll keep to the bridle paths where there is less danger of falling into some unseen hole in the ground. Riding at night has its risks," he said.

"Yes, but taking risks can be exciting."

❧

He smiled. For the first time in their short acquaintance, she was actually able to elicit a smile from him. It transformed him. She had a glimpse of what he must have been like before. His smile was totally sensual, promising heaven. Slightly crooked because of the way his scars had changed the shape of his mouth, it was rakish, yet boyishly appealing. If she hadn't been the hardened whore that she was, she might have found herself tempted by that smile.

As it was, it gave her hope. Before the night was over, she'd have his disdain completely transformed to lust. Then he'd be hers.

❧

The night was soft. They rode in silence along the dark trail lighted only by shafts of moonlight that peeked through the overhanging trees. The quiet thud of hooves on turf was soothing.

Chartreuse was transported back to her childhood. She'd loved riding as a child and had her first pony when she was barely four. Father gave her Pegasus for her tenth birthday. He was much too big for her. Her mother nearly had a fit of the vapors when she saw him. But Father knew that she could handle him.

She and Pegasus became fast friends. She started every day by going out to the stable to feed him and muck his stall. Father had said that if she was to have her own horse, she had to be responsible for him. No servant ever did her chores, and she never asked. She loved Pegasus.

Leaving him had been like losing her father all over again. Pegasus had been a constant reminder of her father's love in those horrible years following her father's death.

Her heart ached. A single tear escaped her defenses and trailed down her cheek. She grieved for that young girl who had once been so well loved.

If she had known that coming to the country would dredge up all these old memories, long buried and best forgotten, she would not have come no matter how much money Bramly promised. She couldn't afford to look back. That way led to misery. She had to keep looking forward. She had to make a better future for herself.

She couldn't erase or escape what had happened to her.

But she could try to change her future.

Lord Chester was the key.

They emerged from the woods and followed the trail through a field. Chester finally stopped in front of an imposing stone structure.

"This place is beautiful," she said when he had helped her dismount. "What was it?"

"We call it the Roman ruin, though it probably dates much later than that time. I suspect it was a medieval chapel built in the Roman style."

He found a spot protected on three sides by crumbling stone wall. Soft grass covered the ground. It was a private alcove perfect for seduction if that was his intent. He retrieved a blanket from his saddle and spread it on the ground.

She explored the ruin, cautiously stepping where shadows overwhelmed the moonlight. It was a romantic setting. If she were truly a lady of quality, she would likely not have been allowed to come out with Chester tonight. She wondered if, had her life unfolded as it should have, she would have had the sense of adventure to flaunt the proprieties and come anyway.

She liked to think that she would. This was just too wonderful to miss. The night sky was abundant with stars. She'd forgotten how many stars there were. In London, in those rare times that she went outside at night, there were too many buildings, too much smoke and fog, to really see the stars.

The air smelled like spring but had a sharp nip to it that reminded one that winter was on its way.

After circumventing the ruin, she joined Chester where he rested on the blanket.

"Oh, this is lovely." She took in the sheltered alcove. Protected from the wind, it felt warm and safe.

Sprawled on his left side so that his unscarred profile

was toward her, she was again struck by how handsome he had been before the fire.

"It must be so hard for you." She said.

"What?"

"To accept your loss."

She reached down and ran her fingers down the left side of his face.

She leaned over and kissed him, trailing kisses from the eyelid that was burned shut over his sightless left eye. Down his cheek that had the consistency of melted wax. Her lips lingered at the corner of his mouth, where the scarring distorted the shape of his lips. He turned his head slightly, so she could kiss the smooth, undamaged side. Then he was kissing her like a man drowning. He devoured her lips like they were his last gasp of breath.

She closed her eyes and savored his kiss. She felt victorious, but at the same time a little disappointed. She had actually found herself liking him.

But now, he was just a man.

She moaned and pressed herself more fully into him. He flipped her over so that now she was on the blanket and he was leaning over her. He kissed her deeply, sweeping his tongue into her mouth. She let her tongue dance with his.

She moved her hands down his back and rubbed her feet along his legs. She knew she should wait until they were back at the house where Nell could walk in on them, but she didn't want to let this opportunity get away from her. If they made love now, they could always make love again back in his bed where they could be caught in the act.

Maybe he wouldn't even need to be coerced into offering for her. Maybe he'd do it on his own out of his sense of honor.

When had she ever known a man to act honorably?

She let her hand drift down to his hip and was about to touch him to let him know she wanted him when he grabbed her wrist. He pulled away from her.

"We'd better be going," he said. He stood up and reached down to help her to her feet.

"You must think me terribly forward," she said.

"I'm not sure what to think about you, Miss LaRue." He bent and picked up the blanket. "We'd best be getting back. Your aunt may have awakened and will be looking for you."

She took his reminder as a gentle rebuke. She had to balance her goal of seduction with the role of lady she was playing. She obediently followed him to where they had hobbled the horses.

"Thank you for bringing me with you tonight," she said when he helped her mount.

"It was my pleasure," he replied courteously if curtly.

She smiled as they rode home. She didn't know why Chester had stopped them at the ruins, but he wouldn't stop when she joined him in his bed. Of that she was certain.

She could practically count the money Bramly was going to pay her. She was on her way to America.

❧

"Are the ladies in their rooms?" Ian asked Dickie, the footman he'd assigned to stand guard outside his guests' doors.

"Yes, my lord," Dickie said.

"Stay alert. I wouldn't want them to get lost wandering the halls during the night."

He'd escorted Chartreuse to her room when they returned from their ride then went down to the library for a snifter of brandy before retiring. His nightly ritual. He'd try to sleep without benefit of laudanum. Sometimes the brandy was enough.

Symmington awaited him when he entered his own room.

"How was your ride, my lord?" his valet asked.

"Interesting," he said. "Miss LaRue accompanied me."

"So I'd heard," Symmington said. "She seems a nice enough woman, if common."

"Is that approval I hear?"

"It is good to see you keeping company with someone. You've been too long alone."

"Yes, well, I'll be alone again tomorrow. The ladies will be returning to Rosemont Cottage at first light. See to it."

"I'll order breakfast trays brought to their rooms as early as possible. Will there be anything else you require this evening?"

"No. Let's get on with it."

Ian sat on the bench at the foot of his bed and lifted his booted foot. Symmington tugged the right boot off with little effort. Then came the left. Ian winced as the fitted leather rubbed against the sensitive skin on his calf and released the slab of red meat that remained of his left foot, which immediately started tingling like it was being stabbed with pins and needles.

He stood so Symmington could remove his jacket, unclasp the links at his cuffs, unbutton his shirt and the placket on his trousers. Stripping him naked, Symmington inspected his skin for blisters and tears, applying ointment on any dry, itchy patches Ian pointed out. He had no modesty in front of Symmington. The man had wiped is arse, for God's sake, when he'd been helpless after the fire. He owed much of his survival to Symmington's meticulous care. So he endured the nightly inspection, which would be repeated in the morning. And he'd try not to resent the man for doing such a good job to keep him alive on those nights when he wished he'd been allowed to die.

"Laudanum?" Symmington held up the dark brown bottle kept on Ian's bedside table.

"Not tonight. Another brandy, perhaps."

Symmington poured him a snifter from the carafe that was always kept full on a cart by the door. Some mornings, after a particularly rough night, the carafe was empty and required replenishing.

"Good night, my lord." Symmington bowed slightly, a habit Ian could not break him of, though he'd told him repeatedly such obeisance was unnecessary between them especially when they were alone. Symmington closed the door noiselessly behind him as he left.

Standing in a shaft of moonlight by the window overlooking the back garden, Ian sipped his brandy, holding the snifter in his right hand and idly fondling himself with his left as he thought about the woman sleeping down the hall.

He couldn't believe he had lost himself so completely kissing her. He had felt desire for her in every part of his being except the part that really mattered. When she'd made as if to touch him, he'd nearly panicked. He didn't want her to know that he was a virtual eunuch. How embarrassing to have a beautiful woman willing in his arms and to have no physical response whatsoever.

Was she willing? She'd certainly seemed so. She hadn't been put off by his scars. She'd even kissed them.

And he had enjoyed kissing her. He had felt his heart race and his blood heat. Perhaps if he had kissed her longer, he might have felt something more.

He was kidding himself. He looked down at his penis, which remained flaccid in his hand. No amount of kissing was going to bring that back to life.

Tossing back the last of the brandy, he climbed into bed and doused the light.

He would never know. Because Miss LaRue and Mrs. Ryan were returning home to Rosemont Cottage at first light. If he was lucky, they would never darken his doorway again. He would make sure of it.

Chapter 4

Chartreuse waited until after midnight to sneak into Chester's bedroom. She had to tiptoe by the footman standing guard outside her own room. Fortunately, he was sleeping soundly. As was Chester.

She removed her shift and crawled naked under the sheets, pleased to find him naked, too. He didn't stir.

She curled her body next to his and stroked him lightly with her fingers. He groaned but didn't waken.

He was soft and flaccid, but she continued to rub and stroke, patiently waiting for nature to take over.

She almost gave up; it was taking so long. Perhaps he'd had too much to drink. Alcohol, she knew, often made men incapable of performing.

She tried using her mouth, taking him in and sucking gently. Finally, she felt him start to stiffen. She sucked harder, and he hardened. She felt him grow and heard his breathing become rapid.

She looked up at him. He was still sleeping though stirring.

Before he woke fully, she straddled him and inserted him into her. She started moving, up and down, tightening her muscles so he'd stay firmly implanted inside her.

His eyes were still closed, but he grabbed her hips with his hands and started moving her faster and faster. His hips joined hers in their rhythm.

Just before he climaxed, he opened his eyes and looked directly at her. He smiled then grimaced as he reached his release.

❧

Ian was dreaming again. The same dream that haunted his sleep almost every night. His mistress, Clarisse, was fondling him. He felt himself grow hard and erect. She straddled him and started the age-old rhythm, up and down, riding him hard. He lost himself in the sensation. Grabbing her hips with his hands, he increased the tempo, joining her in the dance.

The dream ended differently this time. When he opened his eyes, he wasn't horrified to see his mother's burned and charred torso looming over him. Instead, he saw Chartreuse and realized that this wasn't a dream after all. He really was in bed with a woman. He really was stiff and hard and coming inside her.

A final spasm shook him just as the door to his bedroom slammed open, and Nell Ryan stormed in, followed on her heels by Dickie, the footman he'd had posted outside her door.

"What is the meaning of this!" Nell shouted. "How dare you take advantage of an innocent girl, a guest in your house. I demand that you make it right."

Ian laughed. He couldn't help it. He felt so damned good. He'd just had not only an erection but an orgasm. Even Nell Ryan storming into his room couldn't quell his good mood.

Chartreuse slid off him and hid herself under the blankets, like some virginal innocent. Still smiling, he sat on the edge of the bed and motioned for Dickie to hand him his robe.

"Well, sir, what have you to say for yourself?" Nell stood tapping her foot impatiently on his Aubusson carpet.

Standing, he tied his robe loosely at the waist. Of course, now he remembered. Nell Ryan. The infamous madam.

He'd never visited her brothel himself, but many of his friends had. It had been quite the thing when they were at school.

"Please escort Mrs. Ryan back to her room," Ian ordered.

"Yes, my Lord." Dickie grabbed Nell's arm none too gently and practically dragged her out of the room.

Ian turned to Chartreuse, who was still hiding under the covers. In his bed. Naked. He was tempted to crawl back in with her, even knowing what she was. She had accomplished what he'd thought was impossible. He wanted to thank her. He wanted to shout and laugh and dance with her. He wanted to make love to her again.

Instead he said, "How much do I owe you?"

She did her best to look confused, even offended. "I'm sorry, I don't know what you mean."

"Cut line, Chartreuse, if I may be so bold as to call you Chartreuse. We are, after all, intimately acquainted, now aren't we? When I was in school, many of my comrades bragged about their exploits with a notorious madame named Nell Ryan," he said amicably. "What a coincidence that a woman with that name and description should show up in my neighborhood with her—*niece*, was it?"

"You knew all along?"

"I knew something wasn't quite right about the two of you, but I didn't remember where I had heard Nell Ryan's name until just now. Suddenly, everything made sense. Except why you are here. Perhaps you'd care to explain?"

"I should think that would be obvious, Ian." She pointedly used his Christian name. Tit for tat, he supposed. Since they were now intimately acquainted. "I came to seduce you."

"But for what purpose?"

"Why, so you'd have to marry me, of course."

He gave a shout of laughter at that. She became indignant.

"It wasn't that funny. You thought I was a lady, didn't you?"

He realized that for some reason this was very important to her. Since he was feeling amiable, he agreed with her.

"Yes, I thought you were a lady. One with loose morals and an incompetent chaperone, but yes, you could pass for a lady."

"Thank you." She got out of the bed then and casually strolled over to him, shamelessly and gloriously naked. He felt himself hardening again. Before he could act on his response to her, he handed her the shift she'd left lying at the foot of the bed.

"So, tell me, who concocted this scheme?"

"What's it worth to you to know?"

He crossed the room to the writing desk tucked beneath the window on the far side and retrieved his change purse. He tossed her the entire thing, not even bothering to check to see how much was in it. She opened the drawstring bag and peeked inside. Satisfied, she palmed it.

"Your uncle, Mr. Bramly, hired us. The plan was to get you to offer for me. Then he'd have you declared incompetent for wanting to marry a known prostitute."

Bramly. He could have guessed. First Bramly had tried to get power of attorney while he was recuperating. Then he'd spread rumors about Ian setting the fire, rumors that had led to an inquest exonerating him. Now this.

It was time for him to deal with his uncle.

"I would suggest," he said as he escorted Chartreuse to

the door, "that you and Nell Ryan remove yourselves from this neighborhood at the earliest possible convenience. I do not take lightly to attempts at extortion."

⊷ఠ

Chartreuse stormed into Nell's room.

"Get dressed, Nell," she said. "We're leaving."

"What happened?" Nell was sitting on the edge of the bed, a flask of whiskey in her hand.

"He knows who we are, that's what happened." Chartreuse paced, which she always did when she was agitated. "I wouldn't put it past Bramly if he told Ian himself. Maybe this was all some grand practical joke. Well, I don't like being humiliated."

"You mean he's not going to offer for you?"

Chartreuse calmed down enough to sit beside Nell. Nell poured some whiskey into a glass and handed it to her. She downed it in one gulp.

"Offer for me! We'll be lucky if he doesn't have us thrown in prison. Come on, Nell, let's get out of here. Bramly's whole scheme was ill conceived. Ian isn't a monster, and he isn't mad. And he's not stupid. He saw right through us.

"He'd heard of you, Nell. He knew about the infamous madam Nell Ryan. He put two and two together. And we're out the blunt Bramly promised us."

"If this was some kind of joke at my expense, Bramly will pay," Nell threatened.

Chartreuse didn't doubt for an instant that, even with Bramly's position in Society, Nell could do him in. A footpad attack in a dark alley some night when Bramly staggered home well in his cups could easily result in a slit throat.

She hoped it didn't come to that. Much as she despised Bramly, she didn't want to be responsible for his death. His scheme had been foolish, but she and Nell had been party to it. She was feeling pretty foolish herself.

She'd been so desperate for blunt, she'd gone along with the ill-fated scheme. Now she saw no hope of ever getting away from Nell's. She might die there.

❧

They returned to the cottage to collect their things and were ready to leave by first light.

Chartreuse took one last look around. She closed her eyes and drew in a deep breath, inhaling the smell of mud and meadow and spring. She knew what she was and what she was going back to. But for a few days she'd gotten to see what her life might have been like.

A soul-deep sorrow took hold of her. All her plans to get out of Nell's and flee to America seemed so foolish and stale. What was the point? No matter where she went, she'd carry Nell's with her. She wasn't a lady, and she never would be again. She was a whore, so soiled and used that a man like Ian didn't want anything to do with her.

To hell with him, she thought. There were plenty of men who did want her and who were willing to pay for the pleasure.

Chapter 5

It took Ian three days to remove himself from Acton Park to his London town house. His first task upon arrival was to summon his Uncle Bramly.

Bramly's given name was Richard, but to Ian's knowledge no one ever used it. He'd always been just Bramly. Ian's father was known as Chester, and until he had acquired the title, Ian was known as Morely, for his honorary title Viscount Morely. So Bramly had the family surname all to himself. He used it like a title.

When Ian's grandfather died, he'd left Bramly a small, unentailed estate, thinking to provide for his son for life. But Bramly lost that in a card game when he was twenty-one. Since then, Bramly had been totally dependent on the good graces of the reigning Earl of Chester, first Ian's father, now Ian himself.

He had realized from his first dealings with Bramly two years ago why his father was always criticizing him for his profligate ways. Ian knew now that his father's greatest fear was that he should turn out like Bramly.

Bramly had a proclivity for cards and women. He went through his generous monthly allowance in a few days. Ian was constantly paying off creditors on Bramly's behalf.

But it was never enough. It would never be enough. Bramly wouldn't settle for less than Ian's entire estate.

It was time to put Bramly in his place.

"I will no longer tolerate your attempts to discredit me so you can get your hands on my estate," Ian said as soon as Bramly was presented to him in his study.

"Won't you even offer your uncle a drink?" Bramly said affably, putting on his charm.

Ian softened toward his uncle for a moment. He knew too well how it felt to be considered useless. It had been a bone of contention between him and his father. He kept asking for some responsibility, for an estate to run or plantation to manage, but his father would have none of it.

"It'll all be yours soon enough," his father would say. Yet it didn't stop his father from criticizing him for enjoying the pastimes that idleness forced upon him. He had long since tired of the routs and balls, the gambling dens and sporting events that he frequented with other members of his generation of heirs.

He understood how easy it was to fall into debauchery when one had nothing else to occupy one's time.

Bramly poured himself a healthy dose of whiskey then raised the decanter to ask if Ian wanted to join him. He nodded.

"I don't know what you're so upset about," Bramly said. "My plan worked admirably."

"I'll not be posting banns to marry one Chartreuse LaRue any time soon," he said.

"Ah, that was just what I told the gals to get them to go out to the country with me. Cost me a pretty penny renting that cottage. I still owe Nell her fee. But it was worth it. You're here, aren't you? Got you to stop sulking in that house all alone feeling sorry for yourself."

"That was your intent?" He didn't know what to think.

"And to get you laid, of course," Bramly said. "A man needs to get laid once in a while. Chartreuse is a good girl. One of my favorites."

An image of Chartreuse servicing Bramly flashed through his mind. Not a pleasant thought. Rather revolting. He'd come to like her in their short acquaintance and didn't want to dwell on what she was to men like his uncle.

"Maybe you should set her up," Bramly said. "Give her a carte blanche. I'm sure Nell would sell her for a reasonable price."

"It was my understanding that slavery had been abolished throughout the land," he said.

"Think of it as a finder's fee," Bramly said, sinking into one of the two leather club chairs facing the fireplace.

Perhaps he'd been wrong about his uncle. Ian took the other seat, and they sipped their whiskeys in companionable silence.

"My methods may have been unorthodox," Bramly said when he'd finished his glass and got up to pour himself another. Ian declined to have his nearly full glass topped off. "Now we need to decide what to do. You need to let me help you, m'boy. That's all I've ever wanted to do."

"You can help me, Uncle," Ian said. The whiskey worked its magic, easing the near constant pain just enough to make him mellow. "You can take on the Yorkshire estate. The factotum retired last fall, and it needs attention. I'd go myself, but the distance is too great."

In fact, he'd planned to go himself, but this unexpected trip to London changed his plan. The journey from Acton Park had been torture. He'd never survive a trip to Yorkshire. He was still learning to live with his limitations.

"You'd banish me to the back of beyond?"

What he was offering Bramly wasn't banishment, but opportunity.

"Run the Yorkshire estate for me for a year," Ian said.

"It's one of the few not entailed properties I own. If you don't run it to the ground by year's end, it's yours."

Ian would have leaped at the chance to prove himself had his father ever seen fit to offer it to him. But Bramly was not Ian. He had, after all, already lost his own estate.

"I don't need your charity," Bramly spat out, tossing back his whiskey and slamming the glass down on the table. "You're just as bad as your father. I made one youthful mistake, and he never let me forget it."

Ian sighed.

"You offered to help," he said.

"As a matter of fact, I've acquired an interest in a gambling establishment. It wants only a bit of capital to get it up and running. I'm giving you the chance to invest. Get in on the ground floor. Of course, I wouldn't expect you to soil your hands with the actual work of running the place, but it should provide you with a good return."

Feeling charitable and wanting to spare his uncle's pride, he asked, "How much?"

"Ten thousand pounds," Bramly answered.

Ian swallowed his last gulp of whiskey and set down his glass.

"Give me the details, and I'll have my man of business investigate," he said.

"What's to investigate? I'm telling you it's a good investment."

"And I don't make investments blindly."

"Who do you think managed your affairs while you were laid up for six months out of your mind with pain and grief? I did. And I didn't need any man of business sticking his nose in my business, either."

Ian knew exactly how Bramly had managed things. He'd been cleaning up after him for the past eighteen months.

"If you want to help me," Ian said, "take the Yorkshire estate."

"I don't want the damn Yorkshire estate. I'll not have your leavings."

"You are, of course, at liberty to do as you choose. As am I. And I have no interest in investing in your gaming hell." Ian stood, making it clear to Bramly that the interview was over. He went to his desk and picked up the bank draft he'd had prepared. Extending it toward Bramly, he said, "Your allowance, sir. Give my regards to Nell Ryan and Chartreuse LaRue when next you see them."

"Go to hell," Bramly cursed then stormed out of the house.

❧

"That bitch gave the whole deal away," Bramly accused Chartreuse.

The three conspirators holed up in Nell's office for their meeting.

"I told you what happened, Nell. He knew. I didn't have to tell him anything."

"That's a lie." Bramly downed another glass of brandy and immediately refilled his glass. "She told him, Nell. And I plan to take it out of her hide."

"You owe us a great deal of money, sir," Nell said calmly. "As this opportunity did not pan out, how do you intend to clear your debt?"

Bramly pulled a purse from his pocket.

"I'll settle my account, but I want one last romp with Miss High and Mighty here."

Chartreuse looked desperately at Nell. She did not want to be alone with Bramly. Not when he was angry with her. Bramly got his jollies by hurting women. She did not want him hurting her.

Nell held out her palm, and Bramly counted notes into her hand. Satisfied, Nell nodded.

"Take Mr. Bramly to room seven," she told Chartreuse.

"Nell…" Chartreuse started, but Nell stopped her with a sharp look.

"You failed, Chartreuse. Now go take your punishment."

She had no choice. If she didn't go willingly, Bill and Pike would drag her there. Either way, she was going to be hurt.

"Bramly," Nell said as he and Chartreuse were leaving the room, "you are no longer welcome here."

At least that was something. At least this was the last time she'd have to tolerate Bramly's brand of sexual pleasure.

They went into room seven and closed the door behind them.

Bramly locked the door.

"Now, you little bitch, you're going to pay for what you did to me."

Chartreuse assessed the situation and decided that subservience was the safest option.

"It wasn't my fault," she whined. "He recognized Nell. Let me make it up to you." She approached him ready to cajole him with her body. Men usually forgot their problems when aroused.

But Bramly would have none of it. He backhanded her hard across her left cheek. The impact sent her flying across the room. She landed on her knees against the bed and grabbed the bedclothes to keep from falling backwards.

Bramly came up behind her. He flipped her skirts up over her head and groped her. She opened for him. So, he wanted to play rough. She'd play along if it would keep him from hitting her again.

He pushed her head down onto the mattress and entered her from behind. She wasn't ready, hadn't had a chance to lubricate with butter as she usually did, so it hurt. Fortunately, it didn't take him long to climax. When he was done, he stepped back from her. She heard him adjusting his clothing.

She stood up and turned to face him, hoping he was finished with her, but she knew by the crazed look in his eyes that he wasn't.

"Take off your clothes," he ordered.

So now he's going to humiliate me. He could try to, at least, but after working at Nell's for five years, it wasn't easy to humiliate her. Taking off her clothes in front of a man was an everyday occurrence.

She undressed slowly and seductively hoping to arouse Bramly again. If she could keep him sexually aroused, she could control the situation.

Bramly stood still and watched dispassionately, his arms hanging limply by his sides. She didn't notice the belt he was holding until it was too late. As soon as she dropped her chemise and stood before him completely naked, his right hand whipped the belt up. The buckle connected with her face, just missing her eye and opening a gash on her cheek.

She screamed.

Bramly beat her savagely, first with the belt then with his bare hands. When she huddled on the floor curled up in a ball trying to protect herself, he kicked her with his booted feet.

Her screams became whimpers then finally stopped altogether when she feigned losing consciousness. She slowed her breathing and kept her eyes closed, but she felt him standing over her, looking down at her, afraid he would not care that she was insensate and keep beating her for the pleasure it gave him.

"That will teach you to cross me," he muttered. He must have decided that she had been suitably punished, because she heard him straightening his clothing. He unlocked the door and left the room.

She let unconsciousness take her.

❧

Chartreuse heard voices but she couldn't open her eyes to see who it was. She wanted to tell them to stop talking about her, but she couldn't get her mouth to work. It was like she was asleep and caught in a nightmare, the kind where you can't seem to wake up.

"How bad is it?" Nell asked. Chartreuse felt herself being prodded. A moan escaped as someone moved her leg.

"Leg's broken." A man's voice. She didn't recognize it. Pain seared through her, and she nearly lost consciousness again.

"Take her to the river and dump her in," Nell ordered someone. Probably Bill and Pike. They did whatever Nell told them to. "She's no good to me now."

Wake up, wake up! She struggled to open her eyes and had just managed to open them a crack when Bill and Pike lifted her limp body and started carrying it down the back staircase. Excruciating pain had her swooning. What should have been a scream came out as a pathetic moan.

"Hush, now," Bill, holding her shoulders, soothed her. "It will be over quick. We won't put you in the river alive."

They had a wagon waiting for them. They put her in the wagon bed surprisingly gently, then the wagon dipped as they climbed onto the driver's bench.

"On second thought," Nell said when they were ready to leave, "this is all his fault. Drop her off at his house. Let him deal with her."

No, Nell, no! I'd rather be drowned than returned to Bramly.

But there was nothing she could do. She was helpless and hurt. She felt the wagon lurch forward, taking her to her fate.

Chapter 6

Ian's carriage wended its way through the darkened London streets bringing him home. It had been a long evening, and his back ached from the effort he'd made to sit casually erect in a club chair even though the soft, upholstered leather offered none of the support he required. He longed for a warm bath and a soft bed.

The visit to his club had gone as well as he could have expected. There was awkwardness at first. Everyone stared as he made his way to a seat by the fire. Then Sinclair came over. They'd been friends at Eton. Sinclair had made attempts to keep in touch with him in the years since the fire, though such attempts had been rebuffed.

"Good to see you, Ian," Sinclair said, proffering his hand.

"Please join me," he said, motioning to the chair across from him. Their conversation was stilted at first. Sinclair seemed afraid of saying anything offensive. But, after a few glasses of port, they both relaxed a bit. He even found himself laughing as Sinclair regaled him with tales of his recent exploits.

Other gentlemen of his acquaintance came over to say

hello. Everyone carefully avoided any mention of his appearance. No one asked about the fire. All were painfully polite. All avoided looking directly into his eyes, or eye, since he had only one now. They scrupulously looked anywhere but at his face. He felt like waving his hands in front of them and saying, "over here!" But he controlled the urge. He knew what a monstrosity he was. He didn't like looking at his face, either.

But at least they were willing to talk to him. Acknowledge him. It was a beginning. His uncle hadn't been able to ruin his reputation completely. Those who had known him before the fire were willing to befriend him again.

The evening overall had been a success.

The carriage stopped in front of his town house to drop him off before going to the mews in back. He hopped down, a little light-headed from all the port he'd imbibed, and started up the front steps.

There was a bundle of rags on the stoop near the door.

"What's this then?" he asked Griggs when the door swung open on cue just as he reached the top step. He indicated the bundle at his feet.

"I have no idea, my Lord, but I'll have a footman remove it at once."

Just then, the bundle moved and moaned.

Ian bent down and pawed through the puddle of blankets.

"My God," he exclaimed when he uncovered her face. "Chartreuse."

"Miss LaRue? The young lady from Acton Park?"

He didn't know how much the servants knew about what transpired that night. Probably everything since Dickie had followed Nell into his room when he and Chartreuse were in a compromising position.

"Help me get her inside."

"I'll get a footman," Griggs said.

Ian cursed. She was such a small thing; he should be able to lift her himself and carry her inside. But he couldn't. Not anymore.

"We can do it," he said. "I'll take her shoulders if you lift her feet."

"My lord," Griggs said in the same implacable tone he'd used when he'd force-fed Ian broth and laudanum during one of his bedside shifts. "I will get a footman." Ian knew better than to argue.

He eased himself down onto the stoop and cradled her head in his lap while he waited for the strong, burly footmen who were not, as he was, incapable of lifting one small woman, to arrive. He pulled out his handkerchief and dabbed at the blood on her cheek. The cut was deep and would leave a scar. He wanted to roar with outrage. Such perfection should not be marred by violence.

Dickie and one of the new footmen Griggs had hired in London came out to lift her.

"Be gentle with her," he said as Dickie grabbed her under the shoulders and the other footman—James was it? — picked up her legs.

She screamed then went silent.

"Lay her on the sofa in the front drawing room. Careful now."

She remained blessedly insensate as they settled her on the cushions. The blankets wrapping her fell away and exposed her bruised and battered naked body. And a leg that was bent at an unnatural angle.

"Go fetch a doctor," he ordered.

"I know of one," James said and raced out.

"Get a fire lit," he said. Dickie bent to the task as his housekeeper, Mrs. Pitts, entered the room. She took one look at the naked girl on the sofa, turned on her heels, and exited before Ian could tell her to prepare a room. Annoyed, he issued the directive to Griggs, who hovered in the doorway. But he'd underestimated his housekeeper, for she returned a few minutes later with a linen sheet, a bowl of warm water, and a cloth.

"That will be all, Dickie," she said. "You may leave, my lord. I have things well in hand." Draping the sheet over Chartreuse, she sat on the edge of the sofa and started dabbing at her cuts with the wet cloth.

"Where is the blasted physician?" he muttered.

"He'll be here soon," Mrs. Pitts said.

Griggs returned.

"A room is being prepared," he said. "Should I send for a constable? Or her..." Griggs hesitated. "Aunt?" he said.

So, he knew. Dickie must have told him. Which meant the entire household knew. How much of the particulars he couldn't be sure, but judging by Griggs's expression, he at least knew that Chartreuse was not the young lady of quality she'd pretended to be when Griggs first met her at Acton Place.

They'd left her naked and dumped her on his doorstep like yesterday's refuse.

Ah, Chartreuse, what have they done to you? What have I done to you?

This was his fault. He shouldn't have sent her back with Nell. He should have known something like this could happen. She'd failed to deliver him leg-shackled and humiliated. The message had been clearly delivered. Her failure was his responsibility.

"No," he said. "Don't send for anyone. I will deal with this myself."

After what felt like an eternity, James returned with the physician in tow.

"Dr. Ashcroft." The man introduced himself, bowing slightly at the waist. Ian wished he could send for Dr. Pearce, the man who had so expertly tended to him after the fire, but he lived in Chester on Avon and had refused to go even so far as Acton Park after Ian removed himself there. He'd referred Ian to Dr. Hargate, another competent physician. This man appeared competent, if appearances could gauge such a thing. He was dressed neatly and conservatively, his hands and hair were clean, his beard neatly trimmed. At least he wasn't slovenly and drunk.

Ian nodded and motioned to Dr. Ashcroft to proceed with his examination.

"Please excuse us, my lord," Dr. Ashcroft said. "Your housekeeper can remain should I need assistance."

"No," Ian said. "I'll stay."

"The woman is your wife? Your mistress?"

He shook his head. He didn't think one quick tumble qualified her to be his mistress.

"Then I must ask you to leave. For the lady's modesty."

"And I'm afraid I must refuse your request. I am staying. Now, get on with it."

Dr. Ashcroft acquiesced, though he made his disapproval known with a shake of his head and a frown. Ian didn't care what the physician thought of him as long as he stopped wasting time and looked after Chartreuse.

She hadn't regained consciousness since Dickie and James had laid her on the sofa. She remained insensate throughout Dr. Ashcroft's examination.

"The ribs are cracked," he said as his hands swept over her torso. "The gash on her cheek needs stitching. I will need help with the leg."

"What sort of help?" Ian asked.

"Someone to hold her still while I set it. Help me move her to the floor."

With Mrs. Pitts's help, the three of them managed to place Chartreuse gently on the carpet.

Ian's knee screamed as he knelt on the floor next to her.

"Hold her down," Dr. Ashcroft ordered.

Without thinking, Ian lay his chest across hers in a parody of an embrace. With his forearms on her shoulders, he placed his hands on either side of her head.

"Ready," he said.

Dr. Ashcroft tugged and yanked so hard he nearly wrested Chartreuse out from under him, but Ian held firm. Her eyes stayed closed, her breathing steady, though shallow. She didn't even whimper.

"I'll use splints and heavy bandaging to secure the leg," Ashcroft said. "That should be sufficient. It's not a bad break, and it snapped into place easily enough."

Ian's stomach threatened to heave. For all he'd endured, or maybe because of it, he had a weak stomach when it came to blood and gore. And bone setting, apparently.

"I'll go check on the room preparations," Mrs. Pitts said, rising from her hands and knees on the floor with all the dignity of royalty. Nothing flustered Mrs. Pitts, it seemed.

His attempt to stand was quite a bit less dignified. With nothing to grab onto nearby, he had to get his feet under him on his own. After several failed tries, he accepted Ashcroft's proffered hand.

Ashcroft knelt by her head and threaded a needle through her cheek. Ian had to look away, his stomach threatening again.

"Why does she not wake?" he asked the wall he was staring at.

"It's a blessing she doesn't," Ashcroft replied. "Her body is protecting her from pain. Have someone watch over her tonight. Expect fever but notify me if it does not abate or if she does not revive. Else, I shall return in a few days."

She did not wake. Not when the footmen carried her as gently as possible up the front staircase to the guest bedroom that had been prepared for her just down the hall from his own. Not as Mrs. Pitts dressed her in a white nightgown she'd found somewhere, maybe her own chest. Not as he sat up with her all night feeling the weight of responsibility on his shoulders.

She was no innocent, he knew, but she was a victim caught in his war with Bramly.

She may have been playing a role, but she was the first person to look right at him since the fire without turning away in horror or discomfort. She was the first person to touch him. She was the first person to make him feel like a man again, not a monster. For that, he was grateful. For that, he owed her.

When dawn lightened the windows and the house began to stir, Chartreuse's breathing settled into a more even rhythm, deeper, less shallow. More like sleep. Her mouth opened slightly and emitted a light snore.

He smiled. That soft snore comforted him that she would be alright.

"Rest," he whispered. "Sleep." He closed his eyes but opened them moments later when Mrs. Pitts bustled into the room.

"Good morning, my lord," she said. "Mr. Symmington awaits you in your room. I will send a maid to look after the girl."

He could have argued, he supposed. Could have insisted on staying until she woke. But his back had stiffened from the night spent sitting in a chair, and he was desperately in need of a warm bath and change of clothes.

"Inform me immediately when she wakes," he said as he pushed himself up from the chair and hobbled to the door.

◈

Chartreuse startled awake. She didn't know where she was. She'd had some wild dreams, dreams where she'd been falling, dreams where she was being hunted, dreams where she feared for her life.

The room she woke up in was unfamiliar. If she was at Nell's, she was in a room she'd never seen. But even as she thought it, she knew she wasn't at Nell's. The furnishings were too fine and tasteful to be anything Nell would buy.

She wore a white, cotton night rail that never would have found its way into Nell's brothel, either. Though plain, it felt soft against her skin and smelled clean. Not scented by cloying perfumes.

She tried to move, but her leg was immobilized. She threw off the blanket and saw bandages wrapped tightly around her leg. She couldn't bend her knee. She couldn't get up. She couldn't walk. She wouldn't be able to run.

Fear, like she'd felt in her nightmares, coursed through her. She started breathing rapidly; she couldn't seem to get enough air to fill her lungs. Because suddenly she knew where she was.

She was at his house. And he wasn't done with her yet. He was going to torture her.

Just then, a young girl came into the room. She was dressed simply in a black dress that buttoned at the neck and ended just above her ankles. She wore sensible black shoes and black woolen stockings. A white mobcap sat atop her head and white bib apron pinned at her chest and tied at her waist.

"Ah, you're awake then," the maid said cheerily. She brought a chamber pot and helped see to her needs. For someone who had done all manner of unspeakable things, this small act of peeing in a pot under the watchful eye of a girl who could not be more than fourteen was one of the most humiliating experiences of her life. Chartreuse felt embarrassed that she couldn't even get out of bed to tend to her most basic necessities. She felt weak as a kitten and helpless as a lamb.

As soon as the girl removed the pot, she slumped back onto the mattress, sweat beading her brow, thoroughly spent.

The maid fluffed her pillows and brought her a much-needed glass of water. After seeing that all her immediate needs had been met, the girl said, "I'll just run along and tell them you're up."

Chartreuse panicked. She didn't know who 'they' were, but she was sure it would end badly for her.

"No, please," she begged, "please don't tell them."

The maid looked at her oddly, bobbed a curtsy and left the room.

Chartreuse needed to flee. She wouldn't just lie here and take it. She looked for a weapon, something she could use to protect herself. She'd kill him if she had to, but she was not going to let him abuse her again.

She'd taken a lot from men over the years. She'd been a victim long enough. This time, she'd go down fighting.

Using all her strength, which wasn't much she discovered, she pushed herself into a sitting position. She had to pause because she was panting and sweating and feared that she would pass out. But then she heard footsteps coming down the hall and was mobilized again into action.

She maneuvered herself to the edge of the bed. It was a high four-poster, but there was a step stool next to it. She got her good leg out and poised on the step stool then swung the bandaged leg out and pushed herself off. She lost her balance and toppled headfirst toward the floor.

"What the hell do you think you're doing?" She heard a man's voice from the doorway just before she landed with a thud.

"Good God woman, are you insane?" It was Chester, no Ian, she couldn't think of him as Lord Chester anymore, not after bedding him. It wasn't Bramly. Relief so profound poured through her that she felt tears streaming down her face. With Ian she knew she was safe. She didn't know why —he was Bramly's nephew, after all; brutality could run in the family. But he had treated her respectfully even when he knew the truth about her. She knew he wouldn't hurt her.

Maybe because he'd been hurt himself so much. Two victims recognized each other.

She propped herself up on her elbows and looked back over her shoulder at him as he limped toward her.

He settled himself down on the stepstool beside the bed. The one she'd fallen off of. The one she was now lying on the floor next to. He made no move to help her up, which was good. She didn't think she could stand. The bound leg throbbed painfully. Her wrapped chest ached. Her left cheek stung. And her body felt bruised and battered. It took too much energy to hold herself up on her elbows, so she eased herself down and rested her right cheek on the carpet.

And stared at his shoes. With his legs stretched out, his feet were right next to her face.

"Now, Chartreuse," he said as calmly and politely as if they were having tea in the drawing room. "Just where did you think you were going? Is my hospitality such an anathema that you'd try to run away?"

"I thought you were Bramly."

"Ah," he said. "So, it was Bramly who did this to you. I wasn't sure. I'd hoped not. I thought perhaps it was retribution from the unsavory underworld characters you associated with, such as Nell Ryan, rather than my uncle."

"How did I get here?" she asked. She didn't bother telling him that Bramly was only able to beat her because Nell had allowed it.

"You were dumped unceremoniously at my door," he replied.

"So, it wasn't a dream." She closed her eyes as she spoke. "They were going to throw me in the river but then Nell changed her mind. She told them to take me to 'his house since it was all his fault.' I assumed she meant Bramly since he did this to me."

She opened her eyes and looked at his shoes again. They were soft leather. One had a higher heel than the other.

"I'm sorry," she said quietly. Those two words held a wealth of meaning. She was sorry she'd ever gotten involved in Bramly's sordid scheme. She was sorry Ian had been left with the aftermath of its failure.

"I'll deal with Bramly and Nell Ryan. You require rest. That leg needs to keep still. You'll not be going anywhere for several weeks, I'm afraid." He stood. Not gracefully. It involved turning slightly to one side and hanging onto the bedclothes to leverage himself up from the low stool. "Now, I shall fetch some burly footmen to put you back in that bed. Do not try to leave it again."

"Why are you being so nice to me after what I tried to do to you?"

He looked down at her battered body lying prone at his feet like some sort of supplicant. She felt anger wafting off of him in waves.

"You didn't deserve this," he said, waving his hand from her head to her leg, "Even for what you did, or tried to do, you didn't deserve this." He turned and walked away. Moments later, two burly footmen arrived, just as he'd promised, and put her back on the bed. As soon as her body settled, she fell into an exhausted sleep.

❧

The next morning, she was awoken by two different burly footmen—the house must be overrun with them—and a sour-faced woman who could only be the housekeeper.

"We're moving you to the servant's quarters where we can keep a better eye on you," one of the footmen said as he lifted her shoulders off the bed. She recognized him as the young man she'd tiptoed past at Acton Park when she sneaked into Ian's bedroom. He'd been with Nell when she barged into the room.

The other footman grabbed her legs. All thought ceased

as she screamed in pain.

"Be careful with her," the sour-faced woman ordered. "Lord Chester wants her to get better, you ninnies." The footman adjusted his grip and managed to find a not-too-uncomfortable position to carry her in.

They headed up the back stairs, Chartreuse dangling like a side of beef between the two men. The room they brought her to was not as well-appointed as the one she'd left, but it was clean and bright. It contained an iron-framed bed and a chest of drawers. A window set between the eaves let in the morning sunlight.

The footmen dropped her on the bed none too gently and immediately left the room. The woman helped her to get settled under the covers. She wiped Chartreuse's brow, which was wet with perspiration from the ordeal of being carried. Her entire body screamed in agony, every muscle was sore, every bruise alive with pain. Her leg felt like it had broken in two.

"There, there, now, you rest. I'll send Bitsy up in a little bit to check on you."

"Thank you, ma'am," she said.

She lay awake for a while after the woman left. The servants' floor was quiet at this time of day. She felt as if she were all alone in the world. Like Rapunzel locked in her tower, she felt helpless and totally at the mercy of the people in this house.

It was exactly the way she'd felt that first night at Nell's. God, she'd been so scared. All she'd wanted to do was go back home. She'd even have been willing to put up with Mr. Granger if only she could go back home.

But she couldn't go back home then, nor could she now. Where was home now anyway? Nell Ryan's brothel? She'd wanted nothing more than to escape from there.

At first, Nell's had seemed like a safe haven, but it soon became her prison.

No, she would never go back to Nell's if she could help it. And she could never go back home. She had to trust that since Ian hadn't thrown her out on the streets immediately, he was going to let her stay at least until she was well.

She wouldn't look beyond then. She'd worry about what to do and where to go then. For now, she would rest.

Chapter 7

"Can I get you anything, miss?" A young girl stood hesitantly in the doorway, the same girl that had helped her the first morning. Chartreuse came groggily awake. The sun was gone from the window, though it was still light outside. She supposed it must be late afternoon.

"Water, please." The girl left and returned ten minutes later with a stoneware pitcher and cup. She helped her sit up to sip some water. "Thank you."

"Do you need to relieve yourself? I can bring you a pot."

She wanted to refuse, wanted to tell the girl to just leave the pot and she'd manage by herself, but she wasn't sure she could. To her credit, the girl managed the particulars in a matter- of-fact manner that made it easier for both of them.

"Will you be needin' anything else, miss?"

"No, no, thank you."

And the girl was gone.

Her days settled into a routine. Breakfast tray in the morning, lunch at noon, tea at six. It was always the same girl, Bitsy. She was sweet and friendly, and Chartreuse grew to like her. She tried to get Bitsy to linger, to share her meal, but Bitsy was always in a hurry. It was obvious that tending to her had been added to Bitsy's other duties, and she was hard pressed to get all her work done for the day.

She hated the long hours alone. At first, all she did was sleep. But as she healed, she spent more time awake. Awake and alone with her thoughts. Thoughts she'd rather not have to entertain.

One afternoon, the physician came. The sour-faced woman, whom Bitsy had told her was Mrs. Pitts, was with him.

"She's well enough to be moved, I'd say." The physician spoke to Mrs. Pitts, acting as though Chartreuse were not even in the room. "The leg's still damaged. I'd keep her off it, but you can have some men carry her down to the kitchen I would think. Shouldn't do any harm."

After that Dickie, the footman from Acton Park, would come and get her each morning. She was given a dark woolen gown to wear, the same clothing as the maids. Bitsy offered to help her dress, but she was determined to do it on her own. She was hobbling now, at least, and no longer needed Bitsy's help with the chamber pot. She couldn't stand for more than a minute or two before her good leg collapsed beneath her, the muscles tired from disuse and not up to the task of bearing all her weight.

Dickie carried her down and set her in a chair in the kitchen by the hearth.

She felt invisible. Servants came and went. All around her was bustling activity. But she sat like a still pool in the middle of a raging sea. Unnoticed. Ignored.

Finally, when she was alone with just Cook, she asked timidly if there was anything she could do. At first, she didn't think Cook had heard her. Or, if she'd heard, that she chose to pretend she didn't. But then the older woman softened. She handed Chartreuse a bowl of peas.

"Snap these," she said.

Chartreuse smiled. Perhaps she wasn't invisible after all.

❧

For the third morning, Dickie came to get her. And for the third morning, he made sure his hand brushed her breast when he lifted her into his arms. When he set her down in the chair, he cupped her crotch and gave her a lurid smile.

"You've been without a man between your legs for a few weeks now, you must be getting lonely. Dickie'll fill you, just you see," he whispered.

"Mmm, I can hardly wait," she said, running her hand up his arm, giving him what he expected from her. "You're making me moist just thinking about it." She pretended sultry seduction. Dickie wet his lips. She grabbed his crotch and squeezed. "I'm sure it's here somewhere. No, that can't be it. That's about the size of the peas I was shucking yesterday. With a name like Dickie, I expected so much more."

Dickie pulled away from her. "You'll get yours."

Their exchange had happened quickly and quietly. She didn't think anyone else in the kitchen had noticed. But when Dickie stepped away from her, she saw that they did have an audience. Ian was watching them from the green baize door that separated the servants' quarters from the main house.

"Is there a problem, Mr. Andrews?"

"No, my lord," Dickie was quick to answer. He gave her one more look that promised more pain than pleasure.

"Then be about your duties." Ian crossed over to her. Anyone who had anywhere else to be quickly escaped to it. Cook tried to look busy. An awkward hush fell over the room as all conversation stopped.

"How are you getting on?" He stood in front of her chair. She was at a disadvantage, having to look up at him as she did.

"I'm doing much better, my lord, thank you."

"Do not attempt to ply your trade in my house, Miss LaRue, or I'll throw you out whether you can walk or not. Is that understood?"

"Perfectly, my lord." They stared at each other for a moment. She refused to look away first.

He nodded once and left through the door that led to the mews, grabbing a scone from the table laid out with the servants' breakfast as he went past.

"Damn," she muttered. Of course, he'd blame her. Dickie could come into her room and rape her in her sleep and it would all be her fault, of course, for leading him on. She'd only be asking for it. She was a whore after all.

"Here's your breakfast, Miss." Bitsy handed her a tray containing tea and scone. She sat apart, in her seat by the hearth, while the servants gathered around the large farmer's table that sat in the middle of the kitchen to break their fast. Dickie was noticeably absent, but no one commented on it even though Dickie never missed a meal.

In a few minutes, the tension eased, and the usual joking and laughter accompanied the scones and jam. She felt like a voyeur from her spot by the hearth. Back to being invisible again.

"So where is Lord Chester off to this morning, Mr. Symmington? It's not like him to visit the mews so early in the day." Bitsy took a bite of scone lathered in butter.

"His friend, Sinclair, invited him to ride Rotten Row this morning," Symmington answered.

A troubled silence fell upon the table. Chartreuse knew what they were all thinking. Rotten Row was where the quality went to ride and to see and be seen. Ian was putting himself out for all of Society to see and gape at.

"They'd better not laugh at him," she threatened from her isolated chair.

"They won't laugh. They're too well-bred for that," Symmington averred. "They may ignore him though, give him the cut direct, which is worse in his world."

"Why is he doing it then?" she persisted.

Symmington regarded her coolly. "It's all about power and appearances. He's showing himself to the ton so they won't believe the rumors his uncle is spreading about him."

"Well, I know all about that, now don't I," she admitted. She wanted it out in the open, all the gory details of her liaison with Ian at Acton Park. She wanted Ian's servants to know that she sided with him, not his uncle.

"We do not discuss the master's business at the breakfast table," Mrs. Pitts decreed. The rest of the meal was eaten in silence.

♨

Ian kept his back perfectly straight as he rode alongside Sinclair on Rotten Row. It was busy this morning, as Sinclair had anticipated. He couldn't believe he'd agreed to this, but Sinclair was adamant. If he continued to hide, Bramly's rumors would gain credence. He had to show himself, let the ton get over their initial horror and begin to accept him as he was.

He didn't believe that would ever happen. The riders who passed them greeted Sinclair warmly, but averted their gaze from him. It was as if he was transparent; everyone seemed to look through him, but no one seemed to see him.

They rode to the end of Rotten Row and back. No one stopped them for conversation, as was occurring all around them. No one said more than a friendly "Good morning." To Sinclair. It was always "Good morning, Sinclair, good to see you." Then a pause and a curt "Lord Chester" with a slight bob of the head and downcast eyes.

He was the elephant in the drawing room that no one wanted to acknowledge.

It was as if his life had been replaced. He remembered being Viscount Morely, that handsome, charming young rake. But Viscount Morely had died in the fire. He'd been reborn as Lord Chester, the Monster Earl.

Even he didn't recognize himself.

They paused outside the gates of Hyde Park.

"Will you join me for breakfast?" he invited Sinclair.

"Certainly, certainly," Sinclair accepted cheerily. "Now, that wasn't so bad, was it? Like I said, you've just got to give them a chance to get used to you."

"How will they become accustomed to the way I look if they don't look at me?" he countered. He was feeling testy. In his opinion, Sinclair's little experiment had failed miserably. "The only person who ever really looks at me is…"

"Who?"

"Never mind." He was thinking of the way Chartreuse had boldly met his stare that morning. She was the only person who would look him in the eye. She didn't flinch, she didn't dart her glance away. It was as if she really saw him. And she didn't care what he looked like. She saw past the burns and scars.

She could see his soul.

"What are the latest rumors about me?" he asked conversationally as they made their way through the quiet streets toward his townhouse.

"You don't want to know."

"I believe I must know."

"Very well, then. The latest rumor is that you wanted to marry a prostitute, but Bramly put a stop to it. You became so enraged that you beat the woman to within an inch of her life and now have her locked up in your house as some kind of sex slave."

He laughed; he couldn't help it. Leave it to Bramly to mix in just enough truth to make the story plausible. He told Sinclair the real story.

"You actually have her living in your house?"

"What else could I do? She's my responsibility. She got caught in the middle of this feud between Bramly and me."

"She's no innocent, Ian. She got what she should expect. She shouldn't have gone along with Bramly's scheme in the first place."

"I'm not sure how much choice she had. Look what happened to her when the scheme failed."

"So what do you plan to do with her? Set her up as your mistress?"

He thought about the way Chartreuse had been teasing Dickie that morning. She was like a bitch in heat, ready to open her legs to any male around.

"I think I prefer my mistresses a little less…well-ridden."

"So what are you going to do with her? Send her back to the brothel she came from?"

He knew he wouldn't do that. Not after Nell Ryan had considered throwing her in the Thames. He really had no idea what he was going to do about Chartreuse LaRue.

❧

By the end of the month, Chartreuse was able to stand for more than a minute with the help of a crutch tucked under her arm. She did her best to make herself useful, helping Cook wherever she could in the kitchen. Most of the servants seemed to accept her presence; at least, they weren't openly hostile. Dickie continued to harass her, poking and grabbing whenever he had the opportunity. She refused to react to him. She didn't want to give Ian any reason to throw her out. She had no place to go.

Dr. Ashcroft came again one Friday afternoon. He declared her fit, no longer in need of special consideration.

"I'd say you're ready to get back to work," he told her, winking knowingly at her. "Of course, that keeps you off your feet anyway, doesn't it?"

The blood drained from her face. He'd been abrupt and dispassionate in his treatment of her, but she'd never felt condescension from him until now. Even Mrs. Pitts scowled at him. He seemed oblivious to their reactions to his comment. He packed up his bag and left.

That night, she couldn't sleep. As soon as Ian learned that she was well, he'd send her on her way. She had no idea what she was going to do.

She had some funds saved, but they were stored safely under the floorboard in her room at Nell's. Nell's was the last place she wanted to go. If she went back, she might never get out again. No, she'd have to abandon her stash.

It wasn't much anyway, not enough blunt to start a new life. Not enough for passage to America or to settle in a country cottage. She had enough to live on for a little while. But what would she do when her funds ran out?

The notes and coins, she'd miss, of course, but more than that, she hated to leave behind the few personal items she'd managed to secret away. Nothing of any real value. Sentimental keepsakes she should have discarded years ago.

The thought of losing them pained her but they weren't worth the risk of going back for them.

She'd walk the streets before she went back to Nell's. But women who plied the trade alone in alleyways didn't long survive.

The house grew quiet around her. She paced in her room, no longer pretending to limp as she had been for the past few days. Since Dr. Ashcroft had informed Mrs. Pitts that she was completely healed, she needn't hide the truth any longer.

If only Ian would let her stay here. She'd do anything if he would let her stay.

The servants had begun to accept her presence. At least, they weren't openly hostile towards her. Some, like Bitsy, had even treated her kindly.

Somewhere in the house, a door slammed. She heard distant voices. The master returning home from his evening out.

He had gone to the theater this evening. He was trying so hard to get back the life he'd led before the fire had changed everything.

She wished him luck. What she would give for a chance to go back to the way things were. Before her father died. Before her mother remarried. Before Nell's.

No use longing for the past. She needed to think about her future.

She heard Symmington coming upstairs to his rooms. Ian must have dismissed him for the night.

The house settled back into silence.

She should leave before they had a chance to throw her out. She didn't want to leave. She had nowhere to go.

She had to do something. She had to convince Ian to let her stay.

Softly, she opened her door and tiptoed down the back stairs. She entered the hallway where Ian's rooms were and crept silently to his door. She entered without knocking, just as she had that night at Acton Park.

Only tonight she would not take him unawares. She would make him ask. She would make him beg.

The room was empty. The bed had been turned down, but he wasn't in it. Symmington must have decided not to wait up any longer.

She considered climbing into his bed and waiting for him but was afraid that would just make him angry. She didn't want to do anything to anger him.

The wall sconces were still lit on the stairway. She went down the main staircase to the main floor. She had been living in this house for over three months, but she'd never seen this part of it. She'd been relegated to the servants' quarters.

The staircase ended in a marble-floored foyer. A door opened down the hall.

"Good night, then, my lord." Griggs closed the door behind him and went towards the back of the house where his quarters were.

Going to the door Griggs had just exited, she raised her hand to knock, then thought better of it. She turned the knob instead and let herself in.

The room was in semi-darkness, but she could tell from the bookcases lining the walls that it was the library. A low fire burnt in the grate. She hesitated in the doorway. She must have made some sound, because Ian said from his chair in front of the fireplace "Who's there?"

"It's just me, my lord, Chartreuse." He stood and looked at her.

"What are you doing here?" His eyes scanned the soft cotton night gown she was wearing. It covered her from neck to toes, giving her the illusion of innocence though they both knew she was no innocent.

"I need to speak with you, my lord," she stammered.

"Can't it wait until morning?"

He was still in his evening clothes, though he'd removed his jacket and loosened his cravat.

"I'm afraid…" Chartreuse swallowed and tried again. "I wanted to speak with you before you saw Mrs. Pitts in the morning, my lord."

❧

"Oh? What do you want me to know before Mrs. Pitts has a chance to tell me?" He assumed she'd done something Mrs. Pitts didn't like, perhaps she'd had passionate sex with Dickie on the table in the kitchen while the rest of the household staff watched. The image flashed through his mind quickly, but not so quickly that his groin didn't harden at the thought.

"Let me get you some more brandy," she offered, reaching for the near-empty glass in his hand.

He pulled it away before she could reach it. "The brandy is fine. Why don't you just say what you sought me out to say."

"Very well, then. Dr. Ashcroft was here today. He has declared me completely healed."

"And?" he said.

"There's no longer any reason for me to be here, unless…"

"Unless what?"

"Unless you want me here." She closed the distance between them. She ran her hand up his arm. Her other hand cupped his cock. "I can make you very happy, my lord, just like I did that night at Acton Park," she purred.

"I'm not sure I'd bring that up if I were you. That's what precipitated this whole disaster if you recall."

"Please, my lord, let me stay. I'll help Cook in the kitchen all day and warm your bed at night. Don't send me back to Nell's."

"I had no intention of returning you to Nell Ryan's brothel, if that's what you fear."

He needed to put some distance between them before he gave in and let her have her way with him. Already, his cock was waking with her gentle stroking. Walking to the table next to his chair, he refilled his brandy glass himself.

"Sit," he said, gesturing to the matching chair next to his. He poured a glass of brandy and handed it to her.

They sat in silence for a few minutes sipping their brandies.

"I don't really know what to do about you, Chartreuse," he admitted. "What do you want?"

"I've enjoyed helping Cook in the kitchen. Perhaps I could be her assistant?" She sounded so hopeful it pained him.

"And be my bed mate at night?"

"If you want. I'll do anything you want. Anything."

He looked at her then, really looked at her as if seeing her for the first time. The bruises had faded but a scar still caused faint discoloration on her cheek. Her braided hair hung over her left shoulder and she wore a silly-looking mob cap on her head.

She looked young, like the debutante he'd first mistaken her for. She looked virginal, all traces of the seductress he knew her to be gone.

"You must be desperate if you're willing to bed me." He took a long sip of brandy, enjoyed the burn as it made its way down his throat.

Her forehead wrinkled in confusion.

"I've already bedded you," she reminded him. "You're just a man like any other."

"Oh, you see all men as monsters?"

He could see the truth of it in her eyes. It didn't matter to her what he looked like because to her one man was the same as the next.

&8

She looked away, afraid that she'd revealed too much. She changed her tactic.

"That night with you in Acton Park was wonderful. I become aroused just thinking about it." She came over and straddled his lap. "Don't you want that again?" She caressed his face and trailed kisses down his cheek, the damaged, scarred cheek. "I want to feel your hard, throbbing cock deep inside me, pounding away at me." She started rubbing her crotch against him. His body reacted the way she knew it would; she could feel his cock hardening beneath her. "I'll come to you every night. No one else needs to know. It will be our little secret."

He grabbed her hands and pushed her off his lap. She

landed hard on her bottom at his feet.

"God," he said, his voice loathing in disgust. "You'd fuck a dog if it would get you what you want."

She looked up at him and dropped the veneer of innocence, letting him see the drawn, world-weary face of the experienced whore she was. "What makes you think I haven't?"

She hadn't, but she'd witnessed it once. One of the other girls, but it could as easily have been her. As far as he was concerned, it may as well have been. The dirt of Nell's stained her.

He released her hands. She wrapped her arms around her knees. She stayed on the floor at his feet, staring into the fire. She'd lost. He didn't want her. He was disgusted by her.

"I'll leave in the morning," she said softly.

"Where will you go?"

She shrugged.

"Don't worry about me, my lord. There's always a demand for my services, even if you don't want them. I'll get by."

It didn't matter anymore, anyway. Once a whore, always a whore. She may as well just accept it.

❧

Ian's heart softened. Gently, he touched her hair. Her braid was coming undone. He twirled a long golden strand that had come loose, wrapping it around his finger.

"As I said before, I have no intention of returning you to Nell Ryan. You may stay. I'll speak to Mrs. Pitts and have her find a place for you on the household staff. You will be paid servant wages and will not supplement your income with any other activities. Do I make myself clear? And you will not, I repeat, you will not be sharing my bed."

She jumped up and threw her arms around him. It was a

hug, not a passionate embrace but a warm, grateful, enthusiastic hug. He couldn't help himself. He hugged her back. She was warm and solid, and the human contact felt so good.

"Oh, Ian, thank you, I mean, my lord. Thank you, my lord." She pulled away from him and smiled. He was once again taken aback at how beautiful she was, even with the fading scar marring her face. "You won't be sorry. Tell Mrs. Pitts not to worry. I'll be the best damn servant you've ever had."

He must be mad. Maybe Bramly was right. Maybe the fire had cooked his brain. He had just hired a prostitute to serve in his household. And not in his bed. The only woman in all of England who wasn't horrified at the thought of sharing his bed, and he'd banned her from it.

The question was: would he be able to keep himself out of hers?

❧

He sent Chartreuse back to her room. Having finished his brandy, he went up to his own.

He stripped off his clothes, but rather than immediately donning a nightshirt as he'd grown accustomed to doing, he strode over to the cheval glass and stood before it naked. He avoided looking at himself usually. He didn't need to; he could see what he looked like reflected in the eyes of those around him. Mostly, it was reflected in the way they averted their eyes.

He knew he looked like a monster.

Tonight he appraised himself as objectively as possible. His body was a patchwork of scars. There on his torso was the spot where his clothing had stuck to him and was ripped away, leaving a gaping wound that had blackened with infection. The physicians had used maggots to clean it out. His right arm had only been lightly burned and was now completely healed. There was no trace of redness, yet it had been one of the most painful areas while he was healing. His left arm had been less fortunate and showed thick scarring where the burn wounds had contracted. It was rough to the touch.

Both legs were relatively unscarred. A few spots where his clothing had singed him, but nothing too serious. His genitals he'd instinctively protected, but the tip of his penis had been singed.

He turned and surveyed his back. He recalled the months of excruciating pain, when he could find no comfortable position. He could lie on neither his stomach nor his back nor his left side. He'd spent six months trying to stay perfectly still lying on his right side.

He'd cried and railed and begged the physicians to put him out of his misery. He'd lived in an opium-induced stupor.

He'd wished he were dead.

Turning to face the mirror once again, he lifted his eyes to examine his face. His face, yet not his face. In his mind's eye, he still saw himself as he was before. Handsome, confident, with a ready smile of even, white teeth and sensuous lips. He'd had two evenly matched dimples in his cheeks. He was a model of British aristocracy with his high cheekbones and long narrow nose.

Now he looked like a marble bust that someone had smashed with a hammer.

He pulled his hair back, allowing nothing to conceal the awful reality. His left eye was gone, the eyelid burned off, the socket scarred over. His left cheek was gnarled and pebbly with scars. His lips were distorted.

He turned away in disgust. This was what vanity wrought.

He'd been so cocky, so sure of himself. Women had flocked to him. He'd been able to pick and choose.

Now, he was reduced to consorting with prostitutes. And he couldn't even bring himself to do that.

Chartreuse was good. She was quite capable of pretending his body didn't repulse her. She had him half believing tonight that she actually wanted him.

But he saw the truth in her eyes. It was all a lie. She didn't want him any more than she wanted any other man. It was just business. A means to an end. She'd exchange her body for a roof over her head and regular meals to eat.

If all he wanted was to masturbate in a willing body, the transaction would be fine. Lord knew, she could certainly arouse him.

It just wasn't enough. He needed to know that he could bring satisfaction to a woman. He needed her to want him. Really want him, not just pretend to.

He looked at himself one last time before drawing the nightshirt over his head and cursed himself for being nine times a fool. What woman would want him ever again?

Maybe he was keeping Chartreuse near just in case having her pretend to want him became enough.

Chapter 8

Cook insisted that she didn't need an assistant, so Char-treuse became a housemaid and an incompetent one at that. She knew that if Ian hadn't insisted on keeping her on, Mrs. Pitts would have fired her within a week.

She had to wonder at her sanity. She worked from morning until night at all manner of drudgery, from cleaning the coals from the fireplace to emptying slop buckets. She was still treated like an outsider by the other servants, like she was some kind of unclean, disease-carrying leper. And her pay was only one tenth what she could earn at Nell's.

Yet she was happier than she'd been in years. She felt whole again. She'd lost so much of herself in the time she'd spent at Nell's. Even before then, at the hands of her step-father.

The other servants couldn't understand her cheerfulness. It seemed they spent most of their days complaining. She never complained, no matter what task she was assigned. She knew she was here on sufferance and was going to make every effort to stay in Mrs. Pitts's good graces.

Most of the servants, she knew, suspected that she was sleeping with Ian. They made suggestive remarks around her, wondering how the master slept last night, winking and nodding all the while. At least having the servants think she was Ian's personal property kept Dickie and the other footmen from bothering her. They were not about to encroach on the master's territory.

So when Mrs. Pitts ordered her to clean the music room one rainy afternoon, she went eagerly. It was the first time in the three weeks since she'd started that she was going to be working alone. That at least told her that Mrs. Pitts was starting to trust her. With the way everyone had been watching her, she felt sure they expected her to abscond with the silver and sneak off into the night.

She stood in the doorway to the music room, which was adjacent to the second-floor ballroom. The room was magnificent with high ceilings and tall windows letting in the early afternoon light. She carried with her a feather duster and cloth, dust mop, and detailed instructions from Mrs. Pitts on what to do, but more importantly, what not to do.

Since she had made a total mess out of cleaning the hearth in the study the previous afternoon, she felt certain this was the safest place that Mrs. Pitts could think to assign her.

She couldn't think of anywhere she'd rather be. For there, in the center of the room, stood a magnificent instrument. A grand pianoforte. Her fingers itched to touch the keyboard. Surely if she hurried with her work, there'd be no harm in trying it out.

She dusted the chairs and paintings. She ran her cloth over the wainscoting. She mopped the floor.

Then, she sat. She opened the lid that protected the keyboard from dust. Tentatively, she touched middle C. Its rich tone sounded loud and pure in the large room, echoing off the walls. The acoustics in the music room were perfect.

She tried a chord. Then a melody. She played an old favorite of her father's, Mozart's "Moonlight Sonata."

It was such a joy to be playing a piano that was actually in tune. At Nell's, she had often been called upon to entertain the guests at the piano that Nell kept in the parlor, but it was sadly out of tune. The only songs she was allowed to play were bawdy drinking songs or ballads. Occasionally she'd sneak down during the day when the house was asleep to practice some of the classical pieces she'd learned in her youth.

She'd bribed Bill and Pike to bring her sheet music, which she'd hidden under the floorboards in her room along with her bank notes and whatever else she cherished. The girls at Nell's were well known for borrowing—and never returning—each other's possessions. More than one fight had broken out over the ownership of a shawl or trinket.

She lifted the seat of the piano bench and found music. It was like finding treasure. She quickly sorted through and picked out a waltz by Haydn and began to play.

She was so lost in the music that she didn't notice the woman standing in the doorway until she finished and the woman applauded. The woman was fashionably dressed and was obviously a guest in the house.

"Please forgive me, ma'am," she said, quickly gathering her things and preparing to make a hasty exit.

Before she could make good on her escape, though, Ian and another gentleman entered the room. She recognized him immediately and could tell that he remembered her as well.

Seeing Derek Lancaster, Viscount Fontaine, was like a splash of cold water. Too many men knew her.

She hadn't serviced Lord Fontaine himself. She had been entertaining his younger brother, Gordon, when Fontaine stormed in bent on saving his innocent brother from her evil clutches. He didn't know that his brother was no innocent. Master Gordon had been quite experienced and knew just what he'd wanted from her, putting his requests in the most graphic terms.

They were of an age, she and young Master Gordon Lancaster, but his experience of sex was far different from hers. For him, it was just a bit of fun. He was on a quest, he'd told her, to poke a hundred different women by the time he turned twenty. He'd already run through all the willing and available servants and local girls at home. Now he was turning to whores. She was number forty-one.

She warned him about the risks he was taking, the diseases he could catch, but he would hear none of it. They'd just finished up when his brother had burst in on them. The change in Master Gordon was extraordinary. The cheeky lad who had boisterously enjoyed their bed play became a quiet schoolboy totally cowed by his older brother.

She surmised that Master Gordon was using his sexual prowess as a means of rebellion against the controls of his family. Of course, rebellion means nothing if your family doesn't know you are doing it. And Master Gordon's family had no idea what he was about.

Fontaine quickly escorted Gordon out and tossed Chartreuse a sovereign, admonishing her to stay away from his brother. How would he react to seeing her in Ian's household? He'd probably give Ian an earful, reminding him just who and what she was. This respite she'd had of temporary respectability was most likely over. Ian would no doubt let her go.

Face pale, she curtsied and left the room.

❧

"Daphne, why don't you go wait in the parlor. I've asked Griggs to send a tea cart up. I'd like a word alone with Ian, please."

"Certainly, dear. Ian, how unusual to have a housemaid who can play the piano. Did you hear her? She's quite talented."

As soon as his wife was safely out of earshot, Derek turned on him.

"What the hell do you mean by allowing your sister to be confronted by your mistress," Derek seethed.

His first impulse was to deny Chartreuse's past, but he could see that wouldn't work.

"She isn't my mistress," he said calmly.

"The woman's a whore. She works at a brothel. What else would she be doing here if not to service your needs?"

Ian was surprised at how angry he got with Derek for calling Chartreuse a whore. Not long ago, he'd called her the same thing.

"Whatever her past occupation, she is now working here as a servant and will be accorded the respect that position deserves."

"Maybe Bramly was right," Derek said. "Maybe the pain did make you lose your mind. What other explanation could there be for you to have a known prostitute living under your roof, being passed off as a servant."

"So, Bramly went crawling to you, did he?"

"He told me you'd threatened to banish him to Yorkshire."

"Let me tell you a few things about my dear Uncle Bramly. Chartreuse is living here because Bramly beat her to within an inch of her life. This was after she'd failed to carry out his latest scheme to discredit me so he can take over managing my assets. Bramly can go to hell as far as I'm concerned. The offer of the Yorkshire estate is no longer on the table. I would, however, pay one-way passage for him to America, or China perhaps. Anywhere so long as he is far away from me."

"Can you prove that it was Bramly, or do you just have the girl's word? She'd say anything to get a deal like this. Be careful, Ian. She'll rob you blind."

"Chartreuse and I understand each other," he said. "She won't take anything I'm not willing to give. Come, Daphne's waiting for us."

"You're being played for a fool," Derek warned him.

Chartreuse fled to the safety of the kitchen. She returned the duster, polish, and mop to the cupboard. Hoping to steal a few minutes to compose herself, she dawdled at the task of scrubbing her hands.

"Ah, good," Mrs. Pitts said, "you've finished your chores. Put on a clean apron and assist Mr. Griggs with the tea cart. His lordship's sister, Lady Fontaine, is waiting in the front parlor."

Mrs. Pitts's voice softened when she mentioned Lady Fontaine.

"Perhaps you would prefer to assist yourself," she suggested. "I'm sure you'd like to see Lord Chester's sister."

Mrs. Pitts paused as though considering the idea, then Bitsy hurried down the back stairs, soot covering her face and hands, panic in her voice, as she shouted, "Mrs. Pitts, come quick, the chimney in the nursery is clogged!"

"Oh, dear Lord," Mrs. Pitts said, "why on earth were you lighting a fire in the nursery? That room hasn't been used in years." She started to follow Bitsy back up the stairs. "Chartreuse, the tea cart, now!"

Curtsying in acknowledgement, Chartreuse grabbed a clean apron and went through the baize door that led to the front of the house. She caught up with Mr. Griggs as he reached the parlor door. After holding the door open for him, she followed him in.

She kept her head down, hoping she'd be invisible to a woman accustomed to having servants wait upon her all her life. She couldn't be that lucky. Of course, Lady Fontaine noticed her and recognized her from the music room.

"My dear, your playing was quite lovely. Wherever did you have the opportunity to learn?"

Chartreuse knew her place and knew she was not supposed to engage in conversation with the guests. Griggs, who was directing her setting up the tea service, scowled at her. But she didn't want to be rude and not answer a direct question.

"I learned as a child, ma'am," she said.

"Yes, but how? Most servants aren't given music lessons."

She didn't know what to say but was saved from answering when the gentlemen entered the room. Though she'd hoped to avoid seeing Lord Fontaine again—and by the scathing look he directed her way, he felt the same—she was at least grateful his and Ian's arrival distracted Lady Fontaine and allowed her to ignore the question.

"Stop badgering the maid, Daphne," Fontaine said, bending to buss his wife on her cheek.

"I wasn't badgering, I was merely asking," Lady Fontaine retorted, not at all intimidated by her husband.

Ian smiled indulgently at his sister, leaving Chartreuse once more surprised to see how a smile transformed him from monster to rogue. With a nod of his head he dismissed her and Griggs from the room.

Griggs gave her a disapproving look when they entered the hall together, but he didn't say anything. She was certain she would hear about it later from Mrs. Pitts. Servants were supposed to be unseen, and today she had been noticed by both Lord and Lady Fontaine.

❧

Ian had had a bad afternoon. It had started with Derek's reprimand and continued when, after seeing Daphne and Derek on their way, he'd taken out his phaeton and gone for a ride in the park. It was part of his strategy to see and be seen, much like the morning rides to Rotten Row that he'd been enduring with Sinclair. Surely if the haute ton saw enough of him, they would stop being so horrified.

He needed to establish himself as the Earl of Chester, competent, arrogant, and powerful.

He'd made the circuit of the park, nodding to anyone who would glance at him, when he passed her. Lady Hilary Cross, now Countess Cosgrove. He'd known Cosgrove, her husband, since school days. He at least had the manners to stop.

"Chester," Cosgrove said. "Heard you were back in town."

"Good to see you, Cosgrove. Lady Cosgrove."

Hilary turned green at the sight of him. She hadn't come to see him when he was recuperating, and he was glad she stayed away. She was too delicate a creature to be exposed to the horror that he'd become.

But now that he was back in Society, there was no way for her to avoid it.

"My lord, how nice to see you…well," she stammered, unable to disguise her shock at his appearance.

He didn't detain them long, making his excuses as quickly as politely possible. How relieved she must be that he allowed her to cry off and didn't hold her to her commitment to marry him.

She must be having nightmares tonight about the life she could have spent chained to a monster.

He was restless after dining, as usual, alone. He had no invitations for the evening. He roamed the house from room to room, finally stopping in the music room.

He'd probably been heading there all along. He needed music to soothe his soul, and he needed Chartreuse to ease the rest of him. He had Griggs send for her.

Chartreuse wasn't surprised when Ian sent for her after dinner that evening. Mrs. Pitts told her he was waiting for her in the music room. Had she damaged the sheet music she had played earlier in the day? Was he angry that she'd had the audacity to touch the piano? Had Lord Fontaine convinced him that it was totally inappropriate to have her working in his household?

She was prepared for the worst. She was prepared to be sent packing back to Nell Ryan's brothel.

Ian was standing in front of one of the floor-length windows that graced the far wall. It was dark outside, but the curtains had not yet been drawn. The light from the candelabra that stood on the piano reflected in the glass panes. From across the room, she couldn't make out his expression. She couldn't tell if he was angry at her.

"Good evening, my lord," she said as she dipped a curtsy for him.

"Please sit." He indicated the piano bench where Lady Fontaine had caught her earlier.

Nervously, she sat. She noticed that a piece of music had been laid out. It was not the piece she had played earlier. It was not a piece she had ever played before.

"I was impressed by your playing earlier, the little bit I heard of it. I was hoping you wouldn't mind playing a piece for me."

"I don't know this one. I'm sorry, my lord."

"Do the best you can." He moved to one of the benches along the wall and sat to listen.

She read the music over then placed her fingers on the keyboard. She made it through the first page without making too many mistakes, though the tempo was slow. The second page was largely repetitive, so by the end of the piece, she was feeling more confident. She played it a second time, just to be sure she had it right.

The final chord echoed in the cavernous room. She

placed her hands in her lap and waited.

"That was lovely," he said. "You play quite well. Perhaps you could play for me in the evenings when I am at home."

She swiveled on the bench to face him.

"You're asking me to play for you?" She laughed. "I can't think of anything I would rather do. This is such a wonderful instrument. I've never played anything so fine." She stood and walked over to him.

Kneeling in front of him, she took his hands in hers then bent her head to kiss them.

"You can't imagine what a gift you've just given me," she whispered. "How shall I ever be able to repay you?"

&

He bent over her and lightly kissed her hair.

"You don't need to repay me. Just play for me. It will be mutually beneficial," he said softly.

He wanted her, for all his principles about wanting more than base, animal coupling. He might never get more.

His reentry into society was proving difficult. He did not receive the invitations a man of his status should. He knew it was because he made his hostesses uncomfortable. They never knew where to seat him at dinner. They feared his presence would ruin their other guests' appetites.

Where once he'd been highly sought after, now he was spurned. He hated to admit the depth of his loneliness. Was it so wrong to accept this physical, human contact?

He wouldn't force her, but when she moved her hands up his thighs, he didn't stop her.

She unbuttoned his breeches and pulled him out, throbbing and ready.

She sucked on him; he stopped even thinking about stopping her. He stopped thinking about anything but what she was doing to him with her expert mouth.

When she had him near climax, she lifted her skirts and

positioned herself on his lap. Straddling him, she placed him inside her, and he was in heaven. It was better than the night at Acton Park because he was fully awake and fully aroused. She set up the rhythm, and he followed.

It didn't take long before he shouted his release. He pulled her to him and held her while his breathing returned to normal.

"Mmm," she murmured. "That was wonderful."

Ian chuckled. "It was for me, anyway. I can't imagine you got much enjoyment out of it."

She looked at him as though he was speaking a foreign tongue. "It's enough that I satisfied you."

"Have you ever enjoyed making love?"

She didn't answer him. Instead, she got off him and fixed her clothing. He stood and did the same.

"I'm sorry," he said. "I'm not in the habit of accosting my servants."

"But I'm not an ordinary servant, am I? Be honest, my lord. The reason you kept me here was so this might happen. You needn't feel guilty about it. I'm a whore. What else are whores good for?"

He ran his hand over his face. "I have no right to use you this way. I'm no better than…my God, I'm no better than Bramly. I will, of course, compensate you."

"Did I ask you for money? I did this," she waved her hand to indicate what had transpired between them, "to thank you. For not sacking me because I spoke to your sister and for letting me play the piano. Besides," giving him a gamin smile, "you looked like you were in serious need of a fuck."

He burst out laughing. "What the hell am I going to do about you?"

"Right now, you can send me to my bed. I'm about dead on my feet, and Mrs. Pitts doesn't allow any slug-a-beds."

He let her go but determined that he would set her up as

his mistress. He could picture himself visiting her each evening, having her play for him, then sharing her bed.

Chapter 9

Chartreuse hummed as she helped Bitsy clean the soot from the fireplace bricks and hearth in the nursery. Mrs. Pitts had made quick work of dousing the small conflagration Bitsy had caused, at Dicky's prompting. The chimney had been cleaned, and the long-neglected nursery was now being given the same sprucing up as the rest of the house. No doubt in the hope that Lord Chester would soon marry and begin populating the room with his offspring.

"Why would Dicky trick me into lighting the fire in the first place?" Bitsy asked for the thousandth time.

"Dicky likes to cause mischief," she said. "But Mrs. Pitts is on to him. She'll bring it to Mr. Griggs, who will no doubt discipline him."

Bitsy blanched at that. "I wouldn't want to get him into trouble."

"He had no compunction about getting you in trouble."

Bitsy laughed.

"Compunction," she said. "Sometimes when you talk you sound like a right toff."

Chartreuse smiled. "I can teach you if you want."

"No, thank you." Bitsy scrubbed hard at a particularly

stubborn spot of soot. "My Mam told me that book learning would only make me chafe at minding my place."

"Oh, I don't know about that," she said. "I've had book learning, and I am very happy with my current place. There's satisfaction in falling into bed at night after a full day of labor knowing you've done your job well."

Bitsy snorted. "Most days I'm just glad I haven't been sacked."

Chartreuse could agree with that. She'd thought for sure she was being sacked last night.

Mrs. Pitts came in to inspect their work.

"Lord Chester wants to see you in his study," she said. Chartreuse and Bitsy looked at each other.

"Am I being sacked?" Bitsy asked.

"Not you. He wants to see Chartreuse."

"Am I being sacked?" Her heart skipped a beat. Had he changed his mind?

"I have no idea what he wants; he simply requested that I send you to him. Don't keep his lordship waiting."

Wiping her soot-blackened hands on her damp apron, she descended the stairs to the study wondering how she could convince him to change his mind.

"Go and pack your things," he said as soon as she entered the room. "I've found a house for you."

"What? I don't understand." He looked so happy she couldn't help smiling.

"Well, you can't stay here now that you're my mistress. Can't risk having you run into Daphne again. Derek would have my head for sure then."

She dropped her smile and felt the color drain from her face. Her legs shook so much that she lowered herself into a chair to keep from falling to the floor.

"I'm not your mistress."

"I'm offering you a carte blanche. You'll have a house, servants, a clothing allowance. I'll be very generous."

"I don't want to be your mistress." A sick feeling settled in the pit of her stomach. She'd made an egregious mistake last night and now she'd have to pay. She'd been so grateful to him for letting her stay, for letting her play the piano, she'd thanked him the only way she knew how. Bitsy was right. She didn't know her place. And now she'd lost it.

"Can't bear to be my mistress, you mean," he said, looking like a little boy who had just had his favorite toy taken away from him. "I see."

"No, you don't see. If you had offered me a carte blanche that night at Acton Park, I would have leaped at the opportunity. But now, I… I like being a servant."

"No one likes being a servant. At least be honest. Is it the thought of having to bed me every night that repulses you? Or is it that I would expect exclusivity, and you would have to confine your appetites to me?" His anger lashed her, feeding her own.

Of course he'd think she was wanton and delighted in bedding total strangers.

"I don't want to be anyone's mistress." She stood and stalked over to the fireplace. Trying to collect her thoughts, she fidgeted with the ornaments that decorated the mantel, which she'd dusted just yesterday. "Whether it's one man or a hundred, it's still the same thing, isn't it? It's still whoring." She looked at him where he stood across the room. "I don't want to be a whore anymore."

"What about last night?"

"Last night was the first time I ever chose to give myself to a man. I've been taken or sold, but I've never willingly given. I meant it as a gift, not a business transaction."

"Chartreuse…"

She held up her hand to stop him. How could she explain something she didn't understand herself?

"I had a lot of time to think while I was recovering. My stepfather preyed on me, but I chose to stay at Nell's. I could have left if I really wanted to. I didn't because I thought that was all I was good for. My stepfather blamed me because he couldn't keep his hands off me. I guess I started believing that he was right, that it was my fault. That there was something inside me that was damaged.

"But since I've been working here, I've felt whole again. I've felt like I can be something more than a vessel to slake men's lust. I like to make things clean. I like having the respect of the other servants. I like having a purpose. Yesterday, you weren't ashamed to have me meet your sister."

He started to move as though he meant to take her in his arms, as though he wanted to give her comfort, assure her that everything would be alright. She longed for him to but feared if he did, she'd melt and give him anything he asked. She felt like a wounded bird, vulnerable and afraid. Tears welled in her eyes.

But he stayed the motion and remained where he was, across the room, leaving the distance separating them. She missed the closeness they'd shared last night, but she had to refuse him. If she had any hope of reshaping her life, she had to start now.

He seemed to be considering what she'd said and for a moment she hoped he'd accept her explanation, but then his expression hardened. She knew he'd rejected it. And why wouldn't he? She'd lain with hundreds of men, yet she refused him. Of course, it would sting, given his sensitivity about his appearance.

Not as much as his offer stung her. She'd thought, for a moment last night, that he saw her. Not as a whore, but as a person. She'd been wrong. He was just a man. Never satisfied with what was offered. Always needing, demanding, more.

"You can't stay here now after what happened last night. I'll have Mrs. Pitts give you a reference and help you find another position."

His words stabbed her. He was sending her away. Discarding her. Giving her an ultimatum. Be his mistress or serve another household. She should accept his offer of a reference, but the thought of starting anew in another residence terrified her. Did he really think that her past wouldn't follow her? Servants talked. Reference or no, she'd never find another position comparable to the one he'd given her. And he knew it. He was setting her up to fail. Cornering her. Giving her no choice but to accept his offer.

"Please, Ian, please let me stay." She hated begging, but she'd kiss his feet if only he'd reconsider.

He crossed the room and grabbed her roughly by the arms.

"You can't have it both ways. If you stay, I can't trust myself around you. Like your stepfather, I can't keep my hands off you."

His hold on her arms bruised her as he shook her. Tears spilled from her eyes as disappointment more than fear assailed her. Why had she thought he was any different from any other man? From his uncle? That she could say no to a man as powerful as he? To any man for that matter? They always held the power.

She felt herself shutting down, retreating into the protective shell she'd lived in for years, that she'd only recently crawled out of.

He let her go as suddenly as he'd grabbed her and turned his back to her.

Shaking, she rubbed her arms where his hands had dug into them.

"Alright," she said, giving in to him. Feeling defeated. Not brave enough to call him on his offer to find her a new position. Who knew what kind of position that would be? Would he pawn her off on one of his friends who would expect the same services she'd given him the previous evening? Better the devil she knew. "I'll be your mistress."

"I can think of nothing more unappealing than an un-willing mistress," he muttered. He turned to face her, still looking remote and unapproachable. "My offer is rescinded. Just tell me one thing and be truthful. If I were any other man, would you refuse? To be blunt, is it because of the way I look that you don't want to be my mistress?"

How could the man be so obtuse? He looked away so his damaged cheek faced her. She reached up and gently touched it. "I don't notice the way you look, Ian. I see the man beneath the scars. No, I would not accept your offer, even if you were unscarred. Would you have made the offer to me if you thought you could do better? Aren't you the one who can't accept how you look?"

Ian grasped the hand that caressed his cheek and lightly kissed its palm. "I think we both have scars we need to learn to live with." He stepped back from her, putting some distance between them. "I apologize for my behavior. It was unforgiveable. Did I hurt you?"

She shook her head even though she knew she'd sport bruises for a few days. She held her breath, waiting for him to decide her fate.

"You may return to your duties," he said. "I won't bother you again."

Relief flooded her.

"Thank you, my lord." She curtsied and hurried out of the room before he changed his mind.

❧

Ian kept his days full. He spent most afternoons at his clubs where he could participate in political discussions and exert some influence over his peers. He was still undecided about taking his seat in Lords, but at least he was making his opinions known.

Gentlemen seemed ready to accept him, once they got over their initial shock at his appearance. But they weren't willing to introduce him to their ladies. Therefore, his evenings were usually spent at home.

Even though she refused to be his mistress, he still had Chartreuse play the piano for him in the evenings. Listening to her play was balm to his sagging spirit. And, he hoped, made up somewhat for the horrendous way he'd treated her when she'd rejected his offer of a carte blanche.

He always made sure that either Griggs or a footman was present, ostensibly to see to his needs, refilling his brandy or lighting his cigar, but in reality, there to act as chaperone. He didn't want a repeat of that first night in the music room, and he couldn't trust himself to be alone with Chartreuse.

She was too beautiful. When she played, she seemed entranced. She became part of the music. Such a look of peace and joy came upon her, he couldn't help but stare.

He lusted after her constantly, more than once imagining taking her to his room, slowly undressing her, laying her down on his bed, kissing her from head to toe, and making love to her all night long.

He hadn't given in to his urges. Yet.

She finished playing. It was a new piece that he'd picked up yesterday. She'd practiced it all afternoon and had played it more than competently.

"Come, join me in a brandy. You deserve it." He'd had a sofa moved into the music room for comfortable seating. The room's formal furnishings were designed to be decorative, not functional.

Unable to stifle a yawn, Griggs, who had been stoically standing by throughout Chartreuse's recital, poured them each a glass of brandy. Ian realized how selfish he was being.

"That will be all, Griggs. You may retire for the evening. If I need anything else, Chartreuse will get it for me."

Griggs gave Chartreuse a pointed look. Ian sighed. Of

course, the entire household knew of her former occupation. They all knew about the night at Acton Park and probably knew of the incident in the music room three weeks ago.

"How are they treating you below-stairs?" he asked when Griggs was gone.

"Fine, my lord." Then she smiled. "Though everyone assumes that I'm sleeping with you. I think they watch what they say around me in case it should get back to you."

"I retract my rescission. The offer to become my mistress still stands."

"My refusal to be your mistress still stands, also, my lord."

They sat in companionable silence for a few minutes.

"Daphne is determined to find me a wife," he said. "I suppose she'll find some foolish chit desperate enough for a fortune and a title to tie herself to an ogre like me."

Chartreuse sighed. "This self-pity of yours becomes rather wearying after a while."

"You think I feel sorry for myself?"

"You survived the fire, Ian. Don't you think it's time you started living again?"

"Come with me." He grabbed her hand and pulled her through the adjoining ballroom, up the stairs to the gallery that formed a mezzanine around the ballroom. He stopped in front of his portrait.

"That is who I was," he said, pointing to it. It showed a handsome young man, proud and arrogant in his bearing, but with a rakish smile that softened his features. "I was cocky and self-assured. I knew exactly who I was and where I stood in society. I knew that I would be Chester and I understood all the responsibilities that entailed.

"The fire changed me. It didn't harden me like steel. It melted me like wax. It isn't just the way I look; it's the way I feel. I don't know who I am."

She stared at the portrait for a full minute before speaking.

"You are Chester, an earl of the realm. You have wealth and power. You have loyal servants, family, and friends."

"I need laudanum to sleep at night, brandy to make it through the day. I still feel pain though the doctors can't explain why. I am fully healed, they tell me, yet I still feel ill most of the time.

"I was content to stay on my country estate and live out my life quietly until you and my uncle Bramly invaded my sanctuary and forced me back into the world.

"Some days, no, most days, I wish I had died in the fire.

"Have you any idea what it was like all those months when I was totally helpless, so helpless I couldn't even feed myself? I was at the mercy of physicians who scraped and prodded and tortured me. I suffered infection after infection. I was so weak I couldn't even lift my head.

"And when I finally left my sickbed, when I was finally declared well by the best physicians in England, this is what I was confronted with." He gestured at his face and body. "This is what I suffered for. To be left like this."

He sank down on the bench in front of his portrait, head down, feeling utterly defeated. Chartreuse rested her hand on his slumped shoulder, but refrained, thank God, from speaking the usual platitudes.

"Everyone tells me how lucky I am to be alive. How grateful I should be to have survived," he said softly. "God forgive me, but I am not."

She sat down beside him and took his hand in both of hers. She traced the scars and the stubs of his fingers where the tips had burned off.

"Once upon a time, there was a little girl," she began. "She lived like a princess. So well- loved was she, she felt safe and secure. Then, her father died, and her mother remarried. And the man her mother married took the girl's body and used it in vile ways. He took her virginity and turned her mother against her. She ran away but found there was no one to help her.

"She lost her home, her family, her reputation. Most of all, she lost her soul. She did things she was too ashamed to admit even to herself.

"She thought about ending her life many times but was too afraid. She was afraid she would never be able to see her father again in the afterlife. So she stayed among the living, but inside, she was dead.

"She suffered a savage beating and nearly died. But a white knight saved her. He gave her a home. He gave her his respect. He gave her life back to her.

"But her white knight was a wounded hero who needed saving himself."

They sat quietly, each lost in thought, staring at the portrait of the man he had once been.

"You know," she finally said. "If you wore a patch over your left eye, you would look exceedingly dark and dangerous. I would imagine all the ladies would find you appealing then.

"There was one gentleman I used to entertain who enjoyed dressing up like a pirate. He said putting on an eye patch made him feel more masculine."

The long gallery echoed with his laughter.

"A pirate. I like that. I shall have Symmington fashion an eye patch for me in the morning."

Chartreuse yawned then stood and stretched. Bending over, she tenderly kissed his left cheek. "Good night, then, my piratical knight."

He held onto her hand. "Good night, Chartreuse. Thank you."

"I may not be your mistress, my lord, but I would like to be your friend."

He watched her walk down the gallery and slip through

the door at the far end, the one closest to the back staircase that led to the servants' quarters.

His friend. She wanted to be his friend. He snorted. Ridiculous. He had enough friends. He had enough servants for that matter. He didn't need her for that, either, though he'd allowed her to stay. What he needed was a mistress. No, what he needed was a wife. Someone suitable. Not a former prostitute turned Puritan.

He still could not believe she'd refused his offer. But on some level, he understood it. Wasn't he doing the same thing? Trying to restore his reputation, his place in society? Her place in society may be lower than his, but she still had ambitions to improve it. To her, being a servant was more respectable than being a prostitute, or even mistress to a peer. He had to respect her for that.

She *was* his friend. She was the only person who treated him like a normal person. She wasn't deferential to him as a servant ought to be. She wasn't horrified by his looks the way his friends and acquaintances were. Maybe because she hadn't known him before the fire. She didn't know who he used to be.

Which was why he'd brought her here to the gallery. To show her.

She'd been decidedly unimpressed. Because she'd lost as much as he had, if not more. She'd lost her home, her family, her future. Nearly her life.

Unlike him, she was grateful for the crumbs life had left her. She didn't wallow in self-pity. She made choices. She chose to remain a servant rather than become his mistress.

He had choices to make, also.

He sat alone in the gallery staring at his portrait until the early gray of dawn lightened the windows. When he finally sought his bed, it was with the resolve to begin anew.

Chapter 10

"It will be a small affair, only fifty people or so. Just dinner, no dancing. Perhaps a small entertainment after dinner. We'll get some of the reigning beauties to sing and play. Too bad we can't have your girl play. She's far better than most of the current crop, but it just wouldn't do to have a servant showing up the crème de la crème, now would it?"

"Daphne, I haven't agreed to this yet," Ian protested, though he knew it was a lost cause. Daphne, aware of his precarious social position, was doing her best to rectify it. She decided that he should play host for Derek's surprise birthday party. She assured him that she would do all the organizing and planning and send out all the invitations. But the party would be held here at his town house.

"Too late, dear, the invitations went out yesterday. I've already consulted with Griggs and Mrs. Pitts, and they are both quite prepared to make our party a success."

So it was that he found himself a week later at the head of his formal dining room table, which hadn't been used in years, playing host to sixty of his sister's closest friends. All of whom seemed to have a daughter of marriageable age. Of course, none of them would look directly at him preferring, he found, to speak to his cravat. It was a very well-tied cravat, he knew, but certainly not worthy of the attention it was receiving.

Dinner was finally at an end, and the ladies had retired to the drawing room. He could finally relax over a glass of port. The gentlemen that Daphne had invited were all known to him and were all men that he liked and respected. None of the fathers had refused to bring their daughters to his home, either, which was an encouraging sign. Perhaps Daphne would be able to rehabilitate him in society after all.

A few of the gentlemen had already left the table to rejoin the ladies when there was a crash in the hallway outside the dining room doors.

"Get your bleedin' paws off of her!" Chartreuse yelled. Another crash sounded. A woman screamed. The gentlemen poured out of the dining room in time to see Chartreuse smash a silver tray on the head of one of his guests while Bitsy cowered against the wall.

"Chartreuse, stop it at once," he ordered.

She turned on him.

"He was forcing himself on her. How dare he come into this house and try to take advantage of an innocent young girl. Some gentleman he is."

"Sorry, love, didn't mean to make you jealous." Of course, it was Gordon Lancaster, Daphne's brother-in-law.

"You will not count Bitsy among your hundred," Chartreuse said. Ian had no idea what she meant by that, but it didn't matter. She was causing a scene, and he had to contain it.

"Enough," he said. "Bitsy, return to the kitchen. You, too, Chartreuse. Gentlemen, we had best join the ladies. They will be wondering what all the commotion is about."

He lagged behind to have a word with young Gordon.

"If you ever lay a hand on any of my servants again, I will give you the beating you so richly deserve," Ian warned him. It was an empty threat and Gordon apparently knew it judging by the unrepentant smirk on his face. Ian was no more capable of thrashing him than he was at tying his own cravat.

"My apologies, Lord Chester," Gordon said with absolutely no sincerity. Then he winked at him. "Thought maybe you hired all your servants from Nell Ryan's brothel."

Ian wanted to wipe the grin off Gordon's face with his fist. Instead, he grabbed him by the collar, crumpling the dandy's Waterfall cravat, and shoved him against the wall. His back screamed at the exertion, but the shock on Gordon's face was worth it. Ian was nearly as shocked as he was, but hid it, he hoped, beneath his scars.

"I should have let Chartreuse hit you on the head a few more times with that silver tray. I'll have a long talk with your brother about you later. Right now, you may leave this house. I shall give Derek your regrets."

Griggs appeared with Gordon's hat and gloves. Dickie and James ushered him to the front door.

Tamping down his anger, Ian turned toward the drawing room. The evening could not end soon enough.

❧

The kitchen was organized chaos as the kitchen staff worked to clean up after the seven-course meal. The cooks had worked all afternoon to prepare the meal, and now all servants were dealing with the aftermath of the evening's festivities.

Chartreuse sorted silver under the watchful eye of Mr. Griggs. A hush fell over the room, and all eyes turned toward the stairs when Ian descended them.

"I want to thank you all for the effort you gave tonight. You made the evening a great success. I realize it has been quite a while since we've entertained here at Chester House, but one would never have known from the quality of the service you provided. Thank you.

"Bitsy, I apologize for the unpleasant experience you had earlier. Please take tomorrow morning off to recover. I hope he did not hurt you in any way."

"No sir. Thank you, sir," Bitsy mumbled.

"Chartreuse, I'd like a private word with you please."

This is it. Now he's really going to sack me. I crashed a tray over Master Gordon's head.

She followed him to his library. When he closed the door, locking them in alone together, she knew she was in for it. She braced herself for his tirade. She wasn't prepared for his laughter.

"Chartreuse, you were magnificent," he said. "Gordon Lancaster is a mannerless puppy who needed to be taught a lesson. Though I don't condone you going around hitting all of my guests on the head with a silver tray, that young man deserved it."

"You're not mad at me?"

"No. I'm proud of you."

She relaxed the hands that were gripping her skirts.

"I was just about Bitsy's age when my stepfather started forcing himself on me. I remember how helpless I felt. I couldn't let that happen to Bitsy."

He pulled her to him and held her in a comforting embrace. Stroking her hair, he said, "Poor Chartreuse. I wish I could have saved you."

She wanted to stay in his arms. He made her feel safe. It was a dangerous feeling to allow herself. Before she knew it, she'd lose her resolve and accept his offer. A carte blanche would give her safety and security. For a time, at least. Until he grew tired of her.

As a servant, she could find another position when he had enough of his charitable impulses and decided to let her go. Another *respectable* position.

She took a step back, breaking the embrace, putting necessary distance between them. Lifting her hand, resisting the urge to touch his burned and scarred cheek, she gestured toward his face.

"I like the eye patch," she said. The square of black cloth, crisply starched, sat over his left eye attached with two black ribbons that circled his head and tied in back.

"I rather like it myself," he said, turning to go to the sideboard and pour himself a glass of brandy. "Though unlike you predicted, the ladies are not throwing themselves at this pirate's feet."

He returned with a glass in each hand.

"Give them time," she said, accepting the one he handed her.

He motioned for her to sit in one of the leather chairs before the fireplace, the same seat she'd taken several weeks before.

"How much of what you told me at Acton Park is true?" he asked after a few minutes spent in silence staring at the fire.

She took a sip of brandy and enjoyed the slow burn as it made its way down her throat.

"I am a Squire's daughter. At least, I was once. I am also a whore, and now, a servant."

"What about your family? Would you ever want to return to them?"

"No." She said it so emphatically her hand shook, spilling brandy onto her sleeve. She stood and placed the glass on the table between them, needing to end the interview before she revealed too much. "If you'll excuse me, my lord, I'll seek my bed."

"Good night, Chartreuse. Chartreuse LaRue, is that your real name?"

"No. And don't ask what my real name is. I won't tell you. You can't save me, Ian. Not any more than you already have." She bent and kissed him lightly on his lips. A mistake, she knew, but one she could not resist. "Good night, my lord."

❧

Encouraged by the success of his dinner party, Daphne decided to have a ball in Ian's honor to welcome him back to society after his long illness. She planned a masked ball, no doubt so that no attention would be drawn to his face. Ian contemplated whether he should even wear a mask. His face was far more frightening than anything a costume designer could create.

But he had to admit that the opportunity to hide behind a mask for the evening held a certain appeal. The eye patch had helped somewhat, at least with the gentlemen, but it didn't cover his entire face. With a full mask, perhaps he could actually converse with her guests without having them look everywhere but at him. Perhaps he could invite a lady to dance without having her stammer some excuse and running for the retiring room.

Daphne needed additional help for the evening, so Ian had dispatched most of his own servants to her house that morning, Chartreuse among them. He knew Derek wouldn't approve, but Derek didn't know everything that he did about her.

In the weeks since the party, they had gotten in the habit of taking brandy together after she played for him in the evening. He found her to be witty and charming and very easy to talk to.

He hadn't asked her again to be his mistress. He had to content himself with keeping her as his friend, though it nearly killed him to do so. Her trust in him was fragile, and he was loath to do anything to disturb it though that did not stop him from desiring her.

They hadn't spoken again about her childhood in Dorset. It didn't really matter. She was right. There was no way to return her to that time of innocence. All he could do was keep her safe from lecherous men who wanted to take advantage of her. Himself included.

Though she'd grown up as gentry, low gentry though it was, she never balked at any of the tasks assigned to her. She seemed to enjoy the life of service she'd found in his house. Mrs. Pitts assured him that she performed her duties admirably well and that she was well liked by the other servants.

In many ways, she was what many men wanted most in a wife. Competent in running a household, charming in the drawing room, and a whore in bed.

If she weren't so completely beyond the bounds of society and if he didn't have his own position to consider, he might just marry her himself. Wouldn't Bramly love that? Perhaps his uncle's scheme wasn't so ridiculous after all.

Because Ian found himself falling in love with Chartreuse despite her past. It had started the night he took her to the portrait gallery, and she'd called him her white knight though he knew he was unworthy of the title. Then when she stood up for Bitsy after his dinner party. It grew every evening she played for him. He fantasized about lifting her off the piano bench and carrying her to his bedroom.

It was entirely one-sided, of course. She'd never shown any indication that she cared for him beyond the gratitude she felt for him allowing her to work for him.

Which made him feel like an absolute cad. He allowed the woman he was coming to love to scrub his floors and perform the most menial tasks in his household. If he had his way, he'd elevate her to mistress of the house.

Maybe the fire had cooked his brains after all.

∾

Chartreuse stood in the great hall with all the other servants while Lady Fontaine inspected their appearance. Like the other maids, she was wearing a serviceable black dress with a starched white apron and a white cap upon her head. She'd spent the day scrubbing wall sconces and shining the delicate prisms that hung from the chandelier that graced the enormous ballroom in Lady Fontaine's mansion.

Her hands were raw from being in hot water all day, but she didn't mind. The ball tonight was in Ian's honor, and she wanted to do her part to make the evening special for him.

Ian was the only man since her father who had shown her any kindness. She'd do whatever she could to repay him.

The Fontaine's butler walked down the line of servants handing out assignments for the evening.

"You will attend the ladies retiring room," he told her. "Make sure there is clean water in the ewer and fresh towels. Provide the ladies with anything they require. If you don't know where something is, ask one of the regular housemaids."

"Yes, sir."

The ladies retiring room was one of the guest suites in the Fontaine mansion. It had a sitting area with couches and chairs. In the bedroom, there was a vanity with all manner of perfumes and cosmetics laid out for the guests to use should they need to retouch their appearance.

The changing room off the bedroom held a commode. It would be her duty to keep it fresh after each use.

Ladies began visiting the retiring room almost as soon as the first guests arrived at the ball. Chartreuse barely had a moment to catch her breath. She made frequent trips to the linen closet in the hall to restock the supply of fresh towels. She made several trips down the back stairway to empty the slop buckets from the commode.

She was only remotely aware of the music from the ballroom and sounds of laughter and murmurs of voices that found their way up the main staircase. The retiring room was a quiet place where the ladies could have some respite from the crowded ballroom downstairs.

The costumes the ladies wore enchanted her. Jewel-encrusted masks covered their faces. They were shepherdesses and Egyptian queens and pre-Revolutionary French aristocrats.

She longed to be one of them, to be that carefree, thinking only about dancing, gossiping, and flirting. She wondered if Ian had danced with any of the ladies, if the dashing pirate that all the young women swooned over was he. She hoped that hidden behind a mask he could relax and enjoy himself.

While she attended to the ladies' every need, she was invisible to them in her black dress, crisp white apron, and silly mobcap.

She returned from the linen closet with a fresh load of towels to find the room empty save for one young lady. As she placed the towels on the table beside the vanity, she noticed the woman sitting on the stool remove her mask and fix her hair. She admired her gown but didn't really look at her face.

"Shelby? My God, it is you! Shelby!"

Phoebe. Chartreuse looked up and their eyes met in the mirror. Phoebe had gone pale, like she was seeing a ghost.

In fact, she was. The woman she was looking for no longer existed.

Chartreuse fled. She didn't say a word; she didn't think. She just ran. She ran down the back stairway and all the way back to Chester House. Hands shaking, she threw the few possessions she had acquired since coming to the house into the soft carpetbag that Bitsy had made for her.

Only when she was ready to leave did she realize that she was still wearing the cap and apron that belonged to Lady Fontaine. She removed them and, neatly folded, set them in the middle of her bed. She wouldn't take anything that didn't belong to her.

Before the unmasking at midnight, Chartreuse was gone.

Chapter 11

Ian had a wonderful time at Daphne's ball. Wearing a mask, he felt like his old self again. Confident and self-assured, he enjoyed the anonymity the masquerade provided. Young ladies who would cringe at the sight of him flirted outrageously with the daring pirate he'd become. While he lacked his former grace, he managed one dance with Daphne that he executed fairly well, and even with his mangled left foot managed not to tread on hers.

Not wanting the magic to end, he left before the unmasking. He knew Daphne would be angry with him. He should have stayed until the very end, but he was too much the coward. He couldn't bear to see the look of revulsion in the eyes of those assembled when he removed his mask and revealed his horrible face.

When he disembarked from his carriage in front of his house, he noticed a young woman hurrying down the street. Most likely a servant hurrying home after her night off. He wondered if his own servants had returned home yet from Daphne's. Probably not, as the ball still continued. He'd seen Dickie serving champagne and noticed Bitsy at one point peeking into the ballroom, a look of awe upon her face. But he hadn't seen Chartreuse. He had hoped to. Wanted her to see him in the costume she'd inspired. Wanted her to see him in the ballroom as the man he used to be, not the monster he'd become.

Maybe she had, and he hadn't noticed her. He'd ask her tomorrow. For tonight, he needed his bed. The dance with Daphne had been delightful, but his foot throbbed from the effort.

A dose of laudanum awaited.

❧

Ian was just finishing his breakfast the next morning when Griggs brought in a card on a silver salver. He read the card with interest. Miss Phoebe Endicott.

"Is Miss Endicott alone?" he asked with some surprise.

"Her maid accompanied her, my lord," Griggs replied barely disguising the disdain in his voice. Griggs knew as well as he did that it was very bad manners for a Miss, of whatever age, to visit a bachelor alone in his home.

"I'll see her at once," he said.

"She's waiting in the front parlor, my lord. Shall I bring some tea?"

"That won't be necessary. I doubt Miss Endicott will be staying long."

Miss Endicott was standing in the middle of the parlor when he walked in, obviously uncomfortable and, he hoped, regretting whatever impulse led her here. Perhaps she was a curiosity seeker who had heard about the Monster Earl and wanted to regale her friends with tales of how she'd bearded the beast in his den. She was young, no more than seventeen or eighteen, fresh from the schoolroom and no doubt enjoying her first Season in London. Whoever her parents were, they ought to have more of a care for her.

"What can I do for you, Miss Endicott?" He did not motion for her to sit. Miss Endicott appeared too agitated to take a seat herself, so they both remained standing in the middle of the floor.

"I need to speak to the servant who attended the ladies retiring room at Lady Fontaine's ball last night," Miss Endicott blurted out. "I already spoke with Lady Fontaine and learned that the servant was one of yours."

"Was there some problem? Did the maid treat you rudely or steal from you?"

"No, no, nothing of the sort. It's just…it's something of a personal nature. I need to speak with her, if I could please, Lord Chester."

"Did Lady Fontaine give you a name? Did she know which servant it was?" Not being wont to visit the ladies retiring room himself, he had no idea which of his servants was working as attendant last night.

"She didn't know. Perhaps, if it wouldn't be too much trouble, you could ask all your female servants who helped at Lady Fontaine's last night to appear?"

"I could, but I really need you to tell me what this is all about. Are you accusing one of my servants of something?"

"No. Please forgive me, Lord Chester. I realize this is most irregular. I just would rather not say what it's about if I am mistaken. The woman seemed familiar to me. Like someone I once knew. If I could just be certain…"

He rang for Griggs. Perhaps he knew which servant Miss Endicott was yammering about. It seemed the only way to be rid of the woman was to appease her.

Griggs, unfortunately, didn't know which assignments were handed out to Ian's servants since he wasn't at the ball himself. He did, however, know which of the housemaids had worked at Lady Fontaine's masquerade and immediately went off to summon them for Miss Endicott's review.

The woman paced and fidgeted the entire time they waited for his butler to return.

"The maids are assembled, my lord," Griggs announced

a few minutes later.

Ian escorted Miss Endicott out to his main hall where, indeed, his maidservants were lined up ready for inspection. With one notable exception.

"Where is Chartreuse? Wasn't she at Lady Fontaine's last night?" he asked Griggs. Is that why he hadn't seen her? Had she remained at home? Which meant she was here when he arrived home last night. Just as well that he hadn't known. In the mood he was in, he would have sought her out. Would have begged her to reconsider being his mistress.

"She's gone, my lord."

"What? Gone where? When?" He couldn't believe how hurt he felt. Had she just left, without even a fare thee well?

"I'm not certain when she left, but she did not report for duty this morning. Bitsy checked her room and found all her things gone."

While they were talking quietly, Miss Endicott walked up and down the line of servants. The one she was looking for wasn't there. Miss Endicott looked like a puppy that had just been kicked.

"She's not here," she said.

No. She's gone. For he knew with certainty that the servant Miss Endicott was looking for was Chartreuse.

Ian dismissed the servants and escorted Miss Endicott to her waiting carriage. Then he set out to find his missing maid. There was only one place he could think to look for her. He hoped she wasn't there.

❧

Nell Ryan's brothel looked like any other of the row of townhouses on the quiet street about a mile from Piccadilly Circus. Many of the homes housed reputable merchants and tradesmen. He wondered if they knew what went on in their neighbor's establishment.

Though it was only late morning and the brothel was surely not open for business, the door was opened immediately after he released the knocker.

"I'd like to speak with Mrs. Ryan, please," Ian said to the brute who answered the door. He certainly hoped he didn't need to drag Chartreuse out of here kicking and screaming, because he was not at all sure he could get her past this lout at the door. To give the man credit, he didn't give Ian's appearance a second look. The man's face wasn't much more attractive than his. His nose had obviously been broken more than once.

The doorman showed him to a small parlor right off the entryway. The room reeked of stale perfume and spilled brandy. The curtains were drawn so the room was dark and tomblike. It made Ian's skin crawl.

Nell kept him waiting a good hour. He was tempted to start trying doors to see if he could find Chartreuse himself when Nell finally appeared wearing a day dress that was so low cut her nipples were practically showing. Nell Ryan had been blessed with voluptuous breasts that had made her a fortune in her day, but now they sagged to her voluminous belly. It was not a pretty sight.

"How nice to see you again, my lord," Nell purred. "What brings you here to my fine establishment?"

"I believe you have something that belongs to me."

"And what might that be?"

"A certain package you left on my doorstep five months ago. I want it back."

"And if the package doesn't wish to be returned?"

"Then I will have the lot of you thrown into Newgate." Ian had no patience for haggling with whores. "On the other hand, if you return the package to me right now, you will be generously rewarded." Ian pulled a purse from his pocket and jingled it for Nell to hear the familiar clink of gold coins.

"Pike!" she called and the big brute from the door came instantly to do her bidding. "Go fetch Chartreuse. She's leaving."

❧

Chartreuse sat on the bed in her old bedroom. Nell had welcomed her back with open arms, as if nothing had ever happened. As if she hadn't threatened to throw Chartreuse's battered body into the Thames. The new girl, Allie or Ellie or something, was summarily removed to one of the smaller rooms in the attic, and Chartreuse was reinstated in her former chamber.

After the simplicity of the servants' quarters at Chester House, this room was tawdry and overdone. How could she have lived here for five years? Worse, how could she have come back?

She'd panicked when she saw Phoebe. If Phoebe were in London, then Uncle Phillip would be also. She couldn't bear it if Uncle Phillip found her. He would be so disappointed, so angry at the shame she'd brought to the family name. He would never forgive her for the way she disgraced her father's memory.

She could never forgive herself.

While she'd been working at Nell's, the rest of the world had seemed very far away. Another time and place. One totally disconnected and unrelated to the person she had become.

But working at Chester House, the two worlds collided. She was constantly reminded of the life she had once known. The life she had run from. The life she could never return to.

She couldn't return to this life either, she realized now. After the months she'd spent in Lord Chester's household being treated with respect and doing honest work, she couldn't go back to working on her back, spreading her legs for any man who had the price.

She was still wearing the plain black dress she'd had on at Lady Fontaine's ball. Nell had brought in a number of gowns for her to try, but she couldn't bring herself to put one on. The bodices were cut low to expose all her assets, the colors were too bright, the fabric, though not service-able, was not silk either. Plus, they all reeked of perfume and body odor. They were a garish costume for the role she was expected to play.

She'd made a mistake coming back here. If she could no longer stay at Chester House, she would at least find herself another position in service. But she would not go back to prostituting herself.

Chartreuse lifted the floorboard where she hid her most valued possessions. Luckily, no one had disturbed her stash. She pulled out the cigar box that fit snugly in the hole be-tween the floorboard and the studs. Opening the box gin-gerly, she surveyed the contents. It contained very little, re-ally.

There were the few bank notes she'd managed to squir-rel away, such a paltry sum for what it had cost her to earn them.

And the guinea she'd taken from home the night she'd made her escape. She had planned to use it to pay for pas-sage, but the mail coach driver who brought her to London had found another way for her to pay.

She pulled out the locket that she'd hidden that first night at Nell's. She hadn't wanted it to be stolen. She opened the locket and smiled at the miniature hidden inside. Her father. He told her when he gave it to her on her tenth birthday that when she was older, she should replace his picture with the picture of the man she would marry.

Her father's place was secure. No man would marry her now.

Chartreuse put the locket on and put the cigar box in her

carpetbag. She hadn't unpacked yet and now didn't intend to. She wouldn't be staying after all.

Just then, Pike banged on her door. "Nell wants you downstairs now, got a gentleman waiting for you."

Her stomach dropped. Nell wanted her to go to work already.

She grabbed her bag and opened the door. "Tell Nell I won't be able to entertain the gentleman right now, Pike. I'm leaving."

Pike grabbed her arm and hauled her toward the stairs. "Not until Nell gives you her by your leave," he said. Pike was ever obedient to Nell, which was why she employed him. He was like a bulldog she'd trained to her beck and call.

Chartreuse tried to reason with Pike, tried to pull away from him as they approached the parlor door, but her efforts were fruitless. The man was too big and strong and had the personality of a door post.

He delivered her to Nell and the waiting gentleman as instructed.

"Ian!" Relief flooded her when she saw that *he* was the gentleman Nell had waiting for her.

"Don't come back again," Nell said. "You're no longer welcome."

She knew what that meant. If she tried once again to return to Nell's, she'd get a severe beating, or worse. She had no intention of ever returning.

Ian didn't say a word as he escorted her out to his waiting carriage and assisted her inside. He tapped once on the roof with the head of the cane he was carrying, and the carriage lurched forward.

Once they were underway, he said quietly, "Why did you run?"

She didn't know what to say. She didn't want to tell him about Phoebe. If she did, she'd have to tell him everything.

So, she remained silent.

"I had a visit this morning from a Miss Phoebe Endicott."

She gasped.

"Ah," he said. "You do know her. Do you care to tell me why she was looking for you? I take it that is why you ran away. Did something happen at the ball last night?"

She shook her head.

"You may as well tell me. I will find out." But still she refused to say a word. "Very well then." He opened the slider that allowed him to talk to the driver. "Take us to Endicott House, please, John. It's on Grosvenor Square."

"Ian, no, you can't!" she could hold her silence no longer. "Please, I'll tell you everything. Just don't take me there."

"Never mind, John. Just drive around town for a few minutes, please." He closed the slider and looked at her expectantly.

"Phoebe Endicott is my cousin. Phillip, Lord Endicott, is my uncle."

"So, the squire's daughter is also the niece to an Earl. I imagine he would not take kindly to learning of your former profession."

"They think I'm dead. Leave it that way, please."

"I don't think that's possible any longer. Your cousin recognized you."

"Just tell her she was mistaken. I'll leave, Ian. I'll find another position. I can't go back to Nell's, but I'll find another position in service. You'll never need to see me again."

He took her hands in his and gently stroked her palms.

"I find I have this need to be your hero, to try to save you, restore you to your family."

She looked down at their clasped hands.

"You can't. You know what I've been. Nothing can save me."

He looked in her eyes.

"Don't leave, Chartreuse."

She shook her head. "Shelby. My name is Shelby. Shelby Endicott. My father was Squire John Endicott, of Hapshom on Green, Dorset."

"Don't leave, Shelby."

It felt so strange to be called by her real name again. She'd been Chartreuse for so long, she had almost forgotten that Shelby Endicott even existed.

"I must leave. I can't risk seeing Phoebe again. I can't risk hurting her. I don't want her to know the truth about me."

They rode in silence for a few minutes, Ian lost in thought and she waiting expectantly for his decision.

"Take us to 18 Templeton Place, John," he told the driver.

"What place is that?" She couldn't keep the anxiety from her voice.

"It's the house I leased for you when I offered you a carte blanche. I haven't sublet it yet. It's empty of servants and completely private. We can talk at length there."

❧

The house was lovely. If Ian had shown it to her before asking her to be his mistress, she may have accepted. It was just the type of house she had always dreamed of. It even had a piano. He had thought of everything.

They stopped in the music room. It was the brightest and warmest room in the house with sun streaming through the windows overlooking the garden. She sat on the piano bench and idly ran her fingers over the keys. Ian looked out at the garden, which was in full bloom.

"Chartreuse LaRue was a prostitute who became a servant in my house. She disappeared one night, apparently deciding that working as a servant is far too hard and preferring to go back to her old life working in a brothel. I tried to convince her otherwise, even offering her the position as my mistress, but she refused. She went off on her own, and I have not seen her since. She is most likely plying her trade down by the docks." He turned to look at her then.

"Shelby Endicott," he continued, "is someone else entirely."

She just stared at him as if he'd lost his mind.

"Stay here until I get back," he said as he headed for the door. "I trust you can fend for yourself. There's food in the pantry. Light a fire, heat some water for a bath. Make yourself at home. Just don't leave. Don't go out. It may be a day or two before I return."

Upon issuing his orders, he left. She found herself completely alone in the charming little house. Her first impulse was escape. She could run away and no one, not Ian nor Phoebe, would ever find her again.

But if she did that, she would be living out Ian's tale of Chartreuse LaRue. She would remain Chartreuse LaRue for the rest of her life.

She wanted to be Shelby Endicott again.

She knew that they were one and the same, but something in the way Ian said it gave her hope. Shelby Endicott was someone else entirely.

She hadn't been Shelby Endicott for five years.

She rose from the piano bench and explored the house, trying to shake free of the memories that assailed her. She'd avoided thinking about the past for five years. In the quiet of the house, she could not escape it.

She did what Ian suggested and prepared herself a bath. The tasks of lighting the fire, heating the water, and filling the tub she dragged into the kitchen kept her hands and her mind occupied.

But when she sank into the warm water and leaned back against the rim of the tub, she could no longer keep the memories at bay. Closing her eyes, she remembered the abuse she'd suffered at the hands of her stepfather, Mr. Granger, her mother's betrayal, running away, and ending up at Nell's.

At least at Nell's she got paid for what Mr. Granger had taken for free. At Nell's, she learned that Mr. Granger had taught her well. She was in great demand. At Nell's, she was in control. Nell taught her about men and about their desires. Shelby took to her life of prostitution and never looked back. She changed her name and changed her past.

No one knew where she came from, and she told different stories depending on her mood. She was good with accents and could put on a Cockney accent as well as speak like a Lady. Shelby Endicott was gone, and Chartreuse LaRue was in her place. Shelby Endicott was dead. She would no longer bring shame to the family name.

Now, Ian wanted to resurrect her. Could he do it? Should she let him?

Rising from the now cool water, she dried herself off and put the plain black dress back on.

And dared to hope.

Chapter 12

Ian tracked Lord Endicott down at his club.

The porter directed him to Endicott's table. Fortunately, Endicott was sitting alone, sipping tea and reading the afternoon newssheet. He was a middle-aged man with blonde hair that was changing to gray and bushy eyebrows that already had.

"May I join you, my lord?" he asked.

Endicott looked up from his newssheet and flinched when he saw him but recovered quickly.

"Chester, isn't it?" he asked.

"Yes, my lord. I'd like a private word with you."

Endicott gestured for him to have a seat.

"Your daughter, Miss Phoebe Endicott, paid me a visit this morning."

Endicott looked at him sharply. He obviously had no idea that his daughter had gone anywhere that morning.

He continued.

"Your daughter thought that she recognized one of my servants, a Miss Chartreuse LaRue."

He saw the flicker of recognition cross Endicott's face before the older man could mask it.

"The name is familiar to you." With effort, he kept his voice calm, but anger churned in his stomach.

"I may have heard it a time or two." Endicott's discomfort was apparent. He kept darting his eyes away, making sure no one was eavesdropping on the conversation. "What did my daughter tell you?"

"Nothing. And let me assure you, Lord Endicott, that Chartreuse LaRue is not the woman your daughter was looking for."

Endicott visibly relaxed.

"What do you want, Chester?"

"I want to talk about your niece, Miss Shelby Endicott."

"My niece is dead," Endicott said. He spoke emphatically, leaving no room for discussion.

"You know that for a fact?"

"Let me tell you something, Lord Chester," Endicott leaned forward. "After five years, if she isn't dead, she may as well be. As far as I'm concerned, she is dead to her family."

"But she isn't dead, is she?" he persisted. "And you know it. What happened to her?"

He didn't think Endicott was going to answer. The man stared into his teacup as though trying to read the leaves that were left there.

"Helen, her mother, thought she'd run off with the young man she'd been fornicating with. The father of the babe she was carrying," Endicott began.

A jolt went through him. Chartreuse, no, Shelby he corrected himself, had never said anything about a child. What happened to it?

"It didn't take me long to find her," Endicott continued. "Just a few days. But by then it was too late."

"Too late?" He didn't want to believe what the man was telling him. "Too late for what? To rescue her? To bring her home?" He had to unclench his fist so he could pick up his brandy. He downed it in one gulp.

"I couldn't have a woman like that in my house. She was ruined."

"A woman like that. A woman? A child. She was, what, fourteen years old? And you abandoned her."

"She had her mother's looks and her father's willfulness," Endicott said in his defense. "She was no child. Not any longer. I did what I had to do to protect my family."

Gorge rose in his throat. "Shelby was your family. What did you do to protect her?"

Endicott had the grace to look down at his lap.

"What did you tell your precious family?" he spat. "Why is your daughter still looking for her?"

"I couldn't tell Helen what had become of her. I didn't have the heart. So I told her I'd found her and sent her to a convent to have the child."

He laughed at the irony of that. Shaking his head, he said, "A convent with Nell Ryan as abbess."

"Phoebe, of course, didn't know about the child. She thinks Shelby is away at a convent school. At least, she did until we came to London for the Season. She's been insisting that I send for her cousin. She wants to share her Season with her."

"And so she shall." Endicott's face paled, but Ian ignored it. "You will go home and tell Phoebe the good news. That you have sent for Shelby, and she's coming home."

"How dare you…" Endicott started to rise from his chair as if ready to challenge Ian, his pale complexion replaced by reddened fury.

Ian held up a staying hand and Endicott settled back down in his chair.

"Unless you want your daughter's first Season marred by scandal, you had better welcome Shelby home with open arms."

"I'd heard you've become a monster," Endicott sneered.

"I thought they were just referring to the way you look. Now I see that you are a monster inside and out."

Ian left as Endicott ordered a brandy instead of another cup of tea.

❧

It was late when he arrived back at the house on Templeton Place. The house was quiet when he let himself in. For a moment, he feared that Shelby had left. He searched the lower rooms, finding water cooling in the hipbath, which was placed in front of the fireplace in the kitchen. So, she had taken his advice and bathed.

He found her in the bedroom upstairs, sound asleep in the middle of the bed. Curled up on her side, her face smooth in sleep, she looked young and innocent. He tried not to disturb her and quietly started backing out of the room, but he must have made some sound, or perhaps she just sensed his presence, because she woke.

Rolling onto her back, she gave him a welcoming smile, though wariness shadowed her eyes. Setting the candle down on the bedside table, he sat on the edge of the bed and took her hand in his.

"I spoke this afternoon with your uncle," he said softly. "He is ready to welcome you home."

"Did you tell him what I've been?"

"I didn't need to," he forced himself to admit, though he hated hurting her this way. "He already knew."

Shelby's breath caught, and she turned her head away, as though too ashamed to look at him.

"How long has he known?"

He'd rather run through a burning building than tell her, but she needed to know the truth. If this was going to work at all, they at least had to be honest with each other. He squeezed her hand as fire threatened to incinerate his belly, knowing he was about to scorch her heart.

"He's known since a few days after you arrived at Nell Ryan's brothel."

"What?" She tugged her hand from his grip. Sitting up, she pulled her knees to her chest and looked him squarely in the eye. Color infused her pale cheeks as she blinked back the tears that pooled in her eyes, took a long, slow breath and nodded in acceptance "If he wouldn't take me home then, why would he take me home now?"

"Because now I know. And he knows that if he doesn't, all of London society will know that the great Lord Endicott, peer of the realm, abandoned his brother's daughter to the likes of Nell Ryan."

"They'll just blame me, Ian. It won't hurt him at all if the truth comes out."

"No, but it will hurt his daughter. What kind of marriage do you think she'll be able to make with such a connection as you no longer hidden away safely in the skeleton closet?"

"I don't want to hurt Phoebe. Please, Ian, just let me go away."

"No."

"Ian," Shelby pleaded. "Why are you doing this?"

"Why? Look at me, Shelby. What do you see?"

"I see a wealthy, powerful man who is used to getting his own way," she answered.

"You don't see a monster?"

"Of course not. You're not a monster, Ian."

"That's why I'm doing this. Because you see a man, not a monster. Because you look at *me*. You see *me*. Not the aftermath of my trial by fire. If I survived the fire for a reason, maybe that reason is so I can help you. Let me do this. If for no other reason than to repay you for what my uncle did. As reparation for the beating you took at Bramly's hands. For him nearly killing you."

"Too many people knew me as Chartreuse LaRue, knew me intimately. Even your own brother-in-law recognized me as soon as he saw me. No matter what story we tell, the truth will come out."

He experienced a moment of doubt, but he quashed it. He could not allow any amount of pleading on her part to sway him from this course. It would work. It had to work. He needed it to work. As much for himself as for her.

He stood and paced to the window and back, then stopped at the foot of the bed.

"Chartreuse LaRue doesn't exist anymore. She certainly never traveled in the same social circles as Miss Shelby Endicott. Though there may be a slight physical resemblance, no one will make the mistake of confusing the two of you.

"People believe what they want to believe, see what they expect to see. When Miss Shelby Endicott returns from the convent school where she's spent the past five years to join her cousin Phoebe for her first Season, no one will suspect that the convent school was actually Nell Ryan's brothel. No one."

❧

Shelby threw off the covers, unable to stay abed any longer. Her bare feet slammed onto the cold, wood floor. Her hands fisted at her side, she stood next to the bed as anger heated her blood. Anger at her uncle for leaving her to her fate. Anger at Ian for his high-handed, autocratic pronouncements. Anger at herself for actually starting to hope that she could have her life back.

She wanted to fling herself at him, pound him on the chest, and rail at him for putting her in this position. Why wouldn't he just let her go?

But she didn't move, too afraid that if she did, he'd concede to her wishes and that thin glimmer of hope would be snuffed like a candle.

"I just have one question for you," Ian said from his position at the foot of the bed. "What happened to the child?"

All the anger drained out of her, leaving her so weak-limbed that she sank back down on to the mattress.

"Uncle Phillip knew about the baby?"

Ian nodded.

"Did he know about Mr. Granger, my stepfather?"

"He seemed to think the child was the result of a liaison you had with a local boy."

"That's what Mr. Granger told my mother, too. Even when I told her the truth, she chose to believe him."

"Where is the child, Shelby?" He came and sat beside her, but he didn't touch her, didn't take her hand like he'd done before.

She looked down at her hands where they grasped the folds of her chemise, unable to meet his eyes.

"Gone. Dead. Never born. Nell killed it. I killed it. She gave me a potion to drink, and I miscarried. The poison nearly killed me. I wish it had."

She waited for him to say something, but he remained silent. What could he say, really? A hardness settled in her belly. To hell with him. To hell with all of them. She'd done what she had to do to survive.

She donned her armor and became Chartreuse LaRue again. She stood up so she could look down on him. He tilted his head up so that his eye met hers. She smiled at him, the ice-cold smile she used with the patrons at Nell's. She taunted him with the voice she'd perfected as the hard-core whore she used to be and maybe still was.

"Tell me Ian, do you think I'm worth saving now?"

Standing so they were toe to toe, he pulled her into his arms and held her. His tenderness undid her. She started to cry. It was a torrent of tears, which had been dammed up for so long.

He settled himself on the bed, leaning against the head-board, and pulled her to him until he had her nestled on his lap. He let her cry it out, stroking her back and hair as if she were a child in need of comfort. She clung to him until her tears were spent, then rested with her head on his chest.

"I've hated myself for so long," she whispered. She held her breath, waiting for him to say something. The tears had washed away her anger, washed away her shame, cleansed her of the stench of Nell's bordello. Her throat felt raw; her eyes, crusty. Her nose leaked.

Ian handed her a clean, cotton handkerchief and watched solemnly as she used it, then tucked her head back against his chest. She listened to the slow, steady beat of his heart as the silence between them lengthened.

That small glimmer of hope grew to a spark. He hadn't tossed her aside in disgust, hadn't asked her for an explanation, hadn't condemned her. Yet.

When he finally spoke, his voice was soft. He spoke slowly, as though struggling to find the right words.

"When I saw my reflection for the first time after the fire," he said, "I couldn't believe that monster was me. But you tell me that I am not such a monster, after all. Now I'm telling you the same thing. You are not a monster, Shelby. You are still worth saving."

She exhaled in relief. Tears threatened to fall again, but she blinked them back.

He shifted her so that she was lying beside him. Taking a strand of hair in his fingers, he twirled it round and round as he spoke.

"Tomorrow morning, a hired hack will take you to your uncle's house. I borrowed a dress from Daphne so you will be dressed appropriately. I've sent notices to the papers announcing your arrival in Town."

"Oh, God, Ian, I don't know if I can do it. Pretend to be someone I'm not."

"It *is* who you are," he said. "Chartreuse LaRue was the imposter. Not you." He dropped the strand of hair and looked in her eyes. "The next time we meet will be at a rout or a ball. Someone will introduce us, as we've never before met. If anyone suggests to you that you bear a resemblance to someone else, someone of low repute, you will beg their pardon and look confused.

"Through no look, word, or deed will you ever admit to being Chartreuse LaRue. Is that clear? She is dead and gone."

Shelby nodded, that spark of hope growing to a steady flame. She so wanted to believe him, but a wave of doubt washed through her, nearly dousing the fire of hope he'd lit in her.

"But what if…"

He put a finger to her lips.

"Shh…" he said. "I'll brook no arguments."

She kissed the finger he held against her lips and murmured against it, "You are entirely too autocratic."

"I am an Earl of the Realm. I am allowed to be autocratic."

She smiled at him because lying here next to her with his hair mussed and his one good eye drooping in fatigue, he looked far from an imposing peer and more like a mischievous boy.

Her heart fluttered. Could he truly make her past disappear? Did he have that much power?

Then a cold dash of doubt splashed over her. Couldn't her uncle have done the same for her five years ago if he had wanted? If it were possible, why hadn't Uncle Phillip at least tried?

Her heart squeezed, and her stomach twisted, but she kept her thoughts to herself. If Ian believed this plan of his would succeed, she wanted to believe it, too.

He stroked her hair, once again twirling a golden strand between his fingers.

"Eventually, someone will ask you to marry him. Some respectable young mister with an income sufficient to sustain you. You will accept. You will never tell him that you didn't spend those five years in a convent school as everyone believes. You will never tell him the truth.

"You will live a long and happy life. Your white knight has decreed it."

He kissed her forehead, her eyelids, her cheeks, finally settling on her lips.

"Your very battered and scarred, piratical knight has decreed it."

He kissed her deeply then, and she kissed him back with the practiced ease of the experienced whore, but this time, something stirred in her. This was not some stranger paying her for his pleasure. This was not Mr. Granger forcing himself on her. This was Ian. A man she cared about. A man who, against all reason, seemed to care about her.

She wove her fingers in his hair and intensified the kiss, filling it with all the gratitude and hope she couldn't express with words. She swirled her tongue in his mouth, nibbled on the sensitive side of his lips, used all her skill to elicit from him as much passion as she could. She had never wanted so much to give pleasure and surprisingly, she felt a small stirring of desire herself.

When Ian pulled back and ended the kiss, she moaned. Heart racing, she fought to get her breath under control as he leaned his forehead against hers.

"I'd better leave, or I will take you for my ease again. And I will not do that to you. It is time I, too, started treating you like the lady you are."

He started to pull away from her, but she grabbed hold of him. She couldn't let him leave. What she was feeling was too new, too uncertain. She needed him, wanted him in a way she'd never wanted any man before. Desperation had her digging her fingers into his arm.

"Don't go. Stay with me tonight. I will do everything you say. I will deny to my dying day that I was ever Chartreuse

LaRue. But I won't marry. It wouldn't be fair to marry someone I could not be completely honest with. So I will never again know a man's touch. That I promise you.

"Just once, I would like to know the pleasure of that touch. Make love to me Ian. As you would a woman you cared for. Pretend I am someone you could love."

He should decline. If he made love to her the way she wanted, he might not be able to let her go. Because she *was* a woman he cared for. A woman he could love.

She had somehow crept under his skin. His raw, fried, flayed skin. She was a survivor, like him. He recognized that in her. But somehow, for all that she'd been through, all that she'd suffered, all the betrayals she'd endured, she had kept her humanity. And an innocence that had nothing to do with sexual experience.

He'd taken pleasure from her and was never able to give her pleasure in return. This was his chance. His only chance. It may be selfish. It may be harmful to both of them, but he could not refuse.

God help him, he could not refuse.

God help them both.

Chapter 13

Shelby held her breath waiting for Ian to give some indication of what he intended to do. Would he accept her offer or reject her? She kept her eyes open, focused on his face and hands. The scarred side of his face hid behind the curtain of his hair so only the unblemished, achingly handsome side showed. Though his eye gleamed with passion, he remained still. Then he slowly lifted his good hand and untied the ribbon at the neck of her chemise, revealing her breasts.

She exhaled, able to breathe again.

She remained present, not taking herself out of her body as she always had when she was with a man. She allowed herself to feel his touch as he stroked her nipple. To be aroused by it.

He was being so gentle it almost made her cry. She had never felt so cherished. He touched her everywhere, running his hand down her arm, over her stomach, coming back to her breasts, following his hand with his lips. She smiled at the familiar scratchiness, one side soft and moist, the other dry and parched, that only Ian's lips had.

Because it was Ian, she relaxed and enjoyed the sensations he was causing. He suckled at her breast, nipped playfully, then laved it with his tongue. She held his head to her breast as her breath quickened and warmth spread throughout her body. Moisture pooled between her thighs, something she'd never felt before without the aid of lubricating oils.

He moved down her stomach, kissing her through her chemise. He moved lower. Raising the hem of her chemise, he gazed at her pubis and heat seared her. Men had leered at her and pawed at her, but none had ever revered her the way Ian did.

He spread her legs and kissed her intimately, nipping at the nub that she knew was the key to unlocking pleasure for a woman, though she'd never experienced it herself. She had never thought she would. That she could. She thought there was something fundamentally wrong with her. The other women talked about pleasuring themselves or each other, about letting the men they serviced pleasure them as well, but she had never tried. Hadn't believed herself capable of it. Or deserving of it.

But what Ian was doing to her, licking and sucking, nipping and laving, had her squirming on the sheets, head thrown back, an aching need centered at the core of her being.

She didn't shout out when she climaxed as she'd been taught a woman should. She caught her breath and held it, then let it out in a long, satisfied sigh. He looked up at her and a self-satisfied grin spread across his face. Even the misshapen, scarred side of his mouth lifted at the corner.

He kissed his way back up her body then lay down next to her.

"I hope that met with your approval, m'lady," he said as she snuggled under his arm.

"Thank you. It was wonderful." She could not express how wonderful, but she had to try. "I've never before felt that. Never before experienced the little death. I've pretended. I learned how to act like a woman in the throes of passion because that was what some men wanted, but it was an act of endurance, not pleasure. You give me pleasure. But aren't you going to join me?" She stroked the front of his pants where his desire for her was obvious.

"Only if it's what you want. This night is all for you. I will pleasure you however you desire."

"I want you inside me. I want to see how it feels to be with a man who cares for me." She regretted the words as soon as she said them. His reasons for forcing her to return to her family had little to do with caring and more to do with his sense of responsibility and honor after the near-fatal beating Bramly had given her. She should not presume that it had anything to do with love. She amended her words. "Someone I care for, I mean."

He caressed her cheek.

"I do care for you, Shelby," he said.

"Because I am a squire's daughter and niece to an earl," she said. Why else would he make such effort on her behalf?

His lips quirked up.

"When I retrieved you today from Nell Ryan's brothel, at the cost of a hefty purse I might add, I was not aware of your familial relations. I care for you, Shelby or Chartreuse or whatever you want to call yourself. The fact that I didn't sack you for all your impertinences should have told you something."

She smiled.

"You didn't sack me because you enjoyed my playing the piano."

"I will miss that. I will miss you." He kissed her deeply.

"We can still see each other…"

He shook his head.

"No, it would be too risky. You don't know me. Have never met me. And if you do see me, you must act appalled at the sight of me as any young woman of good breeding would."

"I will do no such thing," she said, lightly running her finger down the damaged side of his face. "Even if I had spent the past five years in a convent school, I would still see the goodness in you. Now," she said, having no intention of wasting the little time they had being maudlin. "Let us get back to the task at hand. You, sir, are overdressed."

He divested himself of his clothing while she drew her chemise over her head. It was the first time she had seen him completely naked. Sorrow at the pain he must have felt brought her close to tears.

"Oh, Ian, I'm so sorry for what you suffered."

She kissed every mark on his ravaged body.

"I really can't feel that, you know," he said, but he didn't push her away.

She kissed lower.

"I know you can feel this," she said as she took him into her mouth.

He sucked in a breath.

"Keep that up and I'll spend too soon."

She swirled her tongue in a practiced maneuver then relented. She didn't want him to spend in her mouth. She wanted to feel him inside her. Would it feel any different from any of the other men she'd serviced over the years? Did loving the person matter?

She'd wet him enough, she hoped, to ease his way into her without the lubricating oils she normally used. Slowly, she crawled up his body like a cat stalking its prey. She stretched out on top of him, nestling his cock between her thighs, rubbing her breasts against his chest. She kissed him deeply, plunging her tongue into his mouth, mimicking the thrust and retreat of the act they were about to engage in. His tongue joined hers in the dance.

She eased his cock into her. Between her spittle on his

cock, his own wetness beading the top, and her own miraculous moisture, he slid in without any pain or difficulty. She pushed herself up on her elbows and looked down at where their bodies joined. Sitting back, she sank onto him. The familiar fullness surprised her and for a moment she felt herself shutting down, drifting away, viewing the act as an observer rather than a participant. Well versed in the mechanics, her body started to move on its own, up and down, attempting to wring pleasure out of him as quickly as possible.

He touched her arm, her breast.

"Slowly," he said, reaching between them and rubbing her nub. Pleasure radiated from the spot, warming her whole body, causing her to clench her walls around his cock. He hissed, and she smiled.

She slowed the rhythm, allowing herself to feel his hardness inside her, the building urgency where his thumb rubbed her. He closed his eye, and she watched his face as it relaxed in pleasure. He opened it again and smiled.

She felt herself cresting but resisted the peak, not wanting it to end. He grabbed her hips and started lifting her up and down in a faster pace.

"Now," he growled.

Her release crashed over her. This time she shouted. Throwing her head back, she let loose a primal scream of joy. He was not long after her. Returning her gaze to his face, she watched as he grimaced as if in pain then felt the hot gush of his seed spilling inside her. When he was spent, she collapsed on top of him.

"That was…"

"Shhh…" He put a finger on her lips. "No platitudes. You don't need to tell me how virile I am, how much better than any other man. No lies between us."

She remained silent because he wouldn't believe her. But it *was* better than with any other man. Her heart was engaged, not just her body.

They made love twice more during the night. She used all her hard-won skills to bring him to heights of pleasure, and he returned the favor, using all the weapons in his not insubstantial arsenal to achieve the same result for her.

After the last time, Ian slumped on the mattress beside her and gathered her into his arms.

"I am done for," he said. In a moment, his breathing slowed, and a soft snore escaped.

Shelby fought against sleep, wanting to remain aware, not wanting this moment to end. Dreading the morning. But eventually, with her head resting on his chest, she drifted off to the steady beat of Ian's heart.

❧

Morning came too soon.

Shelby woke early, as she'd become accustomed to while working in Ian's household. The staff started their day before dawn to ready the house for him. Fires needed starting, breakfast needed to be prepared, all before the master roused himself from slumber.

She should get up and light a fire in the cold hearth. She should search through the cupboard for something to break their fast. But she could not exert herself to move. She spent these precious moments looking at Ian's sleeping face. How relaxed he looked. Sated. She smiled knowing that she made him this way.

Why had she refused to be his mistress when he'd offered? Now, she wanted nothing more than to hide away in this house by day and make love to him all night long. What a fool she'd been. Now, he'd concocted this scheme to return her to her family. A family that didn't want her. Well, maybe Phoebe did, but Uncle Phillip, her mother, and Mr. Granger had all been perfectly happy to let her go.

The enormity of what she was about to do settled its

weight on her. How was she going to face Uncle Phillip? How could she lie to Phoebe for the rest of her life?

Ian stirred. His head turned toward her and opened his eye. And smiled, that endearing crooked smile of his that had her heart melting.

"I want to be your mistress," she blurted. "I want to stay here. Please, let's forget this nonsense. It will never work."

"Don't tempt me." He sat up and planted his feet on the floor. Sitting on the edge of the bed with his back to her, the puckered skin testament to the agony he'd endured, he hesitated. She held her breath, hoping he'd renege and see that she was right. "We've talked about this. You agreed."

"I've changed my mind. After last night…"

He stood and padded to the ewer on the far side of the room.

"That was a mistake then."

Pain stabbed her heart.

"So, you're done with me. You're throwing me away. Just like everyone I've ever loved."

The words rang in the room for a heartbeat. She held her breath, wondering if he registered their import. Then he slammed his hand on the wall and turned to face her.

"I'm doing this for you! Giving you a second chance! Do you think if someone offered me a chance to go back to the man I was, I wouldn't take it?"

"I don't want to go back! I want you!"

He strode over to her and pulled her into his arms.

"You don't want me," he said. "You're frightened."

"Terrified."

"Phoebe will be so happy to see you."

"She's the only one."

"The notice has gone to the papers."

"You can send a retraction."

"I'll do no such thing." He gently pushed her hair behind her ear. "You don't love me. No one could."

But there he was wrong. Because she did. He lifted her chin, forcing her to look at him.

"You don't want to be a mistress. Not mine nor any man's. You told me that yourself. It is all the same, you said. You preferred scrubbing floors to earning your living on your back. This is your chance, Shelby. Go back to the life you were meant to have. Be happy. Do that for me."

"What about you? What will you do?" Dared she hope he would court her? Was that why he was restoring her to her family? So Bramly could not accuse him of incompetence if he married her? Hope surged through her.

His next words crushed it.

"Oh, I'll muddle along well enough. Daphne is intent on finding me a wife. I suppose it's time I allow it." He gave her a steady gaze. "We will not be introduced. It would be too dangerous for your reputation to have anyone suspect an association between us."

She stepped out of his embrace.

"So this is goodbye then," she said, donning again the shield of Chartreuse LaRue.

"This is goodbye."

She gave him a cocky, confident smile.

"Thanks, guv, fer the right good turn you've done me. I won't ferget it."

He chucked his knuckles under her chin and gave her a gentle smile that nearly broke her heart.

"No talking that way when you return home." His expression became serious. "Remember."

She nodded.

"I'll remember."

They dressed in silence. He played lady's maid and helped her with Daphne's dress. The fit was almost perfect. She hadn't realized she and Daphne were so close in size. She played valet and tied his cravat.

He left before the cab came for her. He didn't want

there to be anything connecting him to her. He kissed her tenderly before slipping through the door.

She did not tell him that she loved him. She'd show him in the best way she was able. By convincing the world that Miss Shelby Endicott had spent the past five years in a convent school rather than a London brothel.

Chapter 14

Ian had instructed her to have the hired hack take her to
Endicott House, but in this one thing she disobeyed him.
Instead, she had the driver take her to the Pulteney Hotel,
then asked him to bring a note to her Uncle Phillip telling
him she had arrived. She wanted a private word with her
uncle before seeing the rest of the family.

She waited in the lobby sipping cup after cup of tea waiting for him. She was nervous, but she slipped behind the
façade of being a lady. Back erect, never touching the back
of her chair, she played the part better than she had at Acton Park. Now even more than then, her entire future lay in
her ability to play the part.

At precisely noon, a footman wearing the Endicott livery
approached her. He bore a note from her uncle. It was
terse, instructing her to take the awaiting carriage to Endicott House. There was no welcome in the words.

Shelby stiffened her spine. She knew her uncle would
rather that she had remained hidden away in Nell Ryan's
brothel until she died of the pox, never to be heard from
again. Part of her agreed with him.

But that was no longer possible. Through sheer determination and obstinacy, Ian had survived a fire that should have meant certain death. He was not about to let her nor her uncle hide from the truth now that it had been revealed. If he could face all of society as the Monster Earl, then surely she could face her uncle's wrath.

❧

Her uncle was not at home to greet her. Instead, she was met with her cousin's boisterous cries.

"I can't believe you are finally here!" Phoebe pulled her into an enthusiastic embrace. "I have been nagging father for years to send for you. Why did you never answer any of my letters? Oh, never mind. You're here now, what does it matter."

Phoebe chattered nonstop while showing her to her room.

"But where are your things?"

"I have none," Shelby admitted. "The convent where I attended school adhered to a vow of poverty. I took only what I needed for travel. Everything else I left for others to use."

And so it began—the lies and deceit. She hated not being able to confide in Phoebe, especially when Phoebe was so open with her. But she felt ancient compared to Phoebe. Old and tired. She'd do anything to keep her cousin's innocence from being tarnished the way hers had been.

They spent the afternoon together, two girls in their first Season. Aunt Lucia, Shelby learned, was out paying calls and Uncle Phillip was visiting his clubs. He'd probably avoid coming home as long as possible.

Still, he had allowed her to spend time with his precious daughter, so he must not be planning to repudiate her.

When it was time to dress for dinner, Phoebe opened her wardrobe.

"We'll have to get you outfitted for the Season," she said

as she sorted through her dresses looking for something for Shelby to wear.

"Any of your castoffs will be fine," Shelby said. "I am, after all, just a poor relation." A poor relation with a sordid past. She didn't even want to touch Phoebe's things for fear she'd taint them. She was accustomed to the cheap satin gowns she wore in the brothel or the rough homespun wool she'd worn as a servant. Wearing Daphne's muslin walking dress made her feel like an imposter. How would she ever manage one of Phoebe's silk evening gowns?

"You've never been a poor relation to me, Shelby Endicott," Phoebe said with a fierceness Shelby had never before seen in the girl. "You were always my best friend."

❧

Dinner was formal though family only. Uncle Phillip sat at the head of the long dining table that could easily seat twenty. Aunt Lucia took her place at the foot and Shelby and Phoebe were across from each other halfway down the middle. The great expanse separating them should have made conversation with her aunt and uncle difficult, which, Shelby believed, had been the intent, but that didn't stop Phoebe. She regaled them all with stories and gossip until Uncle Phillip nodded to Aunt Lucia for the ladies to leave the table.

"I liked it much better when we used to eat alone in the nursery, didn't you?" Phoebe whispered conspiratorially to Shelby as the three ladies made their way to the drawing room for tea.

And just like that, Shelby came home. They could have been six and seven again, stealing sweets from Cook in the Endicott kitchen and smuggling them to the nursery. Or nine and ten, sharing secrets under the covers after the light had been doused. They could have been eleven and twelve spying on the handsome new footman. What if she had confided in Phoebe when Mr. Granger first started touching her? Shelby, as the elder, had always tried to protect Phoebe. She wanted to protect Phoebe still.

No, she was glad she hadn't told her about Mr. Granger. She hoped Phoebe never learned where she really was the past five years.

The past five years had changed her considerably so it surprised her to find that she and Phoebe could still be friends. That the bond between them had not been lost. She had always liked her cousin very much and found that she liked her still. Phoebe's innocent vitality attracted her, reminding her of who she had once been. Who she would be now if not for Mr. Granger.

"Ah, Phoebe," she said, her voice shaking. "I have missed you so much."

Once in the drawing room, Aunt Lucia instructed Phoebe to play the piano for them as she drew Shelby aside. Phoebe made a face, but dutifully obeyed. She settled on the bench, straightened the music sheets, and hit the keys with plodding authority but little finesse. She struck a discordant note, paused, then continued slowly marching through the piece like a good soldier on parade.

Shelby smiled as she settled on the settee next to Aunt Lucia so they could listen. Phoebe was not the musician that she was; her playing was mediocre at best because Phoebe never felt the music. That hadn't changed. But Phoebe could sew rings around her. Phoebe's needlework was art. They each had their talents and never begrudged the other hers.

"I am so glad that your long separation from your family is over, Shelby," Aunt Lucia said gently. "I hope that it was grief over your father's death that caused your indiscretion and that we have no need for concern about your behavior around Phoebe."

Shelby wrinkled her brow in confusion. Did Aunt Lucia

know about her career at Nell's? Had Uncle Phillip told her? Surely if he had, she would never have invited Shelby into her home. Then her aunt continued in a low, secretive voice.

"I know about the child, though I'm not supposed to. Did the sisters find a family for it?"

Her body tightened. She fisted her hands in her lap to keep from screaming. Uncle Phillip had told Aunt Lucia the same thing he'd told her mother. That he'd sent her to a convent to have the baby instead of abandoning her in a brothel.

Eyes downcast, she struggled to get her breathing under control before she answered. Her voice sounded hollow and empty, devoid of the emotion she was holding inside, trying not to lash out at Aunt Lucia for her husband's actions. She was here now. That's all that mattered.

"The child died before it was born."

Aunt Lucia patted her hands sympathetically, and Shelby's fists relaxed. "I lost a child once, before Phoebe was born. I know how heartbreaking it can be. But in this case, perhaps it was a blessing."

Shelby's eyes filled with tears, her anger defeated by a simple gesture and expression of understanding. Aunt Lucia was so kind and gentle. Why couldn't her own mother be that way? She couldn't imagine Aunt Lucia sending Phoebe away no matter what she thought she had done.

❧

Caught up in Phoebe's enthusiasm, Shelby spent the next week in a whirlwind of activity, being fitted for day dresses, a riding habit, even a ball gown.

Secretly, she reviewed a copy of Debrett's Peerage that she'd found in the library and absconded to her room in order to reacquaint herself with proper forms of address. She watched everything Phoebe did and shamelessly copied her.

Her education in the proper forms of etiquette had been cut short. She caught herself often saying or doing the wrong thing. She'd make a remark that was totally inappropriate or forget which fork to use.

The weeks passed quickly with dance lessons and shopping trips by day and social engagements in the evenings. She told the story about being in a convent school so many times, she almost started believing it herself. When she helped the scullery maid light the fire in her hearth in the morning—the girl really had no skill for it—she covered her gaffe by explaining that they'd had no servants at the convent school so she'd had to tend to her own fire herself. The only reminders of her real past were the scars she bore from Bramly's beating, stiffness in her healed leg when the weather turned wet, and incessant searching for a glimpse of Ian everywhere she went.

She wanted to be worthy of his faith in her. She wanted to make him proud. But how could she show him how well she was doing if she never saw him? Perhaps he had gone back to Acton Park after foisting her on her uncle, finally deciding that returning to society was too much effort. She eavesdropped on the servants unabashedly trying to hear a single word about Chester House. She missed Bitsy and Mrs. Pitts.

At the oddest moments, she'd be reminded of one of the girls she'd left behind at Nell's.

"Rose would love this shade of red," she said when looking at fabrics one afternoon.

"Who's Rose?" Phoebe asked.

Shelby cursed herself for her slip-up.

"One of the girls at school," she stammered, recovering quickly. "She loves flashy colors."

"Then you should send her some," Phoebe said.

Shelby grimaced.

"The girls aren't allowed to wear anything this fine.

Mother Superior would confiscate it."

And so she found a way to talk about the past five years to Phoebe without revealing the truth. Nell was Mother Superior, the girls she worked with were fellow students, Bitsy was a novitiate, and Mrs. Pitts her favorite teacher. And Ian was an anonymous benefactor to the convent.

She attended musicales and soirees and was introduced to a select group of family friends, small gatherings to ease her back into society and make sure she would not be an embarrassment to the family.

The first time she encountered one of her former patrons from Nell Ryan's brothel was at the Pennington's musicale. Shelby held her breath as Lord Hornby was introduced to her. He kissed her hand and made inane pleasantries without a glimmer of recognition. Ian was right, people saw what they expected to see. And no one expected to meet a whore at a Society party.

Shelby relaxed more then and started to believe that maybe she could put her past behind her. Maybe she could just be Shelby Endicott and forget that Chartreuse LaRue had ever existed.

She must have passed the test, because three weeks after returning to her family, Shelby found herself at Almack's assembly rooms. The ladies at Nell's had often joked about Almack's, the bastion of propriety. Who would have thought that one of their own would actually be sponsored there one day? But here she was, being given permission to dance her first waltz.

A pimply-faced boy, some relation to the Baron Ornsby, claimed the dance. As niece to an earl and daughter of a country squire, she had a decent pedigree though no fortune. Her uncle agreed to a small dowry and hoped, she knew, to pawn her off on the first unsuspecting suitor who came along.

She hadn't told him she had no intention of ever marrying. She was far too jaded and cynical to make a good wife. She would eat someone like this green boy alive.

She felt like she was playing a part in a play. On stage, she was the graceful young aristocratic ingénue waltzing in the arms of an eligible young gentleman. Off stage, she knew, she was still the coarse whore. She didn't know who she was anymore.

She loved having her friendship with Phoebe back, but it was a friendship based on lies. Phoebe would not trust her if she knew where Shelby had really spent the past five years.

And even though she'd populated the fiction of the convent school with characters from her real life, it was still a lie. There was no one she could confide in. No one who really knew who she was and what she had gone through. Uncle Phillip, who avoided her as much as possible, chose to pretend her past did not exist.

The dance ended and her partner, whose name she'd already forgotten, immediately, as convention dictated, returned her to her place with her family. He bowed handsomely, but neither of them pursued a conversation. He retreated as quickly as was politely possible, and she wondered if she'd given herself away. If he could smell the stench of Nell's on her and couldn't get away from her fast enough.

Across the room, Shelby saw a familiar figure. Her heartbeat quickened. Ian had come.

He dressed conservatively, as though he did not wish to draw attention to himself. Though she knew it pained him, he stood with a stiff rigidity even though the muscles in his back and shoulders had contracted during his recuperation from the fire, making it difficult for him to maintain a good posture.

The eye patch he wore covered most of the fire-ravaged half of his face. He stood stiffly erect, his tailored black jacket concealing the irregularity of his posture with extra padding on his left shoulder. He wore his hair clubbed back, an emerald stick pin gleamed in his cravat, his formal breeches hugged his thighs and calves, his dancing shoes shone.

She drank him in, quenching a thirst she hadn't realized was so acute.

She waited hopefully for him to come to her and ask her to dance, but he stayed on the other side of the room, not even meeting her eyes though she knew he had seen her.

She danced twice more, and each time the steps brought her close to him, she tried to attract his attention.

But he never glanced her way.

He didn't leave his place. He chatted amiably with the gentlemen around him but never approached any of the eager young ladies hoping for a dance partner. Never approaching her, the most eager young lady of them all.

Before the end of her third set, he was gone.

Perhaps he was just ensuring that Uncle Phillip was living up to his part of the bargain. If her uncle had hidden her away somewhere, would Ian really have brought scandal down on Phoebe? If her uncle had bothered to learn more about Ian's character, he would know that no such threat existed. Ian would not have hurt Phoebe that way any more than he had turned her away when she was dumped on his doorstep. He may be known as the Monster Earl, but she knew the moniker did not fit. She knew monsters, and Ian was not one of them.

⊷

He was a monster.

He should have stayed away. He knew even being in the same room with Shelby could put her at risk. But when Daphne had mentioned the new crop of girls that had been issued vouchers to Almacks and Lady Phoebe Endicott was on the list, he had to make sure that her cousin had been included.

As Ian leaned back against the leather squabs of his carriage, he let the tension ease between his shoulders. Standing for over an hour had been torture. Watching Shelby dance with other men tortured him even more.

It was foolish and unnecessary. He knew she was out, had heard it at his club. It had taken an enormous strength of will not to put his fist in the mouth of Lord Compton when he said that if he couldn't bring Endicott's daughter up to scratch he'd settle for the niece as she was equally as comely and having no fortune would probably be twice as biddable. Fists clenched, he'd had to sit there and pretend an indifference he didn't feel.

He missed her. Wished he'd kept her to himself. He'd sublet the house on Templeton Place the day after she'd left it so he wouldn't be tempted to renege on his promises and set her up there.

Foolishly, he hadn't realized the depths of his feelings for her until she was gone. Or perhaps it was because of the night they spent together not as master and mistress but as lovers.

He'd taken to going out in the evenings because staying home meant hearing the silence in the music room.

She'd brought the light back into his life. She'd made him a man again. She'd forced him to accept himself as he was now.

The only way he could think to repay her was to restore her to her family. But what if he'd been wrong? What if Endicott blamed Shelby for Ian's actions? What if she was worse off now than she was before?

She had seemed genuinely happy in his household. But her cousin had made her continued employment as one of his servants untenable even if her uncle would have gladly left her to it and paid her salary.

No, he'd done what was necessary.

Tonight he had proof that he'd done the right thing.

God, she looked so young. And innocent. Her eyes sparkled like she was amused by some private joke. She flirted; she danced. She behaved like all the other debutantes in the room. No one would suspect that she wasn't the innocent young woman she appeared to be.

He chose to ignore the shadow that crossed her features when she thought no one was looking. Ignored the spark of hope that lit her eyes when she first spotted him. The longing he saw there matched his own.

She would find another. Some worthy young man who could make her happy. Someone who knew nothing of her past with whom she could begin her life anew.

An association between them would be disastrous. Someone seeing them together might recall his servant, the former prostitute Chartreuse LaRue, and put together that she and Shelby Endicott were the same person. Or at least close relations. Either way, it would bring scandal down upon her, and her second chance would be forfeit.

No, he had to stay away from her. But Lord knew if he'd be able to.

He was a monster.

❧

The next evening, she saw him at the Howe's rout. The room was so crowded that by the time she made her way over to where she'd spotted him, he was gone.

At the theater the following evening, he entered the box across from hers, stayed for part of the performance but left before intermission.

It became a pattern then. He would appear at whatever function she attended, then disappear without a word. He never asked to be introduced to her. He never acknowledged her in any way. He never gave away by even the slightest glance that they were acquainted.

But he was always there.

She came to depend on it. She couldn't begin to enjoy the evening until she saw him. He was still her knight in shining armor watching over her.

She was glad to see that he was receiving invitations. Society seemed to be accepting him even though his appearance was still shocking to some. She thought he looked quite dashing with his dark clothes and eye patch.

A week after Almack's, last-minute preparations for the Endicott's ball occupied the household. Final invitations were being sent out.

"I think we should invite Lord Chester," Phoebe said over breakfast only days before the big event. "He was very kind to me when I mistook his servant for Shelby, and he is responsible for encouraging Father to bring her home."

Shelby nearly choked on her toast. Phoebe had never mentioned recognizing her at Lady Fontaine's masquerade.

"I don't think your father wants to be reminded about that," Aunt Lucia reprimanded Phoebe.

Shelby pretended ignorance.

"I visited Lord Chester at his house very inappropriately," Phoebe confessed. "But the woman I saw looked so much like you, Shelby, I just had to find out. I had been begging father for years to let you come live with us. And even though I sent letter after letter to you, I never got any response. I was afraid that there was some conspiracy afoot to keep you away from me."

Phoebe was not as naïve as everyone assumed.

"If seeing someone who looks like me caused Uncle Phillip to bring me home, then I am very grateful," Shelby said. "Maybe we should invite this Lord Chester. I don't believe I know him."

She managed to keep her voice steady as she lied to Phoebe, even though her heart was racing and her breath caught at the prospect of Ian coming to the ball. He wouldn't be able to avoid her there; he'd have to be introduced. No doubt he wouldn't even come, she oughtn't get her hopes up. But the prospect exhilarated her.

"You must have noted him. He's everywhere we are it seems. He wears a patch."

Shelby appreciated Phoebe's description. Rather than calling attention to his injuries, she merely distinguished him by the eye patch he wore to conceal them.

"I will discuss the matter with your father," Aunt Lucia said, putting an end to the conversation.

Chapter 15

Shelby stood in the receiving line at the entrance to the ballroom. She felt like a princess in a fairy tale, dressed in a satin ball gown that flowed around her like water. She even wore a tiara on her head. She and Phoebe looked more like sisters than cousins. Their yellow hair, Shelby's just a shade or two darker than Phoebe's, was done up in the identical style. Even their gowns were similarly cut, though Phoebe wore blue to match her eyes and Shelby's was a lovely shade of lavender with oversized flowers embroidered on the hem that swirled when she walked. She could hardly wait to dance.

Shelby had grown complacent. It seemed that no one who had known her as Chartreuse LaRue would ever make the connection that she and Miss Shelby Endicott, Lord Endicott's niece, were one and the same person. Even she had difficulty believing it now.

But not all her former patrons would be fooled. And when Mr. Gordon Lancaster bent over her hand, Shelby's stomach sank. He held onto her hand for too long. When he looked up, he gave her an insolent grin and a familiar wink.

"So nice to see you again, Miss Endicott." Gordon put special emphasis on her name, telling her he knew her to be a fraud.

Shelby decided to brazen it out as Ian had told her to. "Have we met, sir?"

He just smiled knowingly.

"I hope that we can meet that way again," he said suggestively before moving on.

Shelby's knees were shaking. If Gordon exposed her, she'd bring ruin on her family. On Phoebe.

Somehow, she managed to keep her composure. She continued smiling and greeting guests, even though her stomach churned at the thought of what Gordon might do. At this very minute, he might be spreading the awful truth about her.

The number of arrivals was dwindling. Phoebe and Shelby were just about to leave the receiving line so the dancing could begin when Ian approached them. Shelby feasted her eyes on him. Surely Ian would know how to handle Gordon.

Phoebe introduced him to her. Ian took her gloved hand in his and held it to his lips.

"Miss Endicott, how very nice to meet you."

"And you, my lord." Shelby grasped his fingers briefly before he released her hand. "Do you dance, Lord Chester?"

Ian looked as though he wanted to reprimand her for her boldness, but simply nodded.

"The first set is as yet unclaimed, and the dancing is about to begin. Would you do me the honor of partnering me?" Shelby knew that she was not allowed to ask a man to dance, but she hoped no one was close enough to hear her.

"It would be my pleasure." He smiled at her and held out his hand.

The dance allowed them only brief moments for private

conversation as they moved through the steps, but Shelby used each available instant to convey her distress to Ian.

"Mr. Gordon Lancaster is here," she said the first time they clasped hands and performed the turn the dance required. Then the steps separated them again.

"He thinks he knows me," she said the next time the dance brought them together.

"But like me, he's only just met you," Ian said as the dance ended. Giving her a warning look, he returned her to Aunt Lucia's side where none other than Master Gordon Lancaster was waiting to pounce on her.

"Can't say I'm surprised to see you here, Lord Chester," Gordon said knowingly. "Miss Endicott, may I have this dance?"

Without waiting for her reply, Gordon pulled her onto the dance floor.

"What game are you and Chester playing, Chartreuse?" he growled in her ear. "You know, I still have a bump from where you crashed that tray on my head."

"If anyone crashed a tray on your head, sir, I'm sure you deserved it. Who is this Chartreuse? What an unusual name."

She hoped that pretending ignorance would deter him, but it only seemed to spur him on to greater boldness.

"You know perfectly well who she is. Meet me in the garden for a quick tumble, Chartreuse, and I'll keep your secret. I'll let you and Chester play Endicott for a fool. But if you're not there in ten minutes, I'll announce to the world who and what you really are."

Mercifully, the dance ended. Ian had remained in conversation with Aunt Lucia. Gordon gave Ian a cocky smile before pointedly heading for the French doors that led to the garden.

"Do you know that young man, Lord Chester?" Shelby asked, amazed that her voice was steady since the color had drained from her face and her insides quivered.

"He's my brother-in-law's youngest brother. Why?" He arched his eyebrow and narrowed his eye.

"He just insulted me, and you. He kept calling me some other name and threatened me with public scandal if I didn't meet him in the garden."

Aunt Lucia gasped. "He dared insult you in this house where you are under our protection? The cheek of the man! I shall see to it that he is no longer received."

"I believe he has mistaken you for someone else, Miss Endicott, just as your cousin did a few weeks ago. I shall speak with him and disabuse him of that misapprehension."

"Please do, Lord Chester," Aunt Lucia said. "Or there will be consequences."

Oh, Aunt Lucia, if you only knew.

❧

Ian found Lancaster lounging on a stone bench hidden in a dark corner of the garden near the back wall.

"So, she sent you," he said when Ian approached him.

"She isn't Chartreuse LaRue, though I admit there is a resemblance. Her cousin Phoebe looks remarkably like her, too. But if you look closely, you'll see the difference. Chartreuse's blonde hair came out of a bottle. She didn't have Miss Endicott's refinement. Perhaps she was some Endicott by-blow, but there is no mistaking either Miss Endicott for her."

"And where is Chartreuse LaRue tonight?" Lancaster persisted.

"I have no idea. She left my employ over a month ago. Perhaps you should check Nell Ryan's brothel."

Lancaster stood and made to take the path back to the house. Ian blocked him.

"What if I go in there and announce to all assembled that Shelby Endicott is a fraud. She's nothing but a common whore who used to work as a servant in your house. What will you do then, Chester?"

"Go right ahead," Ian said, moving out of the way and waving his hand toward the house in invitation. "You'll only embarrass yourself. Miss Endicott has spent the past few years living in a convent school. I'm sure her uncle would not take kindly to you implying anything else. He may even be forced to call you out.

"If you persist, I will take insult myself. Once Endicott is done with you, if there's anything left, *I* will call you out. Are you prepared to meet me on the dueling field, Lancaster?

"You're awfully protective of someone you hardly know."

"I will not have you bring embarrassment on your family, which now, however unfortunately, includes my sister. Go home, Gordon."

"I'm not the only one who will recognize her," Lancaster threatened. "It's going to come out. Half the men in London have fucked her."

That's when Ian hit him. Glass-jawed Gordon Lancaster fell to the ground like a stone.

❧

Ian managed to get Lancaster loaded in his carriage without too much fuss. To the few people they passed as he spirited the now-groggy young man out the garden gate, he explained that he had obviously imbibed too much champagne. With Lancaster safely on his way home, Ian went back to the ballroom to allay Shelby's fears of exposure.

She was dancing. He didn't recognize her partner, but it really didn't matter since he focused solely on Shelby. She was beautiful, young and radiant. She looked exactly what everyone here supposed her to be: a convent-educated, innocent young lady enjoying her first Season.

As her self-appointed knight-errant, he would do any-thing he could to preserve that illusion. Watching her now, even he could hardly believe she was the same woman he had lain with only a month before.

Since their last night together at Templeton Place, Ian could not stop thinking about her. He knew he had to stay away from her to protect her reputation. Thanks to his Un-cle Bramly, his association with the common prostitute Chartreuse LaRue was well known in all his clubs, if not in a few drawing rooms as well. He didn't want anyone to sus-pect, Gordon Lancaster notwithstanding, that Chartreuse LaRue was now being launched into Society as Shelby Endi-cott.

Coming here tonight had put her at risk. Perhaps Lan-caster wouldn't have made the connection if Ian hadn't danced with her. He should not even have been frequenting the same social functions that she was going to, but he couldn't help himself. He had to know how she was faring.

As the dance ended, Ian sought Shelby out. He would take his leave and try to avoid meeting her again. He would have to follow her progress in Society through the newssheets and his sister's gossip. He would do nothing to jeopardize this second chance she'd been given.

He made his excuses to Lord and Lady Endicott. Lord Endicott looked relieved to see Ian on his way. They had not spoken since the day Ian had threatened him at his club, but he knew Endicott was well aware he was watching Shelby's progress. He had been quite surprised to receive the invitation to Endicott's ball. He thought for sure the man would give him the cut direct after the way he had co-erced him to accept his responsibility to Shelby.

Miss Phoebe was reluctant to let him part.

"Lord Chester, I have to thank you for encouraging my father to send for my cousin Shelby," she said far too loudly. "If not for you, she would still be hidden away in that awful convent school."

Ian wanted to put his hand over her mouth to keep her quiet. If anyone within hearing range started putting the pieces together, Shelby's position would become precarious.

He merely nodded and turned to say good-bye to Shelby.

She looked at him with such trust, he wanted to pull her into his arms.

"The matter you mentioned earlier has been rectified, Miss Endicott," he said as quietly as he could. She nodded her understanding.

"Must you go so soon, Lord Chester?" she asked hopefully.

"I'm afraid I have another obligation," he lied. He wanted to tell her that he wanted nothing more than to stay, to dance with her again, to be with her again. He wanted to tell her how much he missed their evenings in the music room. But he could say nothing.

They must keep up the pretense of being new acquaintances. If she were truly what Society thought her, he could politely call on her the next afternoon. But he would not allow himself that luxury.

Giving her hand a slight squeeze, he tried to tell her with his gaze that this was good-bye.

❧

The joy went out of the evening for Shelby as soon as Ian departed. She wanted to talk to him. She wanted to know what had transpired between him and Gordon Lancaster out in the garden.

She wanted to tell him how much she missed him.

Now that they had been properly and publicly introduced, there was no reason why they couldn't be seen talking together. Surely now he would call on her or at least approach her the next time they were at the same social gathering.

Maybe he would even court her.

But the week after the ball, Shelby saw no sign of Ian. She continued to look for him everywhere she went, but he did not appear. She asked Phoebe if they could ride on Rotten Row in the mornings in the hopes that she might run into him there, but Aunt Lucia forbade it.

Finally, the realization hit her. Ian was done with her. He had seen her safely launched into Society, safely restored to her family. The task he'd set himself was completed. And he wanted nothing more to do with her.

Even though she knew it was for the best, she couldn't help but feel hurt. Even though she knew he should marry someone unmarred by a tarnished past, she had secretly hoped he would want to marry her.

He was the only man she could marry because he was the only man who knew the truth about her.

But because he knew the truth about her, she could never marry him. He deserved better, she reminded herself. He deserved a woman who would come to him a virgin on their wedding night.

She tried to be happy for him, therefore, when she learned at the Marstons' ball that he was betrothed to Miss Penelope Furbush.

Chapter 16

Shelby hadn't been aware that Ian even knew Penelope Furbush. And as a servant in his house, she thought she knew every one of his associates. Servants talked, after all. Even close-mouthed Mr. Symmington, Ian's intrepid valet. Obviously, unbeknownst to her and all his staff below stairs, he had been paying court to young ladies of good ton.

Miss Furbush seemed to be a good enough match for him. She was in her third Season, so she was getting a bit long in the tooth and needed to find a husband soon, or she'd be left sitting on the shelf. Her father was a Baron, so it was a good match for her, becoming a Countess as she would. Most importantly, Miss Furbush had a sterling reputation. She'd never been associated with a hint of scandal.

Unlike Shelby. If she couldn't have Ian herself, she supposed Miss Furbush would do as his wife.

She was a pretty enough young woman, Shelby supposed, as she watched her dance a country set. She had plain features and ordinary brown hair, but her eyes were a deep, dark chocolate. She was quite pretty when she smiled, as she was smiling now at her dancing partner, Lord

Leighton.

Lord Leighton was a lecherous lothario. Shelby knew him well as he'd been a regular customer at Nell's. He was married, but it was well known that he had never made a practice of fidelity.

Shelby wondered what Miss Furbush found to smile about. She must be an innocent, Shelby decided. None but a complete innocent could be fooled by Leighton's flirting. He'd tried flirting with her a few times, but she just brushed it off. At first, she thought that he had recognized her, then she realized that he behaved that way with all the ladies.

Shelby watched with interest as Lord Leighton escorted Miss Furbush to the French doors leading to the terrace. They stepped outside together, which, Shelby assumed, was a respectable thing to do since they were still in full view of the ballroom, but she didn't think it was wise for a newly betrothed woman to go off alone with another man. Especially that man.

Feeling that it was her duty to Ian to protect the woman he intended to marry, Shelby discretely made her way over to where she had seen the couple make their exit. They stood just outside the doors, their heads very close together, whispering. Miss Furbush appeared to be upset.

Shelby slipped behind a potted fern out on the terrace so she could eavesdrop on their conversation. So, she wasn't such a lady. One thing Nell had taught her: information was a valuable commodity. Nell traded in information as much as she did in flesh.

"How will I endure being married to such a monster?" Miss Furbush was saying.

"Hush, my sweet," Leighton reassured her. "Once you are married, you will have more freedom. I doubt Chester will even come to your bed. I've heard he's incapable of performing his marital duties."

"He'd better come to my bed, or he'll know the babe

isn't his."

"It won't matter once you're married. He'll have to claim the child. Just think, my son may be the next Earl of Chester." Leighton laughed. Shelby wanted to punch the smirk off his face. "Come, let us return to the ball."

They went back inside. Shelby stayed behind the plant until she stopped shaking. They were duping Ian. Innocent Miss Furbush was nothing but a lying harlot.

Shelby had to warn Ian.

At last she had a reason to go see him. She hadn't realized how much she wanted some excuse.

❦

Shelby pleaded a headache, so Uncle Phillip escorted her home early from the ball. Riding home in the carriage, she realized it was the first time the two of them had been alone since she'd come to stay at Endicott House.

"Uncle Phillip," she tentatively began, "why did you leave me at Nell's?"

"We won't speak of it," he said with finality.

Something cracked inside her. All the shame, self-loathing, and pain she'd trapped inside released through the fissure, leaving only a rage so overpowering it nearly choked her.

"We must speak of it. Why did you leave me there?" She forced the words out of her tight throat, so they sounded guttural and vicious.

"Why did you run off to London? Why didn't you come to me?" he countered.

"I did come to you. You sent me back."

Phillip Endicott squirmed uncomfortably in his seat. "I sent you home as your mother requested."

"You sent me home to the bastard who was raping me."

"I didn't know he was raping you. I would have seen him hanged." In the dim light of the carriage, she saw tears glistening in his eyes. "I failed you. I failed my brother. I'm sorry. It was easier to think that you…"

"It was easier to think I deserved what I got, that the fault was in me. That way, you couldn't be responsible. The only one responsible for me ending up in Nell Ryan's brothel was my dear stepfather, Martin Granger."

"Granger? I thought it was…"

"Some local boy? That's what my mother wanted to believe. No, it was Granger."

"You should have told me. I would never have sent you back if I had known."

"I'm sorry, Uncle Phillip. I was too ashamed. You see," she said, spitting the words out like a bitter pill, "he'd convinced me that it was my fault. Working at Nell's just confirmed it. I'm nothing but a whore."

Uncle Phillip drew her into his arms, giving her a comfortable pat on the back.

"You are not. Not anymore." His voice sounded hoarse, and she felt a tear splash on the back of her neck.

The comforting gesture that reminded her so much of her father, the words of absolution, and her uncle's show of emotion broke her. Her anger collapsed, her heart squeezed, and she let loose a wail of grief for the frightened girl who had thought herself alone and without redemption.

❧

Uncle Phillip saw her inside then returned to the ball for Phoebe and Aunt Lucia. Knowing she had several hours before they would return, Shelby dismissed the maid who helped her undress. Rummaging through the bottom of the wardrobe where she had hidden the few things she'd brought with her, she retrieved the plain black dress she'd worn as a servant in Chester House. After quickly donning the dress, she slipped silently down the back staircase and let herself out through the kitchen door. She walked the few blocks to Chester House, as though she were just another servant returning home after her night off.

She let herself into the kitchen. The door had not yet been locked for the night. Mrs. Pitts was sitting at the farmer's table where Shelby had shared many a meal with the other servants.

"Good evening, Mrs. Pitts," she curtsied.

"Chartreuse, whatever are you doing here? Lord Chester said you'd run off."

"I'll only stay a short time. Is he in?"

"He is," Mrs. Pitts said. "I'm just preparing a tray for him."

"Please let me bring it," Shelby offered. "I need to speak with him about a most urgent matter."

"You'll not be getting your old job back," Mrs. Pitts warned. "His lordship was quite upset with you when you returned to your old life." Even as she was saying it, Mrs. Pitts was handing Shelby the tray laden with a cold collation for Ian's midnight snack.

Ian was immersed in a book when Shelby brought the tray into the room, so he didn't notice that it was she.

"Just leave it on the desk, Mrs. Pitts," he said without looking up.

Shelby set the tray down but didn't leave.

"Ian, I need to talk to you," she said. He jumped up as if he'd been burned.

"What the devil are you doing here?" he shouted. She put a hushing finger to her lips. There was no need to in-form the entire household of her presence.

"You can't marry Penelope Furbush," she said, getting straight to the point of her visit.

"Why the hell not?" She couldn't believe he was angry at her. She was trying to save him. "You risk everything just to tell me I've made a poor choice of bride?"

"She's carrying Lord Leighton's bastard."

"I know." That stopped her cold.

"You know? And you're marrying her anyway? Why?" Then realization dawned. "You love her then."

"Of course, I don't love her. I barely know her. Her father offered her to me when he found out about her predicament. In case you haven't noticed, I don't have a great number of women wanting to marry me. It seemed like a good solution for both of us."

She felt like throwing something at him. How could the man be so obtuse?

"You don't care that she has no intention of being faithful to you?"

"She may not intend to be faithful, but I assure you she will be. I will not allow her to continue her association with Leighton, if that's what concerns you."

"What concerns me is that you are throwing your life away on a woman who has the morals of a bitch in heat. For God's sake, Ian, if you want to marry a whore you can marry me!"

Her voice had risen during their exchange. Her last words rang in the room like a sounded gong.

"I can't marry you," he said so softly she could barely hear him. She understood, though.

"No, of course you can't. You can do much better than me. But you can do much better than Miss Penelope Furbush, too. Don't belittle yourself, Ian. Marry someone who loves you."

"Who could love me?"

"I love you," she confessed. He turned away without responding. She knew when to take her leave. "I did what I came here to do. Marry her if you wish."

"Shelby." He stopped her as her hand reached for the door latch. "I love you too. But if I married you, too many people would put together that Chartreuse LaRue and Shelby Endicott are the same person."

"I should have stayed Chartreuse LaRue. At least then I could be your mistress. Oh, Ian, I miss you so much." She launched herself into his arms. They felt like home to her.

His arms tightened around her.

"You wouldn't be my mistress, remember?"

"What a fool I was." Her voice was muffled as she buried her head in his shirt. She breathed in the scent of him, musk and brandy and bay rum.

"You have to go," he said, but he continued rubbing her back and made no effort to push her away from him.

"I know." She didn't move. They continued to stand by the door, just holding each other, reveling in the familiar sanctuary of each other's arms.

A knock on the door broke them apart.

"Will you be needing anything else this evening, my lord?" Mrs. Pitts asked when Ian opened the door. Shelby moved to the tray which remained undisturbed on the desk where she had left it.

"No, thank you, Mrs. Pitts. I will be escorting Chartreuse back to her new employer momentarily. I'll lock up when I get back."

"Good-bye, Mrs. Pitts," Shelby said from her place across the room. "Thank you for all that you did for me. I won't forget you."

No doubt wanting to ensure that she didn't make a habit of returning to the house posing as his former servant, Ian added, "Chartreuse is leaving England tomorrow, going to America with her new employer."

Shelby went along with his falsehood.

"Yes," she said. "We sail with the morning tide. I just had to come and say good-bye before I left. You have all meant so very much to me."

In an uncharacteristic display of emotion, Mrs. Pitts crossed the room and embraced her. "You're a good girl, Chartreuse," Mrs. Pitts told her. "Don't you ever forget that."

⁓

"So now that you've shipped Chartreuse LaRue off to America, what do you intend to do?" Shelby asked as Ian escorted her back to Endicott House. It was well past midnight. The streets were filled with carriages carrying members of the ton home from their various balls, routs, and soirees. A few eyes noted the renowned Monster Earl walking beside a servant girl.

Ian sighed in response to her question.

"I suppose," he said, "that I could call on Shelby Endicott if you are willing to risk it. Though your uncle may not welcome me."

"Uncle Phillip and I have made our peace." She told him about her talk with her uncle in the carriage on the way home from the ball earlier that evening. "I think he would welcome you. But you have to end your engagement to Penelope Furbush."

"Yes, I suppose I must. It was an ill-conceived notion." They had almost reached the alleyway that would take her to the back door she would use to sneak back into the house. Ian pulled her into the shadow of a neighbor's stone wall.

"Are you sure you want to risk your newly restored reputation by publicly associating with me? We can say all we want that Chartreuse LaRue is safely en route to America, but that won't stop some people from speculating."

"Ian, my new-found reputation means nothing if I can't share my life with the one person I care most about."

"It will take me a few days to clear up the Furbush matter, then I will call on you."

They reached the alley that ran behind the row of houses.

"A few days, then," she said, stopping when he looked

as if he would escort her all the way to the door.

"A few days."

She reached up and touched his cheek with her bare hand.

"I love you."

"I love you, too."

"Good night," she said, turning into the alley. She made her way quietly to the door. When she reached it, she turned to see him still standing at the top of the alleyway watching her. She lifted a hand in farewell and slipped into the house.

Chapter 17

Ian called on his intended the next morning. The staid butler showed him into a formal parlor to wait while he asked if Miss Furbush was ready to receive visitors, his censorious tone clearly conveying his disapproval of anyone calling at such an unfashionably early hour.

The parlor was well appointed if a bit ostentatious for his tastes. It bespoke a tendency toward excess and a desire to flaunt wealth. The furnishings were heavy and ornate, the carpet thick and tightly woven, the paintings on the walls framed in gold. Every available flat surface contained an abundance of figurines, vases, and other bric-a-brac so that he was afraid to move lest he topple something to the floor.

Even the mantel over the fireplace sported an assortment of china boxes that seemed to have no practical purpose other than decoration.

He stood in the middle of the room with his hands behind his back, awaiting Penelope's arrival.

He shouldn't have involved her in his plans. Though she was no innocent and, as Shelby had discovered, had no plan to be faithful to him, he had no right to use her for his own purposes. It was not well done of him.

But, in the weeks since Shelby returned to her family, when she was lost to him, he had turned his attention to his uncle. He still had not forgiven Bramly for his brutal beating of Shelby nor for his attempts to undermine him.

He had not seen Bramly in months. He continued to keep track of him, both through Society's gossip and the Bow Street Runners he employed to monitor his uncle's movements. Bramly had refused his offer of the Yorkshire estate, and Ian had refused to pay any more of Bramly's bills.

They appeared to be at a standoff. Bramly used his position as Ian's heir as collateral for his debts. He kept assuring his creditors that Ian's health was failing and that he would soon be in control of the Earl of Chester's estates and resources.

Ian's engagement to Penelope had been calculated to quell Bramly's contention. Especially since Penelope's pregnancy would become known shortly after the wedding. With an heir in the oven, Bramly's cachet as the heir apparent would certainly be put to rest.

But his plan had failed.

His engagement to Penelope had only caused Bramly to increase his attacks on Ian's reputation. Perhaps Bramly realized that it was only a matter of time before Ian did marry and produce an heir, leaving him with no claim to be in line to the earldom.

Ian knew he would have to deal with Bramly soon, but this subterfuge was not the way to do it.

Penelope was a foolish young woman who had fallen for Leighton's seduction. She was well and surely ruined; he would not add to her distress. She thought he didn't know about the babe in her womb, but half of London knew of it because Leighton had a tendency to brag about his conquests. That was how she had come to Ian's attention. Oh, Leighton thought he was being clever and not using names, but he gave enough clues that any idiot could figure out who he meant. And seeing them together at a social event just confirmed it.

Penelope was foolish but not stupid. He hoped he could convince her to cry off. He would use a combination of threats and bribes if he needed to.

Shelby was right. His ill-conceived plan was not worth sacrificing his life. He would not subject himself or Penelope to a lifetime of misery merely to enact vengeance on his uncle.

His only excuse was that he'd been so miserable at losing Shelby he thought his life was over. But now she'd given him his life back.

Courting Shelby might be as foolish as his engagement to Penelope, but the prospect filled him with hope rather than despair.

Penelope kept him waiting an hour, just punishment for coming early and unannounced, which he took as his due.

"My lord, what an unexpected pleasure," she said when she finally entered the room. "Have you been offered refreshment?"

"I have not," he said. "Though none is desired. I wanted to have a private word with you. I heard that you were overly friendly with Lord Leighton last evening. He is not the sort of man you should be associating with. He is a scoundrel of the first order."

She blanched a bit but was not cowed.

"Lord Leighton is a gentleman and an old family friend," she said.

"Nevertheless, I expect my betrothed to behave with circumspection when out in society. Your actions are a reflection on me." He crossed the room to her and reached up to caress her cheek. She flinched and took a step back from him. He smiled. He had purposely left off the eye patch today. He wanted her to view him in all his disfigured glory.

"I require fidelity in my betrothed. And in my wife."

"Surely once I have produced an heir, we can go our separate ways," she said.

"No. We will not." He stroked her cheek with the crooked index finger on his mangled hand. "You are mine. I do not share what is mine. As soon as we are married, we will remove to Acton Park. Where we will remain. I have no love of town life."

"But you will need to come for Parliament…"

"No. I do not intend to take my seat. Parliament will function quite well without me. No, Penelope, dearest, we will live quietly in the country for the rest of our lives." He looked pointedly at her slightly rounded stomach. "I want all our children to live where the air is clear and easy to breathe. I've inhaled far too much smoke. London is filled with smoke, don't you agree? It's far too hazy here to see things clearly. I like things to be perfectly clear."

"But even in the country, we will have guests. Parties. We will not be cut off from all society."

She was trying so hard to find some way to salvage her hopes. It almost pained him to dash them completely, but he had to get her to cry off from their engagement. Even knowing the desperate situation she found herself in, he had to convince her that marriage to him would be worse than no marriage at all.

He felt like a cad.

"We will welcome no visitors. We will not entertain. I prefer seclusion."

"You are mad," she said.

"So I've been told."

"A monster."

"Yes."

She pulled away from him and sank onto the nearby settee. He knelt before her. Taking her hands in his, he rubbed them gently.

"When we marry, Penelope, there will be no lovers. Especially not Lord Leighton. You will make love to me and only to me."

She pulled her hands away and recoiled against the back of the settee.

"No," she said. "No. I can't marry you."

He should have felt satisfaction at achieving his ends, but all he felt was compassion. He stood and looked down at her where she sat cowering on the cushions.

"You deserve better than Leighton," he said. "Better than me, since I repulse you so much."

Her eyes narrowed. She dropped all pretense of civility between them.

"You were supposed to be grateful to me. To anyone who would be willing to marry you."

"I'm sorry to disappoint you. I hold myself in higher esteem than you do. Unfortunately, it took me a bit too long to realize it." He reached out his hand to assist her to stand. She ignored it and stood on her own.

"You are wrong about Leighton," she said. "He loves me. And I love him. We will be together."

He bowed.

"I wish you all good fortune in that regard. I will go speak to your father."

❧

A week later, Ian's carriage made its way to Endicott House so he could pay his first call on Shelby. He'd settled matters amicably with Baron Furbush, especially as he assured the man he would not sue for breach of promise. The family left Town early and went quietly back to their country seat for the remainder of the Season, though Penelope was not with them. She and Leighton had run off to the continent together, leaving his wife and his debts behind. Perhaps he did care for her after all.

Ian wished them no ill. He could not believe how close he had come to leg-shackling himself to a woman who thought so little of him. She probably believed Bramly's tales of his mental deficiencies, else she would not have thought she could continue her affair with Leighton unimpeded by marriage.

He had come so far in his recovery, but apparently not far enough.

He had re-established himself with his peers and was slowly coming to terms with his permanent disabilities, to the point that he could even look in the mirror without cringing or wanting to throw a rock at it. But it wasn't until that moment in the Furbush's formal parlor that he realized he did deserve a chance at happiness.

It was all because of Shelby. Even when she was trying to deceive him back in Acton Park, she had always treated him with a casual respect without any concessions to his horrifying appearance. She didn't allow him to wallow in self-pity, nor did she coddle him with sympathy. She accepted him as he was, scars and all.

He accepted her as well. Even with her unsavory past that, if known, would ostracize her from Society. He would do his best to make sure it never became known, but even if it did, he would stand by her. They could live quietly in the country if need be the way he had been living for the past two years. What he'd said to Penelope was not an idle threat. He actually preferred living in the country.

He knew that being respectable was important to Shelby; for her sake, he wanted her to remain so. But after what he had endured, Society's opinion didn't matter as much to him.

In the past few months, since returning to London, he had realized just how unimportant the opinions of others were. He had put up with rude stares and even ruder comments. He had entertained curiosity seekers who enjoyed

hearing every gory detail of his experience, the more grue-
some the telling, the better. He had even learned to accept
being invisible to those who could not bring themselves to
look him in the eye.

Through it all, he finally understood that the only opinion that mattered was his own. He spent hours in front of
the looking glass coming to terms with this new body that
housed him. He had developed a respect for the resiliency
that had enabled him to survive.

He found that the process of healing was ongoing, not
only in his body but in his mind as well.

He had needed his time of isolation in Acton Park and
had been forced out of it sooner than he would have liked
by his uncle's scheme.

Though if not for his uncle's ill-conceived scheme, he
would not have met Shelby. So he supposed he should
thank Bramly for that.

The carriage slowed and stopped. Ian bounded out.

As he skipped up the steps of Endicott House to pay his
first call, he felt lighter in spirit than he had since the awful
night of the fire just over two years ago. The door to Endicott House was opened to him, and he was shown to the
drawing room where the ladies of the house were greeting
their afternoon callers.

Shelby looked radiant in a yellow day dress that was almost the same color as her hair. She smiled when she saw
him but made no indication that she knew him any better
than she was supposed to. Lady Endicott accepted his
greeting and invited him to sit in the seat next to her, which
had just been vacated.

Lady Endicott was a gracious woman who managed to
hide her discomfort at his appearance. Ian knew many of
the other gentlemen paying their respects to the ladies this
afternoon, most of whom hovered around Phoebe. Shelby
was sitting quietly by herself a little outside the circle of ac-

tivity, plying a needle in a most inexpert fashion.

Ian remembered her telling him once that needlepoint was not her greatest skill. He wished she would instead seat herself at the piano sitting idle in the corner and entertain the assembled party with her playing. Then he felt sure all the gentlemen would abandon Phoebe and rush to Shelby's side.

Perhaps it wasn't such a good idea after all, he thought, as a stab of jealousy went through him.

After a suitable period of time exchanging pleasantries with Lady Endicott, Ian went to join the assemblage around Phoebe. Several of the gentlemen greeted him warmly. Phoebe herself welcomed him most enthusiastically.

"Lord Chester, how good of you to come," she said. "My condolences on your broken engagement," she said quietly.

"Thank you, Miss Endicott, but there is no need for concern. The lady and I realized that we would not suit. It is for the better."

Finally, Ian felt that he could approach Shelby without drawing undo attention to himself or her.

❧

Shelby immediately put her needlepoint down. She had wanted to jump up and run to Ian as soon as he entered the room but had maintained her composure.

He had come, and the world had not ended. No one stood up and decried her as a whore. No one even noticed as he took a seat beside her.

They behaved as decorum dictated, though Shelby craved to run her hands over him. She had to settle for drinking him in with her eyes. At last, someone who really knew her. Someone she could be herself with without any pretense or lies. Even though convention limited their conversations to polite, impersonal inquiries and topics of general interest, she could be at ease with Ian in a way she could not with anyone else.

"I am pleased to see you, Lord Chester."

"How do you fare, Miss Endicott?" His words were polite enough, but she could tell by his tone that he wanted the truth, not just a courteous reply.

"I am well, thank you. But what of you?" She knew his engagement to Penelope Furbush had ended. The lady had cried off, as was her prerogative. What she didn't know was how Ian had engineered it so quickly. It had been only a week since she'd warned him of the lady's perfidy.

Ian just smiled and winked at her with his good eye. Anyone observing would have thought it merely a blink since his other eye was concealed by a patch, but Shelby knew that Ian was giving her a private, wordless message.

The visit was interminable, having to maintain an air of politesse when all she really wanted was to be alone with him, to really talk to him.

After ten minutes, which was all that Society allowed, Ian took his leave. Shelby felt like she'd had a confection waved in front of her and just as she was about to take a bite, it was whisked away.

On a sunny summer afternoon, when the sky was as blue as cornflowers with not a cloud to be seen, Ian took her for a drive in his open carriage. He dismissed his tiger so that for a blissful hour she could enjoy being completely alone with him.

She loved seeing him out in society. Loved that he was receiving invitations and accepting them. Loved that he came to see her regularly at Endicott House. But she loved most this stolen hour of having him all to herself.

"I have missed you so much," she said as soon as they were underway and could not be overheard by any prying ears.

He laughed.

"You've seen me every day.

He had become a regular visitor at Endicott House, coming each afternoon that she, Phoebe, and Aunt Lucia were at home. He'd attended two balls in the past week and asked her to dance at both of them, claiming two dances each night, one of which was a waltz.

"I've seen you, yes, but I haven't been able to talk to you. This whole business of being perfectly polite at all times grows tiresome. I may have spent the past five years in a brothel, but at least when we weren't working, we could be ourselves and talk about anything we wanted. I feel like I am constantly constrained even when I am alone because I'm never really alone. Having worked in your household, I know that servants observe everything, and I'm so afraid of making a mistake. I realize now what a failure I was at pretending to be a lady at Acton Park. Ian, proper ladies are the most boring lot. Ladies of the night are much more interesting."

"Are you thinking of returning to your former profession?" he teased.

"I'm just not sure I'm cut out for this one. Maybe Mr. Granger was right. Maybe I am not a real lady."

"I'll hear none of that," Ian reprimanded her sternly. "You are as much a lady as your cousin Phoebe. You would not be feeling constrained if you had actually spent the past five years in a convent as everyone supposes. You'd be feeling delirious with freedom."

The reminder of what it was like living at Nell's sobered her.

"While they may not have to adhere to all the rules of propriety, Nell's ladies enjoy very little freedom," she said. "I would not want to return there and should not have made light of it. Five years in a convent would have been preferable. I have had a rather strange education, haven't I?"

"Indeed," he concurred.

Ian slowed the carriage as it neared the entrance to the park, handling the ribbons expertly as he maneuvered the horses through the crowded street. As expected, the park was crowded on such a beautiful day. She and Ian greeted many mutual acquaintances. Shelby was surprised at how many people she knew now as Shelby Endicott. She realized that the portion of Society that frequented Nell Ryan's brothel was very small indeed, and, in general, those were not the men who courted young ladies.

All of Society knew Ian was courting her. The Monster Earl of Chester was enamored of the daughter of a simple country squire. More amazingly to Society's eyes, she seemed to be enamored of him, too. If society only knew the truth, it would realize that she was the more fortunate. She still had trouble believing that he was willing to over-look her past and court her.

"When do you want to announce our engagement?" Ian asked as he steered the carriage around a gentleman on horseback.

"Are you sure you want to marry me?"

"I am," he said.

"But I'm not a proper lady. You can do so much better than me."

"Like Miss Furbush?"

"Well, not her, but someone."

His hands tightened on the reins.

"Perhaps I presumed too much. I thought you wanted to marry me."

"Of course I want to marry you. I'm just not sure I'm the best choice for you."

"Because you're not a proper lady."

"Precisely."

"You are quite right, of course. You do not demur as a proper young lady would. You are much too straightforward." His mouth quirked in a mischievous grin. "You are every man's dream, you know."

"A lady in the drawing room, a whore in the bedroom?"

He shrugged, but that smirk remained. She laughed, not the quiet titter of a proper young lady, but the loud guffaw of a bawd. Had they not been surrounded by half the ton, she would have thrown herself into his arms.

"Very well, my lord. You will get what you deserve. I will marry you."

"I still need to speak to your uncle."

"Please speak to him today. Engaged couples enjoy ever so much more freedom. Why, we could even ride in a closed carriage without a chaperone. Just think of the mischief we could get into then."

The moment of levity ended when Gordon Lancaster rode up to their carriage and walked his horse beside them. Shelby noticed the fading bruise on his chin and braced for a confrontation.

"Lord Chester, Miss Endicott." He surprised her by greeting them politely. "I owe you an apology, Miss Endicott. It has been brought to my attention that I mistook you for someone else."

She exhaled in relief.

"It's quite alright, Mr. Lancaster. Lord Chester explained that I resemble a servant he used to employ, with whom you had an altercation one evening. My cousin Phoebe also noted the resemblance between that servant and myself. It's an understandable mistake."

"Quite." Lancaster still appeared unconvinced. But he merely tipped his hat and rode on.

"I asked Derek to impress upon his brother just how inappropriate it was to insinuate that a young lady in her first Season had once been employed in a brothel. It could ruin her reputation for life. I hope that Lancaster will let the matter rest and not stir up any more trouble," Ian said as Gordon rode away. "But I think that I had better marry you very soon. I may have other miscreant puppies against whom I must defend your honor."

Though he was trying to make light of it, she sobered at the thought of Ian challenging other former clients on her behalf.

"I won't have you fighting for me, Ian. If the truth comes out, so be it. I won't have you hurt on my account."

"There is no reason for the truth to come out. Chartreuse LaRue should be halfway to America by now."

Chapter 18

Phillip Endicott was more than happy to give his permission for Shelby to marry him.

"So, this was your plan all along then," Endicott said to Ian as they shared a brandy in Endicott's study. "Turn a whore into a lady so you can make her your wife."

Ian had to contain his anger at Endicott's callous phrasing.

"Actually, that wasn't the plan at all," he confessed. "I never had any intention of marrying Shelby. I just thought she deserved to be restored to her family and place in Society after the wrongs that had been done to her."

Endicott squirmed in his seat at the reminder of the part he played in Shelby's downfall. Shelby may have forgiven him, but Ian never would. Even now, he was more than happy to pass her off on the first man who offered for her, even if that man was a monster like himself.

"It would be better for her if we didn't marry," he continued. "But she appears quite determined that we should." He could not help but smile. "Far be it for me not to give her what she wants."

"She'll be a countess. That's not nothing," Endicott said.

"Yes, I can give her that at least." He hoped it was enough. Because he feared they were making a terrible mistake by marrying. If he had been able to stay away from her, no one would ever associate a servant girl in his household, albeit one who had a colorful past, with a young lady of Society. But he hadn't been able to stay away. He needed Shelby.

And Shelby needed him. And so, here he was, asking for her hand. A slight smile curved his lips. It seemed almost comical to be observing the proprieties now after all that had transpired between them. What would he have done if Endicott had refused him? Probably elope with her to Gretna Green.

"It really doesn't bother you? The countless men who have come before you?"

His smile dropped.

"There were no other men," he said. "I am the first man she has ever loved."

"So she says." Endicott twirled the brandy in his glass, then raised it in a toast. "You are either a saint or a fool."

"I am no saint, I assure you," he said. "As for being a fool, I think I have been one. I've allowed the ugliness I see on the outside to seep into my soul so that I felt as ugly and disfigured on the inside as I am on the outside. It's taken me a long time to realize that I am still the same man I was. No, a better man than I was. Before, I was shallow and judged by appearances. Judged by the rules that had been bred into me. Had I encountered your niece two years ago, I would not have been moved to help her. I would have thought, like you, that she had gotten what she deserved, that she used her beauty to entice men, that she had broken the rules and so must be punished. But now I know that sometimes what you deserve and what you receive are two different things. I didn't deserve to be burned in a fire, and Shelby did not deserve to be preyed upon by her stepfather and abandoned by her uncle.

"Sometimes we pay a terrible price for beauty. If she can look past this," he waved his disfigured hand toward his face, "I can look past any of her perceived imperfections, though when I look at her, I see none."

❧

Shelby awoke on the morning of her wedding day with a sense of foreboding. It didn't help that it was raining buckets on this late June morning with a wild wind whipping through the streets. The weather merely confirmed Shelby's fears. Fate was not going to allow her and Ian happiness.

They both had been tested by fire, he literally and she the moral fires of hell. Ian had come through his test with strength and courage. Shelby found herself lacking both.

At least the Season was over. Much of Society had already returned to their country estates, but there were still enough people in Town to give the occasion the honor it was due.

Marrying in London eliminated the necessity of inviting her mother and stepfather as would be required if they waited and married at Holling Hall, the Endicott estate in Dorset. She refused to entertain the idea of having either of them at her wedding. She would elope first.

Ian wanted her to have a fairy tale wedding, even if it was prepared in haste. Uncle Phillip agreed to have the wedding breakfast at Endicott House and to give her away.

Her hands were shaking as she sipped her morning chocolate, causing her to spill some on her dressing gown. The dark brown stain looked like dried blood on the snowy white bodice.

Ian assured her that Bramly would not be in attendance, thank goodness. But could she avoid him for their entire married life?

She didn't think she could carry it off. She didn't think

she could greet Bramly as a new acquaintance and pretend that their past association did not exist.

He'd recognize her. If anyone would, it would be Bramly. He'd see it in her eyes. The fear. And he would not have any qualms about announcing it to the world.

He would decry her as a whore and have Ian declared incompetent for marrying her, just as he originally planned.

The realization slammed into her. How could she have placed Ian in such danger?

She had to cry off. She couldn't go through with it. She would not jeopardize all Ian had accomplished over the past seven months. He was accepted now, not just by the gentlemen at his clubs but by their ladies as well.

It was very rare these days to hear him referred to as the Monster Earl.

Now, Shelby heard notes of sympathy when people talked of him and the tragedy he had suffered. He was no longer held in suspicion. He was recognized as being an equal victim with his parents in the fire that had killed them.

She could ruin it all.

Just as she was about to don her old servant's dress again to make a clandestine visit to Ian's house, Phoebe and Aunt Lucia descended upon her to help her dress. Seeing their excitement only caused her anxiety to grow. So many people would be hurt if Bramly exposed her.

Uncle Phillip would be ridiculed, Aunt Lucia would not be accepted in any of the best drawing rooms. And Phoebe, poor Phoebe, would never make a suitable match.

How had she ever thought she deserved a happily ever after? Why had she coerced Ian into marrying her?

She should have stayed hidden away at Nell's where Uncle Phillip wanted her. Instead, she was about to destroy all of their lives.

Phoebe and Aunt Lucia accepted Shelby's anxiety as normal pre-marital jitters. They laughed when she begged them to send a message to Ian telling him she couldn't go through with it.

"All brides feel nervous," Aunt Lucia reassured her. Sending Phoebe out of the room on some trivial errand, Aunt Lucia asked, "Is there anything you need me to tell you about the wedding night?"

Shelby almost burst out laughing until she saw that her aunt was serious. If Aunt Lucia realized just how much Shelby knew about what went on in the bedroom, she'd be shocked. Seeing how uncomfortable the topic was making her, Shelby immediately assured her that she knew what to expect.

Shelby was thankful for her aunt's naiveté.

Between Aunt Lucia and Phoebe, along with a bevy of servants, she was buffed and polished and made presentable. They wouldn't let her look until they were done with her, then turned her triumphantly toward the mirror.

She gasped at the image reflected there.

She looked like a fairy princess. Or a virgin bride.

Aunt Lucia had selected the dress for her since Shelby had no idea what was appropriate to wear. Her aunt had selected wisely. The dress was in a medieval style, with a high collar that plunged to a V, revealing just a hint of cleavage. The sleeves were long but puffed at the shoulder and belled at the cuff.

The underskirt was silk covered by a layer of intricately designed lace. Blue ribbon decorated the sleeves and neck.

Her hair had been left down and brushed out to a satiny sheen. It fell in waves all the way to her waist.

Atop her head, they'd placed a wreath of baby's breath.

Shelby felt like Guinevere on her way to marry King Arthur.

Or like Anne Boleyn on her way to the chopping block.

Ian waited nervously at the church. He wanted the ceremony to be over, the social niceties to be done, so he could whisk Shelby away with him. He had a wedding trip planned that surprised even him.

They were going to travel to Worcestershire to visit Chester Hall. He hadn't been there since he'd been removed to Acton Park after the fire.

It was time for him to face his nightmare. He couldn't start his life with Shelby while still being plagued with memories of that night. He had to go back to grieve and to accept.

He needed to say goodbye to his parents, to see the ruin and move on.

Shelby looked radiant as she walked down the aisle. She looked like a fairy-tale princess, a maiden from some long-ago time when there were still dragons to slay.

She looked so composed walking toward him that it wasn't until she was finally standing next to him at the altar that he realized she was shaking. He resisted the urge to put his arm around her in a protective embrace. Instead, he reached out and lightly squeezed her hand. She grasped his hand and held on when he would have released hers, so they greeted the celebrant with hands clasped.

❦

Shelby barely heard the words the rector recited, so terrified was she. Somehow, she managed to utter the correct responses in the appropriate places. She was tying herself to Ian for the rest of her life and, for better or worse, he was shackling himself to her. She only hoped that he didn't later regret it.

They had reached the part of the ceremony she had been dreading, when the rector asked the congregation if anyone had reason to object to their union. She kept her back to those gathered, holding her breath. She didn't have to wait long. Right on cue, as though it were a play that they'd re-hearsed, the door to the sanctuary slammed open. She felt the stirring of the crowd and looked over her shoulder to see Bramly standing at the top of the center aisle.

"I object to this union," Bramly said in a theatrical voice, loud enough so all could clearly hear. "I cannot allow my nephew to marry this…" Bramly paused for dramatic effect. By this time, he was making his way down the aisle toward them. She turned fully around to face him. Ian grasped her hand, and they stood side by side waiting for him to finish his sentence. Which word would he choose? she wondered. Whore? Harlot? Prostitute? Did it matter?

"…innocent young woman…" She expelled her breath with a whoosh. She felt light-headed with release. But Bramly wasn't done yet. She couldn't relax too soon.

"…knowing him to be a murderer!" Murmurs erupted among the congregation. Ian's hand relaxed its grip on hers.

"We've been through this already, Uncle," Ian spoke over Bramly. "The inquest cleared me."

"I'm not talking about that, though I still believe you set the fire that killed your parents because, in your greed, you couldn't wait to get your hands on your inheritance. No, I'm talking about a young woman who was recently in your employ who has mysteriously disappeared. And you were the last person seen with her. I accuse you of murdering Chartreuse LaRue."

The tension in the church was palpable, but Ian re-mained unperturbed.

"This is neither the time nor the place for leveling such an accusation, Uncle. I suggest you take your suspicion to the proper authorities. In the meantime, if no one has any valid reason for objecting," Ian turned back to face the rec-tor once again. "I suggest we get on with the ceremony."

The rector looked at her questioningly. Did she still want to marry a man who had just been accused of murder? She nodded once.

To give him his due, the rector, though flustered, continued from where he'd left off in a clear, unshaken voice.

Like a staccato beat in time to the officiant's words,
Shelby heard Bramly's footsteps echoing on the marble
floor as he marched his way back up the aisle. The heavy
wooden door slammed loudly behind him when he left.

The remainder of the ceremony was finished without
further incident. When they went into the sacristy to sign
the marriage papers, Shelby's hand was shaking so much
her signature was barely legible. The rector assured her it
was perfectly legal. She and Ian were married in the eyes of
the law and in the eyes of God.

Chapter 19

The wedding breakfast at Endicott House was less festive than it should have been. Though all the guests tried to make light of Bramly's accusations, Ian could sense their doubts. He had to hand it to Bramly. If he'd come out and attacked Shelby directly, it might have backfired on him. Lord Endicott was a powerful man and wouldn't take kindly to the public humiliation of his niece.

By accusing Ian of murdering Chartreuse LaRue, Bramly put him in an impossible position. If he produced the living, breathing, Chartreuse LaRue, he would ruin Shelby. If he didn't produce her, Bramly would ruin him by casting the shadow of a murder accusation on him. It would never be proved, of course. There was no body to produce, and without a body one could not prove a murder had taken place.

But it would put doubt in people's minds. The old accusation of starting the fire would be resurrected, as Bramly so aptly had done today. All Ian's hard work over the past few months to repair his reputation and establish himself as the new Earl of Chester would be for naught.

What did Bramly hope to gain? Or was it, at this point,

merely for spite? Ian had thwarted Bramly, so Bramly was taking his revenge.

"What do you intend to do?" He'd been so absorbed in his thoughts, he hadn't noticed Derek come up beside him.

"I doubt I'll have to do anything. The charge won't stick. I haven't murdered anybody."

"It doesn't matter. Bramly probably won't even bring it to the House of Lords. The damage has been done simply by the accusation."

"Then I shall ride it out."

Ian caught Shelby's eye from across the room and smiled.

"I hope she's worth it." Derek walked away.

❧

Finally, the toasts were all made and the congratulations were all given and Ian and Shelby could take their leave. They would spend their wedding night at Chester House and leave for Worcestershire the following morning.

It was the first time she had ever entered Chester House through the front door, Shelby realized. Except for that first night, but she'd been unconscious then, so she didn't remember it. The servants were lined up in the hall waiting to greet the new Countess.

She didn't think she could pretend that she didn't already know each and every one of them. Would they recognize her? Or would they, like most of fashionable society before them, merely see what they expected to see? An upper-class woman, innocent and refined. Would any of them see in her a resemblance to Chartreuse LaRue?

Nervously, she allowed Ian to introduce her to Mr. Griggs. He bowed formally and presented her to Mrs. Pitts. Mrs. Pitts's eyes widened when she saw her, but she quickly recovered and made her curtsy as required. Mrs. Pitts introduced the maids while Mr. Griggs did the same for the footmen and other male servants.

Bitsy barely even looked at her, Shelby noticed. The girl was nervous, fidgeting with her skirt and looking down at the floor. Shelby wanted to hug her and tell her not to worry. But she couldn't, of course. The lady of the house would never be so familiar with a mere servant.

Dicky Brown was suitably subservient. He showed none of the cockiness he'd shown her when she'd first arrived.

It seemed like such a betrayal to these people who had been her friends to deny that she knew them. There was a gulf separating them now, the gulf of class and position. Never again would she be able to sit in the kitchen and have a cup of tea with Mrs. Pitts while sharing in the day's gossip. She wouldn't hear of Bitsy's sister Mary's baby or Mrs. Pitts's brother Jim's gout.

Now, she would give orders to Mrs. Pitts rather than take them. It made her feel sad and terribly inadequate. What did she know about running a house? The only house she knew how to run was a house of ill repute.

The magnitude of what she'd done overwhelmed her. She'd been transformed from whore to lady. With a short interval as a servant. She had gone from being held in lowest esteem to highest.

Yet, she was the same person. She was the same person who had sold her body for money. The same person who had scrubbed these very floors. Now, she was being looked at with respect and reverence, as though she had done something to deserve it.

Ian dismissed the servants and personally escorted her to her room.

"You'll need a maid," he said as they made their way up the stairs. "Did you see anyone who might do as a lady's maid, or do you want to hire someone else?"

"Bitsy should do nicely," she replied.

"Do you think that's wise?" He looked around to make

sure none of the servants was near enough to overhear. Lowering his voice, he spoke so softly she could barely hear him. "You and she had a particular friendship. She may recognize you if you spend so much time together."

Shelby sighed.

As soon as they were alone in her room together, she started pacing.

"I can't do this, Ian. Lying to Phoebe was bad enough, but she never knew about the other and I wanted to protect her. Duping my former clients, like Gordon Lancaster, held a certain degree of satisfaction. But I can't deceive these people. Ian, they were my friends. They accepted me when no one else would. How can I deny them now? How can I pretend it never happened, or happened to somebody else? Just months ago, I was their equal, but now by an ironic twist of fate, I am in charge of their lives."

Her mother would say that she was restored to her natural station. Shelby didn't quite see it that way.

Her mother had always taught her that their position and status was a God-given right. She was raised to believe in her innate superiority over those lower than she on the social scale. Until Mr. Granger taught her that vile baseness was not limited to the lower classes.

Her customers at Nell Ryan's had reinforced that teaching. Many of the so-called gentlemen who had the most bizarre tastes were from the highest echelons of society.

She knew Bitsy to be a kind-hearted, generous person, Mrs. Pitts a wise, level-headed woman, Mr. Griggs a staunch and loyal man. And she knew herself to be no better than any of them.

"You better than anyone knows how servants talk," Ian said. "The staff is loyal now but may not always be. If you let them know, it will get out. Are you ready to face that?"

"I don't know. But I don't know if I can face them day in and day out and act like we've just met. Act like I really am a lady when inside I know I am not."

Ian caught her on her return from the windows and hauled her into his arms.

"Lady Chester, my Countess, you most certainly are a lady."

❧

Ian undressed her reverently, slowly exposing every inch of her body and kissing her clear, unblemished skin as he revealed it. She was perfect. From her crown of golden hair, the arch of her slightly darker brows, her full, pink lips, the rosy nipples on her pale, plump breasts, to the soft, golden down covering her pubis, which proved that her coloring did not come out of a bottle as he'd led Gordon Lancaster to believe.

He pushed the thought away. He would not invite other men into this chamber. He wasn't coming to her a virgin any more than she came to him one. While he'd never been considered a rake, he'd had his share of exploits. All his partners had been willing, and he'd tried to give as much pleasure as he received, but he'd never given his partners a thought once he left them. Had any of them been abused as she had?

She had never asked about his partners. He would not inquire about hers. He did not want to know any more than he already did. He knew too much already of how men had used and abused her. His uncle included.

Her past was her past. Chartreuse LaRue was dead according to Bramly. May she rest in peace. Now there was only Shelby, Countess of Chester. His wife.

When she stood naked before him, he took a step back so he could see all of her. His gaze swept her up and down then up again. His breath caught at the sheer beauty of her. He stopped at her face and his heart skipped a beat.

Her lower lip was caught with her teeth and her eyes

welled with tears. She looked vulnerable and frightened.

"What is it?" he asked.

She released her lip and blinked the tears into submission. A familiar hardness settled on her features.

"Like wot ya see, Guv?" she said in a credible Cockney accent.

"Stop it," he said. "Yes, I like what I see. I love what I see. My wife is beautiful. You are beautiful."

She dropped her chin and looked down at the floor. He held his breath while he waited for her to gather herself. When she raised her eyes to him again, her brow furrowed.

"I thought you wanted a whore in the bedroom."

He pulled her to him.

"I want you, Shelby. Just you."

"That is me," she said. "It's part of me."

"But not all of you. It's who you were, not who you are now."

She wrapped her arms around his waist and squeezed, hugging him to her.

"Forgive me. I don't know why I'm so maudlin on our wedding day. Perhaps because Bramly said I was dead. And that you killed me."

He rubbed his hand up and down her back.

"He said Chartreuse LaRue is dead. And for all intents and purposes, he's right. She's gone, sweetheart. You aren't her anymore."

She lifted her head from where it rested on his chest and smiled up at him.

"Except for you. You may as well benefit from my years of experience entertaining gentlemen in the bedchamber."

She reached up and untied his cravat. Slowly, she undressed him with expert ease, teasing him with light touches and sensuous licks of her tongue. He should object. Tell her he wouldn't take advantage of her hard-won expertise, but he remained silent.

Because she was right. This side of her was part of who she was. It was part of why he loved her. That she could still be so innocent and loving after all that had happened to her amazed him. The years at Nell's hadn't broken her. They'd made her stronger. Resilient. Everything he wished he could be. Where the fire had melted him like wax, the years at Nell's had forged her like steel. In her, he found his strength.

It took her slow, excruciating minutes to undress him completely, but when she tossed the last stocking over her shoulder to join the pile of crumpled clothing on the floor behind her, he could only imagine how Symmington would pale when he saw them. He could wait no longer. He needed to be inside her now. To claim her as his wife. To worship her with his body as he'd promised.

He grabbed her hands and tugged her toward the bed. He wished he could pick her up and toss her on it, but instead he guided her to the stool so she could climb up onto the high mattress. He followed.

The scent of rosewater wafted off the clean linen sheets. His staff had prepared his nuptial bed with care. Shelby rolled onto her back in the middle of the bed and beckoned to him.

"Come, my lord," she said. "Let us consummate."

His shaft was so engorged he wanted to consummate without delay, but he wanted more for her to enjoy the experience. He held himself in check as he set about arousing her as much as she aroused him.

Hating the limitations his injuries placed on him, he shifted so that he lay next to her partially on his stomach. He could not support himself on his left arm, and he wanted to touch her with his right hand. The one that could feel the softness of her skin. But his current position did not allow him to kiss her. He groaned his frustration.

"Lie back," she said, pushing him onto his back. "You

are the musician. I am your instrument. Tell me what you need me to do so you can play me, my maestro."

While he suspected she'd used that line before—it sounded too well-rehearsed to be spontaneous—he was grateful that she was willing to make a game of his inabilities.

"Lean down so I can kiss your breasts," he said, touching her waist as she straddled him. She leaned forward and teased him by keeping her nipples just out of reach of his mouth. He playfully slapped her bottom, and she acquiesced. He suckled and nipped, kneading one breast with his good hand while his mouth nursed the other.

"Now move up toward the headboard so I can taste you." She immediately followed his instruction, settling her knees on each side of his face and slowly eased herself down so he could feast on her. She grabbed the headboard to steady herself and soon found a rhythm while he laved and sucked, paying special attention to the nub at the top of her slit. He inserted two fingers and massaged while her rhythm increased in urgency and suddenly ceased as she moaned in satisfaction.

"I am melting," she said as she slid down his body and lay on top of him. "You have turned me into liquid."

He stroked her back while she recovered herself, hoping it would not take her long because his own need was urgent.

"Sit up now and ride me," he said when her breathing slowed.

She obeyed, raising herself up and sliding him into her. Her wet heat surrounded him. He closed his eye for a moment to fully enjoy the feeling. When he opened it, she was smiling down at him. His breath caught at how happy she looked. He wanted to keep that look on her face for the rest of her life. Then as she started to move, all thought fled as his whole entire being focused on the feel of her. Playing him like a maestro.

His release hit him with the force of a summer storm, pouring over him, drenching him with pure, clean pleasure. He felt her contract around him and again she moaned as she reached her release a moment later.

She flopped down on top of him, as though she could no longer hold herself up.

"Now I am completely undone," she said.

He stroked her hair.

"The feeling is mutual."

"I love you, Ian," she whispered.

"I love you, too."

Whatever doubts had possessed him earlier were gone. Whatever had happened in the past didn't matter. She was his. And he was hers. And that was all that mattered.

❦

"Shall I send for a tray?" Ian asked when they awoke after their second—no third—bout of lovemaking. She could call it that now—making love. Being with Ian, her husband, was different from any other encounter she'd experienced. While she knew how to elicit a response from any man, she enjoyed making Ian react to her touch. She found herself toying with him, delaying his release where always before, she tried to bring a man to completion as quickly as possible. Now, she played. He seemed not to mind. And she received as much as she gave. They were attuned to each other.

The room was cast in shadows. The sun had set, and twilight filtered through the windows. She stretched and felt a delicious soreness between her legs.

"Mmm," she said. "As much as I would enjoy continuing these activities, I know that Cook has likely spent the entire afternoon preparing a special wedding feast for us. We cannot disappoint her by not giving it the honor it deserves."

They dressed for dinner and ate in the formal dining room. Shelby's prediction proved correct. Cook had outdone herself. The meal was lavish and succulent and reminded her of the meal she and Ian had shared at Acton Park.

They were just starting on the second course of stuffed squab with baby mushrooms when Griggs interrupted them to hand Ian a note waxed with Sinclair's seal.

Ian read the note and calmly put it aside.

"Please tell Bitsy to unpack Lady Chester's trunks. We won't be leaving for the country in the morning after all." Ian resumed eating.

Shelby gave him a questioning look.

"As it turns out," he explained when Griggs left the room and he'd dismissed the footmen serving them, "Bramly had another card up his sleeve yesterday when he accused me of murdering Chartreuse LaRue. A body had been recovered from the Thames the day before our wedding."

Shelby grabbed the folded paper he'd set aside.

According to Sinclair's note, it was a young woman with blonde hair. Though her features had been marred by the time spent under the water feeding the fish, she resembled Chartreuse LaRue closely enough for the House of Lords to launch an investigation.

Since many members of Parliament were still in London after the end of the last session, it was decided to expedite the matter and hold a hearing immediately rather than wait until the next year. Ian was asked to remain in Town and appear at the House of Lords the next morning.

"I should have taken my seat this session," he said when she'd finished digesting what Sinclair had written. "I might have made some allies."

They finished their meal in silence, each lost in thought. Shelby barely tasted the food after that and doubted Ian did, either. Cook's efforts had been wasted after all.

❧

"There's only one thing to do," Shelby said the next morning as their carriage made its way through the crowded streets on its way to Westminster. "I must testify. I'll simply tell them that you couldn't have murdered Chartreuse LaRue because I am Chartreuse LaRue and I am very much alive."

"First of all," Ian said as the carriage once again came to an abrupt halt, causing him to lurch forward in his seat and grab hold of the strap to keep from landing on the carriage floor, "there's no reason for them to believe you. A wife can't testify against her husband, nor does she make a very good witness on his behalf. There is the assumption of bias.

"Secondly, I will not have you putting your reputation at risk. Quite honestly, I wouldn't mind for the world to believe that Chartreuse LaRue is dead and buried. Then she could never come back to haunt us again.

"We need only prove that I did not kill this woman they have found, which I most assuredly did not; we need not prove that she is not who they think she is. A murder has taken place, no doubt about it."

The carriage lurched forward again.

"I can think of a couple of likely suspects," Shelby said. "Your Uncle Bramly and Nell Ryan topping the list."

"I've had Runners following Bramly for months. If he's involved, they should be able to prove it."

Shelby admired how calm and unperturbed Ian appeared. She was not so confident. She had learned that an inconvenient truth was often rejected in favor of a more palatable belief.

The House of Lords may be predisposed to view Ian as a murderer because of his monstrous looks and the rumors of madness that Bramly had spread about him. They could argue day and night that the woman found in the Thames was not Chartreuse LaRue, that Ian never knew her, that the obvious candidate for prosecution is the man who stood to gain the most from Ian's demise, but if his peers chose not to believe him, Ian could very well be convicted of a crime he did not commit.

❧

Shelby was escorted to the gallery from whence she could watch the proceedings. Women were not allowed on the floor of the House of Lords unless called to testify. Though Ian had told her she would not be able to testify on his behalf, she would not allow them to convict him of murdering her without making them aware that Chartreuse LaRue was alive and well and sitting in the balcony. She'd shout from the rafters if necessary.

Ian was being ably represented by his friend Sinclair who had read law at Oxford.

The first witness was called. Nell Ryan approached the bench. She was dressed flamboyantly as always in a bright red satin gown with a plunging neckline that exposed her copious cleavage. Though it caused quite a stir among the gentlemen below, Shelby thought it quite restrained for Nell. She'd obviously dressed for the occasion.

Nell gave a tearful account of how Lord Chester had burst in on her one afternoon and dragged Chartreuse away, never to be seen again. Shelby had to pinch herself to keep from laughing out loud at Nell's obvious overacting.

"Why did you allow Lord Chester to take the girl off?" Lord Darrow, who was acting as prosecutor for the case, asked Nell.

"Because he threatened me, my lord," Nell answered obsequiously. "He threatened to have me and all my poor girls sent to Newgate, or worse."

"You are the one who identified the body recovered

from the Thames River on Thursday last, were you not?"

Nell nodded.

"Are you sure the dead woman is the same woman who left with Lord Chester that March morning?"

"I am positive, my lord. Looks like she'd been in the river since then, too."

Sinclair rose to question Nell on Ian's behalf.

"How did Miss LaRue come to be acquainted with Lord Chester in the first place? Was he a customer at your brothel?"

Nell looked decidedly uncomfortable.

"I don't run a brothel, my lord, I run a gambling house. What arrangements some of the girls who work there make with the gentlemen is their own business."

"I meant to cast no disparagement on your obvious good breeding, Mrs. Ryan. Could you just answer the question, please."

"Well, the first time they met was in the country. We'd gone out to have a brief holiday and happened to be staying near Lord Chester's estate. We met him then."

"At whose expense were you staying in the country?" Sinclair pursued.

"Mr. Bramly was kind enough to lease a small cottage for us," Nell admitted.

Sinclair pointed out that she was referring to Mr. Richard Bramly, Lord Chester's uncle.

"And how did Miss LaRue come to be in Lord Chester's employ?"

"I don't know about that," Nell hedged. "I brought her to his house after she'd been hurt by a gentleman at the gambling house." Perspiration appeared on Nell's upper lip. She was obviously regretting her decision to throw her lot in with Bramly.

"Why did you bring her to Lord Chester's house? Who was it that hurt her, do you know that Mrs. Ryan?"

"Well…" Nell hesitated. Looking around the room at the assembled company, who represented the most powerful men in England, Shelby held her breath, hoping Nell would lose her nerve and slink back to the gutter where she belonged. Then something in her attitude changed. She sat up straighter, getting her confidence back. She must have realized that she could ruin many of the men in this room. They wouldn't be calling her a liar for fear of what she might say about them.

With an air of defiance, Nell continued her testimony.

"He'd been sweet on her when we were visiting in the country," she said. "Almost asked her to marry him, he did. So I thought he'd want her, that's why I dumped her there. She was no good to me anymore, beat up the way she was."

"Who was it that beat her, Mrs. Ryan?" Sinclair repeated the question.

"I don't rightly know." Nell lifted her chin arrogantly, daring him to call her a liar. Sinclair wasn't interested in disputing her on that point.

"But it wasn't Lord Chester, was it?"

"No sir," Nell was forced to admit.

"Did you ever see Lord Chester harm or threaten Miss LaRue in any way?"

"Well, he took her off, he did."

"Did Miss LaRue object to going with him when he took her off as you say?"

Nell gave it up at that point. Shelby could tell she wanted nothing more than to get out of there and back to where she wielded the power.

"She went willingly enough, I suppose," Nell grudgingly admitted.

Ian's coachman testified that he dropped Chartreuse and Ian off at the house on Templeton Place after leaving Nell Ryan's establishment and the driver didn't see Chartreuse again.

Mrs. Pitts was called to testify about the night, two months later, when Chartreuse came to Chester House. She reluctantly admitted that Lord Chester and Miss LaRue appeared to be arguing.

"But she said she was leaving for America the next day with her new employers," she argued.

Lord Cantwell volunteered that he had seen Lord Chester walking with a servant girl along Marypole Street that same night. The girl matched the description given of Chartreuse LaRue. She appeared to be fine, and Lord Chester seemed to be on friendly terms with her. She went down an alley between two houses, he couldn't remember which, and Lord Chester turned and went back down the street in the direction from whence he'd come.

There were no eyewitnesses to the murder. No one could place Lord Chester near the river. There was some dispute about when the murder had taken place.

Very quickly, the lords determined that there were not enough grounds to hold Lord Chester over for trial. He was free to go. The murder of one Chartreuse LaRue, prostitute, would remain unsolved.

Shelby heaved a sigh of relief from her seat in the gallery. She said a silent prayer for the poor young woman who had been found dead in the river. She knew how close she had come to being like her. Whoever she was, Shelby would be eternally grateful to her. Because as long as the world thought that the dead girl was Chartreuse LaRue, no one would suspect that Shelby Endicott, now Countess of Chester, had once plied her trade under that name.

Chapter 20

Shelby waited in the carriage for Ian to join her. He was being congratulated and apologized to by his fellow peers. It seemed none of them had ever entertained the possibility that the charges against him might be proved.

Of course, they hadn't. Justice worked differently for those with wealth and power. More than one man had been hanged with less proof of guilt than that presented against Ian. While she was grateful he'd been spared, since she knew for a fact he was innocent, she wondered if he would have been had the trial been held at the Old Bailey instead of in the House of Lords.

The day was gray, the sky overcast, and a light mist covered the window. She wiped the glass with her sleeve, clearing away the condensation that had collected on the inside, trying to spot Ian among the dark-clad throng of gentlemen crowding the portico.

Instead, she saw Nell Ryan making her way down the street toward her own carriage. She looked old, worn, and tired. And worried. A sharp ache stabbed Shelby's heart. For all Nell had done, her casual cruelty and remorseless selfishness, she was a survivor and had taught Shelby how to survive in a world that had turned against her

She ruled her house with an iron hand, keeping her girls virtual prisoners. She was not above stealing children off the streets to satisfy the request of a customer. She made her fortune by pandering to the tastes of the wealthy, no matter what those tastes might be. Whatever your sexual preference, women, men, boys, or girls, it could be accommodated at Nell's if you had coin enough. She frequented the posting inns, or sent her minions, to lure poor country girls into her clutches to provide her jaded clientele with fresh meat. Nell was even suspected of murder on more than one occasion, though it had never been proved. The poor woman found in the Thames most likely was one of Nell's girls, killed either by Nell or one of her customers.

For all that, Nell had given Shelby a home when she needed one and for that she'd always be grateful. And when Nell could have dumped her own battered and beaten body into the Thames, she'd instead brought her to Ian, saving her life.

She couldn't hate Nell, only pity her, because Nell had failed at the task Bramly had set for her. Shelby had no doubt that he would make her pay for that failure.

The door to the carriage opened and she smiled, expecting it to be Ian. But it wasn't he.

As though her thoughts conjured him, Bramly pulled himself into the carriage and sat on the seat beside her. Instinctively, she cringed and shifted away from him, grabbing for the latch on the opposite door. Before she could get the door open, he had his hand at her throat.

"You think this is over, don't you?" he snarled. "It's not over. It will never be over as long as that whelp lives."

She struggled against his grip; her ears roared, and black dots danced in front of her eyes. She couldn't breathe and started losing consciousness. Then he was gone as quickly and unexpectedly as he'd come.

Gasping for breath, she inhaled deeply, coughing with the effort. The dizziness that had assailed her cleared. Her throat ached. Lightly, she touched her neck where Bramly's hand had held her.

She was still coughing and having difficulty swallowing when Ian entered the carriage.

"What's wrong?"

"Bramly." She choked out the word.

Ian disappeared. She could hear him shouting orders, running feet, stomping horses. Then he returned.

"He's gone," he said. Fury laced his words. At that moment, he looked capable of murder. She'd never seen such rage even as his fingers gently stroked her throat. She was grateful his fellow peers could not see him now, or they would be convinced he had done in that poor girl. "I had men watching him, but there's no sign of them, either. I'll find him. And when I do, he will rue the day he was born."

"I believe he means to kill you," she said. "He hates you so much."

"At this moment, the feeling is mutual."

❧

As soon as they returned to the house, Ian sent Dicky to Bow Street to get a report from the Runners he'd hired to follow his uncle. How had they allowed Bramly to accost Shelby? Where the hell were they when he scoured the area trying to locate his uncle after the assault? He saw no evidence that Bow Street was even present. And they should have been. Bramly had expected victory today. He'd expected Ian to be remanded for trial. He would have wanted to witness his nephew's humiliation. He had probably been sitting in the gallery with Shelby the entire time.

The thought sent ice-cold daggers through his heart.

After dispatching the footman, he searched out his wife. He found her in her bath. Dismissing Bitsy, he knelt by the tub and took up the sponge. The bruises on her neck stood out in stark contrast to her pale skin. Already purpling, the imprint of Bramly's fingers circled her throat.

He could barely breathe. He'd nearly lost her.

"I'm so sorry," he said as he gently rubbed the soapy sponge up her arm, across her chest, and down the other arm, carefully avoiding the bruises.

"It's not your fault." Her voice sounded rusty and hoarse.

"It is my fault. I knew what he was capable of. My God, he beat you to within an inch of your life before. I should never have allowed him to get within a mile of you."

She was quiet. He put his forehead on hers.

"I was so frightened," she whispered. A single tear escaped to make its way down her cheek.

Ian sprang into action. He pulled her from the tub; water splashed everywhere but he didn't care. Wrapping her in toweling, he ushered her to the rocking chair in the corner of her room and settled her on his lap, the need to hold her, to feel her, overwhelming all others. He rocked and rubbed his hands on her arms and back. She shivered and he covered them both with the afghan that hung on the arm of the chair.

"I was back at Nell's, the night he beat me. Helpless. Alone. So afraid I would never see you again. Never again get the chance to tell you how much I love you."

"Shh," he said. "Bramly will pay for this. He will pay for all his sins. I should have dealt with him earlier. I let my fear of the damage he could do to your reputation hold me back. But reputation be damned. The man is dangerous. He must be stopped."

"Nell looked worried when she left today. The girl in the Thames was likely one of hers. If Bramly is holding a charge of murder over Nell's head, I wouldn't be at all surprised if she takes it upon herself to eliminate the threat. Nell is a survivor. Bramly had better watch his back."

To Ian's relief, Shelby's voice sounded stronger, less raspy. At least the damage to her throat was not long lasting.

"Whichever one of us gets to him first, Nell or I, Bramly's days of wreaking havoc are over. Poor sod. He may realize that his best option lies with me. I am less likely to kill him outright, though that remains to be seen."

Shelby shifted, nuzzling at his neck, kissing his cheek.

"Make love to me," she said. "I need to feel you inside me. I need to feel alive."

Sliding from his lap, she reached out her hand to him. He did not need to be told twice. Grasping her, he rose from the chair and let her lead him to the bed. She dropped the towel and settled herself in the bed. He quickly discarded his wet clothes and climbed in beside her. He set out to banish Bramly from her mind. Soon, he would banish Bramly from their lives.

❧

He left his sleeping wife and, dressed in fresh clothes thanks to Symmington, had dinner in his study while he pondered what to do about Bramly and how to protect Shelby. And himself since his uncle had threatened to kill him. He was sipping his brandy when Griggs showed in a scruffy little man with shabby clothes and odiferous breath who claimed to be a representative from Bow Street.

The man, Atkins, looked longingly at the glass in Ian's hand. Reluctantly, Ian poured him a snifter and passed it over. He downed the liquid in one shot, a waste of perfectly good brandy.

"Sorry, gov," Atkins said. "We lost him."

"What do you mean, you lost him?"

"We had a man at Parliament today, followed your man there he did, but couldn't get inside so he waited for the bloke to come out. He must have snuck out another door, because next thing my man knew, you were shouting fit to raise the dead, and there was no sign of your uncle any-where. My man checked all his usual haunts, Nell Ryan's house first and foremost—she sends her regards by the way, hopes there's no hard feelings—but no sign of him. He's gone to ground. He'll show up in a few days, I expect. We'll nab him then. What should we do with him?"

Truss him up and toss him in the Thames. He kept the thought to himself, afraid he would sound like the monster Bramly had created through rumor and innuendo.

"Haul him before a magistrate and hold him for trial. He attempted to murder a peeress," Ian said.

Bramly had become unhinged. Levelling false murder charges against him was bad enough, but nearly strangling his Countess, that was a hanging offense. The sooner his uncle was safely locked away—either in prison or in Bedlam —the safer they would all be.

He decided that proceeding with their wedding trip was the wisest course of action. With Bramly's whereabouts un-known, he wanted to get Shelby out of London in case Bramly took it into his head to hurt her again.

"Send word to me at Chester Hall when you find him." He stood, indicating that the interview was over. Mr. Atkins made a cursory bow and exited the room.

❧

Four days after the hearing dawned warm and sunny for the first leg of their journey to Chester Hall. Ian had hired some extra men, former soldiers who weren't afraid of a good fight, for added protection. He was damned if he was going to let his uncle disrupt his life any more than he al-ready had.

He'd sent some servants ahead to make the dower house on the estate at Chester Hall ready for them. It was where

he had stayed the first six weeks after the fire before remov-
ing to Acton Park. He had no real memory of those first
weeks except for excruciating pain. He'd spent most of the
time in drug-induced sleep plagued by nightmares.

The trip was pleasant and unhurried, unlike his last visit
to Chester Hall. He'd been so excited to share the news of
his engagement to Lady Hillary Cross with his parents that
he'd made the trip on horseback, riding as far and fast as he
could each day so he could get there speedily. He'd made
the trip in two days rather than the four it would take them
now with their heavy coaches, luggage, and entourage.

For three days and nights, Ian relaxed and allowed himself the happiness of a newly married man. He and Shelby
slept in the coach by day and kept each other awake at
night. They ate in private parlors so he could avoid the
stares of the common folk, but he found that the common
folk stared far less than the upper crust. Perhaps because
burns and scars were more common among their peers than
among the peerage.

Shelby took to lovemaking, now that she found pleasure
in it, with great enthusiasm. He was more than willing to ac-
commodate her. He benefitted greatly from her years of experience in the matter.

On the fourth day, as he started recognizing the vicinity
near the Hall, he was besieged by childhood memories. He
regaled Shelby with stories of his youth, most of which was
spent at Chester Hall. His parents preferred the country to
London. He'd been allowed to run free across the estate
and into the environs beyond.

Even after he went to school, holidays were always spent
at the Hall. Approaching in the coach as they were brought
back the anticipation he'd felt when coming home from
school at Christmastime. The house was always decorated
with holly boughs and pine wreaths. His mother would be
waiting at the door to greet him.

But the closer they came to the Hall, the more agitated he grew. He felt trapped in the overheated coach. Could not catch his breath. Sweat poured down the back of his neck. A mile from the drive, he tapped the roof and ordered the driver to stop. Throwing open the door, his feet hit the ground as soon as the wheels stopped rolling. He retched against the stone wall that lined the road.

He felt a gentle touch on his shoulder.

"We don't have to go on," she said. "I saw a lovely inn at the last village we passed through."

With a shaking hand, he wiped his mouth with his handkerchief. He straightened and turned to her.

"I'm fine," he said. "The movement of the coach made me ill. That or the meat pie I had at lunch." He looked down the familiar road, sighting landmarks he knew as well as his own name. "We are almost there." He took a deep breath, then took her hand and led her back to the coach. "Come. Let us continue."

The coach turned into the drive. The grounds had been maintained even in his absence and neglect. They looked as they always had, the lawn lush and green spreading out on both sides of the drive. Closer to the house, a garden surrounded the fountain that marked the main entrance.

To his surprise, the front of the Hall looked unscathed. Its yellow-brick façade stood stolidly just as he remembered it. He had imagined it to be smoke-blackened and decayed. The coach passed the main Hall and continued on the drive to the dower house. As they went along the west side of the main structure, he saw where the fire had been.

It seemed so small and minor. Self-contained. The fire had only damaged the new wing that his mother had insisted they use for the family quarters. It was warmer, she'd said, than the drafty old hall that had been built during the reign of Queen Elizabeth. The new wing was less than fifty years old and beheld all the modern conveniences his mother desired.

Though the exterior walls were scorched, even the new wing had sustained far less damage than Ian anticipated. The roof was blackened, the windows blown out. He could see that the rooms were ruined, but it wasn't the irreparable damage he was expecting. Only the people in the building had been irreparably damaged. The house itself had survived.

By the time the coach came to a halt in front of the dower house, he was panting like a dog after a long run, struggling to get air into his lungs. His stomach alternately rolled, fluttered, and clenched. A horrified scream lodged in his throat, but he swallowed it back. His hand gripped the door handle so he could make his escape as soon as the coach came to a halt, but there was no escape. Why had he thought he needed to come here? The house may still be intact, but he certainly was not.

Shelby had not said a word during the long ride down the drive, but she'd held his left hand, his damaged, deformed, scarred left hand, in both of hers the entire time and now gave it a gentle squeeze as the coach finally, blessedly, stopped.

He leaped from the coach, desperate for air. He staggered a few feet away and fell to his knees. The horror of that night confronted him as though it had just happened. He felt Shelby's hand on his shoulder.

"I couldn't save them," he gasped. "Why couldn't I save them? Did you see? It looks like nothing. A small bonfire. Not the conflagration I recall. But I couldn't save them."

He wept uncontrollably.

"It haunts me. They haunt me."

"Ian, there was nothing you could do. You told me they were already dead when you reached them, that they died in their sleep," Shelby knelt beside him on the grass, reaching her arm around his shoulders. "What more could you do?"

He shook her off and stood, striding away from her as though the very devil was at his heels. When he'd gone a few feet, he turned.

"I lied," he shouted. "I lied to you, I lied to everyone, even to myself. They weren't dead when I got there. They were alive. And burning. My God, I watched them die. I can still hear them scream. I was paralyzed, helpless. My mother…" His voice trailed off, the horror he'd witnessed too awful for words. But he forced himself to continue, more calmly now, as though reciting a practiced piece from memory.

"When I reached their room, I had trouble opening the door. The doorknob was so hot it scorched my palm. But I could hear screams, a high-pitched, otherworldly sound. I finally forced the door open and saw the bed engulfed in flames. My mother was always cold at night, the Hall was a drafty place, even in the newer wing, so she kept to the old-fashioned custom of bed hangings, creating a warm, safe cocoon for her and my father. When I was a child, she'd let me and Daphne join her for her morning chocolate. We loved pretending we were gypsies and Mother's bed was our caravan tent."

Shelby closed the distance between them. The servants were busily unloading the coach, dutifully ignoring his embarrassing breakdown. She took his hand and started walking along the gravel drive, away from the activity in front of the Dower House—a relief to all of them, he was sure—up the way they had come, toward Chester Hall. Closer to his memories.

He didn't want to go any closer. Like a stubborn toddler, he stopped, forcing her to stop, too.

"But that night, Mother's bed was no safe haven," he continued. He was grasping her hand like a lifeline, afraid that if he let go, he would be plunged back into the past, into the fire. "The bed hangings fed the fire, and there was no way out. At first, I couldn't see them behind the wall of flames, but I knew they were there. I could hear their screams."

Shelby tugged on his hand, forcing him to take a few steps forward. He stumbled on an uneven patch in the drive. She directed him toward a bench placed along the walkway. He didn't remember it, wondered when it had been added. Before or after the fire. His entire life was now divided between before and after. He sank onto the stone slab.

He should stop talking, shouldn't tell her the rest. Should keep his demons to himself. But now that he'd started the exorcism, he couldn't seem to stop.

"I tore the bed hangings down, catching my own clothing on fire when I did so. I had to roll on the floor to put it out. Smoke was everywhere. I could barely breathe. When I looked up, I saw my mother standing in the middle of the bed. Her nightgown was on fire. She looked like a lighted torch. Her hair caught. It just…disintegrated.

"I pulled her to the floor, using my hands and body to put out the flames. I tore her clothes off, embarrassed for both of us, but I needn't have been. Her skin peeled off with her clothing. I caused her more harm.

"She wasn't screaming anymore. She was whimpering. And then she made no sound at all."

His throat closed on the words, a silent sob choking him. Finally forcing him to stop talking. They sat in blessed silence.

"And your father?" she prodded after a few moments.

He shouldn't tell her the rest, but he'd told her the worst. What did it matter now? He coughed, cleared his throat, and began again.

"When I knew Mother was dead, I crawled back to the bed. I couldn't find him. He wasn't on the bed. By now the room was black with smoke; I couldn't see anything. I crawled forward, trying to find the door or a window, any means of escape. I was coughing uncontrollably.

"I found him by chance. I crawled into him. He was on the floor. He must have been trying to escape, too, when the smoke overcame him. He wasn't breathing."

Ian paused, the long-buried memory playing in his mind like a scene on the stage. His throat closed as if he were again in that room, suffocating.

"By then the flames had died down a bit, but the smoke was choking me. I crawled to the nearest wall and threw open the window to let some air into the room. I hung my head out gasping for breath, but there was no air to be had. Smoke billowed all around me, pouring out the window in waves, thick, black, and dense. I tried to call out to the servants on the lawn below, but my voice was hoarse from coughing. No one heard. In desperation, I nearly threw myself out the window, more afraid of the fire than of a fall, but it was a casement window and I didn't fit. I was trapped."

More than once during his long recuperation he'd wondered if he would have fared better had he taken that leap. If he had tried harder to rip the casement from its hinges and squeezed himself through the opening.

"But you found your way out," Shelby said. "You survived."

"Yes," he said. "I survived. And they didn't. I've not been able to forgive myself for that."

Calmer now, he became aware of his surroundings. Of Shelby's hand in his, the sound of the carriage pulling away from the Dower House, an early cricket chirping in the grass behind the bench.

"How did you get out?" she asked.

"I'm not really sure," he said. He closed his eyes to bring the memories into focus. "I dropped to my hands and knees trying to get below the smoke. To find the smallest breath of air. Above my head, with a giant whoosh like a dragon's breath, fire roared out the window and the room ignited once again into flames.

"I was surrounded by fire. Heat seared my lungs. It felt like I was in the very depths of hell. I remember crawling. I kept one hand on the wall, staying to the perimeter, seeking some means of escape. Away from the open window, which was now filled with flames.

"Somehow, I found a door. I opened it and crawled through it into darkness as black as pitch. The fire hadn't reached this room. I slammed the door behind me and lunged forward blindly, seeking egress. I knocked over the ewer and realized I was in my parents' changing room. I passed through it into the Countess's room on the other side. My mother never used it, preferring, instead, to share my father's chamber.

"Smoke followed me like a relentless shadow. Through the windows, I could see flames licking at the glass like a lover seeking entry, but the fire hadn't reached its tentacles into the room yet.

"I ran through the door into the hallway. The hall had less fuel to burn than my parents' bedchamber, but still fire slithered up the walls and ate at the carpet. Blinding smoke made the familiar hallway an unknown passage. Disoriented, I staggered right, back toward the conflagration, when I should have gone left to safety. But I was a ravening beast at this point, lost to reason, my one thought to find a way out."

He gave a soft chuckle.

"The stairs found me. I tumbled down them, stopped on the landing. That's when the tapestry fell on top of me, I guess. I really don't remember the rest, thankfully."

Only the pain. He remembered the pain.

"I told everyone that my parents were dead when I found them. I never wanted to relive the horror of watching my mother die, though I've relived it every night in my nightmares. I failed her. I failed both of them."

"You didn't fail anyone, Ian," Shelby said sternly. She moved from her seat beside him on the bench and knelt in front of him, taking his hands in hers, turning over the palms where she could see the scarring left by the burns he'd sustained. "You did all you could. All anyone could. You need to forgive yourself."

He looked down at his hands.

"I cannot forgive myself for hating them. If I had not tried to save them, I would not be like this. It was all for nothing. I hate them for dying when I risked all to save them."

"Come," Shelby said, pulling him up from the bench. "Let's go see them."

He had no idea who she was talking about. She led him up the path toward the Hall.

"Shelby, I…" *Don't want to go there. Don't make me go there.* "I think we should get back to the Dower House. It will be dark soon."

She looked at the sky. While the sun was low, it had not yet set. Full darkness would not fall for hours yet. He'd been so lost in his memories, he could have sworn it was night.

"There's time," she said. "This shouldn't take long."

He trudged beside her on leaden feet. If he just stopped, she would not be able to move him. He should just stop. Turn around. Go back to the safety of the Dower House. Why was he allowing her to bring him here? She had to know how difficult this was. Did she have no care for him at all?

They emerged from the path to an expanse of lawn. The burned-out hull of the west wing stood before them. The smell of charred wood tickled his nose. Damp charred wood. He should have had the place torn down years ago.

While the stone walls stood strong, the windows gaped empty holes; the collapsed roof littered the ground with debris. A remnant of staircase climbed to nowhere as the second floor had tumbled to the first. It was unsightly. Dangerous. Animals were no doubt nesting inside.

He crossed the lawn and peeked inside.

Anything of value had been removed, either by his servants or by vandals, after the fire cooled. Any wood not burned through had been harvested for cottage fires. What was left of the wing was a mere shell.

He touched the cold stone wall. So solid under his fingertips. He looked up and walked backwards.

"There," he said, pointing at the hole in the wall where a window had been. "That was their room."

The wall around the window was blackened with soot.

He sank to the ground. Shelby sat beside him and touched his arm.

"Do you need to rage at them? Shout your anger and disappointment?"

He shook his head. All the rage had drained out of him. All his hatred and anger.

"I wonder if it started in their room. If a candle caught the bed hangings perhaps. I blamed them for so long. But they were trapped. Helpless. Terrified. They were victims just like I was. I can't hate them for that. I miss them." He took Shelby's hand and rubbed her palm with the stubs of his destroyed, burned fingers. "Thank you."

She stared at the ruin for a few minutes, studying it as though searching for some truth that eluded him.

"I felt the same fruitless hatred myself," she said, her words barely above a whisper on the breeze. He bent his head toward her so he could hear her better. "Toward my father. For leaving me at the hands of Mr. Granger." She pulled her hand from his and pressed her palms against her skirts, smoothing the fabric. "Unreasonable, I know. But no less real."

"Do you feel the need to rage at him?" he asked.

She took a deep breath and let it out slowly. Then shook her head.

"I think we need to forgive them. Sometimes, even the worst sins need to be forgiven in order for you to heal."

He got the sense she was no longer talking about his parents or her father.

"Can you forgive them?"

She stood and shook the grass off her skirts. Still, she stared at the remnants of the west wing. Rising, he put his arm around her shoulders and watched the sky change from blue to purple as the sun descended behind the Hall.

"Let's go back to the Dower House. I'm sure Bitsy and Symmington have everything settled there by now," he said, turning her back toward the path up which they'd come.

"When we are finished here and ready to travel again," she said as they crossed the lawn. "There is someplace that I need to go." She stopped walking and turned into his arms. Lifting a hand to his face, she cupped his chin. "You faced your worst fears. I think it's time for me to face mine."

"You never have to face anything alone," he said. "Never again." He kissed her lightly on the mouth. "Let us get ourselves fed, bathed, and bedded."

She laughed.

"Does it have to be in that order?"

His tension eased, and his maudlin spirits lifted.

"Not necessarily."

"Good," she said. "I think the bedding should come first." She spun out of his arms and, lifting her skirts, took off at a run down the path to the Dower House. Ian followed at his own pace behind her.

Chapter 21

"Where is Lord Chester?" Shelby asked Bitsy when she returned to the Dower House eager to tell Ian all the wonderful things the tenants had to say about his parents and him, as well. Even though he hadn't been able to bring himself to Chester Hall before this, he had not neglected his responsibilities to the people. They were grateful for it.

"He's still at the Hall, m'lady," Bitsy said.

During the two weeks they'd been staying in the Dower House, Ian had thrown himself into repairing the Hall. Having exorcised his demons from the night of the fire, he was able to recall the happier times he'd spent there. He wanted to restore the Hall to what it had been.

While Ian was busy at the Hall, Shelby spent her days visiting the local tenants and villagers. She didn't know yet where Ian would want to call home, Chester Hall or Acton Park, but she wanted to perform her duties as Countess.

She learned a great deal about the former Earl and Countess of Chester from talking to people in the neighborhood. They had been well-loved and were sorely missed. But everyone sympathized with Ian. And no one thought him mad or a monster. In fact, because many of the people she talked to had known Bramly since childhood, none had given any credence to the rumors he'd spread about Ian.

"Mr. Bramly was always a spiteful young man," one old cottager had confided to her today. "We were quite grateful when he hied off to London and refused to return to the neighborhood. No offense, my lady, but good riddance to him, I say."

Shelby couldn't agree more.

"I think I'll walk up to meet him," Shelby said to Bitsy. "There's still a good bit of daylight left. You go have your dinner. We'll eat when we get back."

She expected to find Ian in the west wing. Incredible progress had already been made. Once all the debris was removed, they'd found that the first floor was relatively unscathed. Even the walls were barely scorched. Though the elements and the locals had done damage to the contents, the structure was sound.

Apparently, when the second floor collapsed, the fire smoldered rather than reignited, allowing the servants time to fully douse it. And then it rained; a good soak according to the master builder Ian had hired to oversee the restoration work. He regaled them with a detailed description of the conflagration that he'd determined from talking to servants who'd witnessed it and from his own assessment of the damage.

"It really wasn't that big a fire at all," he concluded.

Ian had turned his back on the man and walked away, leaving Shelby to discuss the work that needed to be done.

Work that was coming along nicely.

After shoring up the flooring, the workmen under the master builder's supervision repaired the roof and started rebuilding the second floor.

The workmen had gone for the day, and she found no sign of Ian. She called out to him as she picked her way through the rooms, avoiding tools, tarpaulin, and scaffolding. The second floor was naught but open framing above her head.

"Drat, I've missed you," she said aloud. She started making her way back toward the door she'd come in when she saw that the entrance to the main hall was ajar. The huge double doors were always kept closed and locked to keep dust from the construction site from getting into the main house.

Ian must have gone out through to the main hall. She followed suit, locking the doors behind her.

The Hall was eerily quiet when she entered. The staff she'd hired to begin cleaning the main Hall had returned to their own homes to enjoy their evening meal.

She wandered the halls of the main building searching for Ian in the shadowed rooms, wishing she'd brought Bitsy with her.

Though she'd been in the Hall many times in the past two weeks, she'd never been alone before. The hallways and stairways seemed alive with ghosts. More than once she jumped when she felt a presence behind her, yet when she turned, no one was there.

She couldn't find Ian anywhere. She started down the back stairs planning to exit through the kitchen and return to the Dower House when she heard a soft step behind her. Turning quickly on the stairs, she caught a glimpse of a shadowy figure two stairs above her. Before she could react, she was pushed and fell down the long flight, landing with a thud, cracking her head on the brick floor at the bottom. Too stunned to move, she lay helpless as the figure descended the stairs to stand threateningly over her. Bramly.

"You won't be so high and mighty when I'm done with you, Countess." The way he said her title sounded like more of a slur than when he'd called her a whore.

She willed herself to move, but her limbs would not cooperate.

"No, no, no," she moaned.

She watched in horror as he aimed his booted foot at her head, kicking her hard against her temple. Then the world went black.

❧

Ian tugged at the shackles that bound his wrists, but a spike secured the connecting chain to the stone wall well above his head. All his struggles did not loosen it. The dungeon was a remnant of the Hall's medieval past. The circular room two stories below the main hall was now used as a wine cellar. Cells with barred doors that now imprisoned bottles and casks lined the granite walls. Interspersed between the cells were chains and shackles.

He and Daphne had played knight and damsel down here when they were children. Until they were banned because he'd chained Daphne to the wall with a lock so rusted that the key would not turn to release her. He'd had to go for help.

His father used to bring guests down to tour the cellars and regale them with tales of his ancestors torturing their enemies.

His family's bloodthirsty past had come back to haunt him. Bramly now held him prisoner in his own home.

The last thing he remembered was being in the main Hall. He'd gone through the connecting door from the west wing because he'd heard something. He'd thought all the help had gone home for the day. No one should have been there. Unless Shelby had come to meet him. He picked up his pace and followed the sound to the front foyer. It was more museum than home. The walls were guarded by armored knights. His father had been a collector and had added several to what had been passed down to him.

As a child, Ian had been afraid to come to the foyer after sunset because he believed the knights came alive in the nighttime. His father had to dismantle one to show him that the armor hung on stands; no human inhabited it.

But even now, he felt unease. Perhaps it was time to donate the armor to a proper museum and decorate the foyer in sculpted statues of frolicking nymphs instead. He smiled at the thought. Perhaps Shelby could model for the artist. He'd like to see her immortalized that way.

A sound behind him like a knight unsheathing a sword had him whirling around, half- expecting to have his childhood fears realized. But no knight in armor stood behind him. Instead, his uncle, armed with a broadsword he'd liberated from one of the sets of armor, stood a few feet away.

"So, you've come home," Ian said.

"Where else would I go?" Bramly answered. "You've set the dogs on me."

"You threatened my wife."

"Your wife is a common whore I hired to seduce you. She succeeded beyond my expectations. You are clearly incapable of making rational decisions. I shall have you declared incompetent, for the good of the earldom."

"The whore you hired to seduce me is dead. Don't you remember? You accused me of murdering her." Ian managed to keep his voice even, so he projected an air of calm he was far from feeling. He didn't like the look in his uncle's eyes. They were bloodshot and glassy, like he'd been drinking, but he held the broadsword steady. Ian took a step back. Bramly matched him with two steps forward. "Tell me, uncle, did you kill Chartreuse LaRue?"

"We both know she's alive and well and purporting to be a countess. How did you convince Endicott to pretend she was his niece? I hope you didn't bankrupt the estate just so you could buy respectability for a prostitute."

"Shelby is Endicott's niece," Ian said. "And now she is my wife. I believe you are suffering from delusions."

It was more than drunkenness he detected in Bramly's

eyes. It was madness.

Ian weighed his options. Before the fire, he could easily have overpowered Bramly, wrested the broadsword from his hands, and rendered him powerless. At the very least, he could have simply run out the door and left Bramly far behind.

Neither of those choices was available to him now. The burns on his left leg had contracted his knee to such an extent that he walked with a noticeable limp, and running was out of the question. His months of recuperation had weakened him. Though he'd regained a bit of his strength, he still lacked the speed and dexterity he'd need to make the first move.

He'd have to try to put himself in the best defensive position he could and wait for Bramly to attack him.

He edged himself closer to the nearest wall, moving slowly so as not to startle Bramly, who tracked his every movement. Bramly held the broadsword in front of him with both hands. Less steadily, now, the weight of it taking its toll. Perhaps if he stalled long enough, Bramly would faulter and drop the sword, allowing Ian to get the upper hand. The sword had not been sharpened in centuries. Even if it struck him, he didn't think it could do much damage.

He was wrong.

When Bramly made his move, he didn't strike with the sword's point. Instead, he swung the broadsword like a club. Ian raised his arm to block it, but he could not raise the blasted thing high enough. The sword whacked him on the temple. The ancient steel hit him with tremendous force, causing him to stagger. Of course, his left leg buckled. Before he could regain his balance, the sword struck again. And again.

Until he lost consciousness.

He'd awoken in the dim dungeon, lit only by a few ancient torches placed in iron brackets interspersed along the wall. The flames flickered and threatened to die out and leave him in complete darkness. He had been trying to free himself ever since.

He sensed movement in the narrow hall that led to the chamber. His uncle returned. But not alone. He entered the room backwards, dragging a body by gripping it under its shoulders. Dear God, not a dead body, please. She could not be dead.

"What have you done?" he shouted. "If you've killed her, I will see you in hell." Ian renewed his efforts against the chain that bound him with increased vigor and urgency.

"Calm yourself," Bramly said. "She isn't dead. Not yet, anyway."

Ian watched Bramly drag Shelby to the opposite wall and secure her in shackles similar to his own. He raged at his impotence. Bracing his feet against the wall, he lunged his upper body forward, pulling on the chains with his full weight. With his arms raised over his head, his damaged shoulder screamed at the effort. Tears leaked from his one good eye. But it was worth it, because he felt a slight movement of the spike that nailed the chain to the wall. He was loosening its grip.

The dungeon room was old, the stone walls crumbling. The spike and chains were rusted. A few more tries and he should be able to get free.

Leaning back to rest against the stone, he eased the tension on his shoulders, regaining his strength so he could try again.

"They'll come looking for us, you know," he said conversationally, trying to draw Bramly's attention away from Shelby. It worked. Bramly left her sitting on the floor without attaching the length of chain connecting her shackles to the wall.

"They won't find you," Bramly said with the confidence

of a madman. "Not alive, anyway."

Cold terror settled in Ian's veins. With a burst of energy, he lunged forward again, straining his muscles against the restraints, chafing his wrists on the metal cuffs constraining them.

Bramly laughed at his efforts. He sat calmly down at the lone, wooden table in the center of the stone floor atop of which sat several lanterns and wax candles stuck in holders. He put flame to wicks, setting the room ablaze with light.

"You should have died in that fire," Bramly said. "Not to worry. There's always another."

Bramly rose from the table and started placing lit candles in a semi-circle around Ian's stockinged feet. When had he lost his boots? Bramly had been busy while he'd been unconscious.

"This time, I'll stay and watch to make sure the deed is done." He started pushing candles closer to Ian's feet.

As the flames came closer, panic seized him. He was back in his parents' burning bedroom. Fear paralyzed him. Then Shelby moaned, bringing him back to the present. He kicked the candles over, dousing the flames.

Across the room, Shelby came to, wincing at the brightness of the room. She moaned again. This time, Bramly heard her. Grabbing a lantern off the table, he practically danced over to her.

"Ah, the bitch is awake," he said, sounding almost happy to see her. He stood in front of her. "Just in time to watch your beloved husband go up in flames."

Setting the lantern on the floor near Shelby's feet, Bramly grabbed one of the lighted torches from a wall sconce.

Ian froze as Bramly approached, gut-wrenching fear settling in his belly. Bramly swung the lighted torch at him, and he cowered like a trapped animal, a whimper escaping his lips. His joints went weak. His legs couldn't support him.

He would have begged had he been able to formulate a clear thought. But he was mindless with terror.

"I imagine that fine, linen shirt would burn rather nicely," he heard Bramly say as though he were speaking down a long corridor, the sound echoing inside his head, as the flame drew closer and closer. He couldn't breathe, heat seared his lungs. Finally, one thought fought through the smoky haze. *Escape!*

He kicked out, but Bramly was safely out of reach. Mindlessly, he pulled at the chain over his head. The spike moved another blessed inch. Not enough. He couldn't get away from the relentless heat, couldn't take his eye from the nearing flame.

Bramly tormented him with it, bringing it close to his face then drawing it away.

"The mistake I made was thinking you were in your room when I started the fire in the hall. It was well after midnight. You should have been abed. I didn't find out until the inquest that you fell asleep downstairs in the library. That's the only reason you survived."

Bramly's voice took on a sing-song quality, like he was telling a bedtime story to an infant. He swayed in front of Ian, waving the torch in a figure eight, each motion bringing it closer and closer to him. If he could have melted into the stone wall, he would have. As it was, he was plastered against it as closely as he could be. Feeling the heat of the flame scorching his skin. Waiting for a chance to kick out again, but Bramly remained tantalizingly out of reach.

"If only you hadn't gotten engaged. I could tolerate being third in line; my brother could not live forever. But if you'd had a son or two, I would lose all claim to the earldom. My creditors would come after me. I couldn't have that. And then I decided, why be in line at all? Why not just take it?"

"You started the fire," Ian said, his suspicions finally

confirmed. "And you tried to put the blame on me."

"I wasn't even at Chester Hall that night," Bramly said. "How could I have done it? No one saw me arrive or leave, did they? But leaving was a mistake. I should have stayed. Waited, made sure the deed was done. I won't make that mistake twice."

Ian flinched as Bramly shoved the torch at his chest, burning his flesh, his shirt smoldering as a spark caught the fabric and died.

When he opened his eye, a movement across the room drew his gaze. Shelby—dear, sweet, wonderful, foolhardy woman. Bramly had forgotten her. She crawled forward and grabbed the wire handle of one of the lanterns Bramly had abandoned at her feet.

"If anyone is going up in flames, Bramly, it will be you," she said as she swung the lantern and let it fly right at Bramly's back. It hit its mark. Enraged, Bramly turned to face Shelby. Ian could see that though the flame went out when the lantern hit, the oil spilled onto Bramly's jacket.

Not wasting a moment, Ian kicked again, this time catching Bramly in the thigh and pushing him forward. He lost his balance and crashed into the table, knocking lanterns to the floor. The lanterns broke and a ring of fire formed at Bramly's feet. Before he could stop it, a spark caught his oil-soaked jacket and ignited.

Bramly screamed and hurled himself at Shelby.

No! With a surge of power, Ian pulled with all his strength and wrenched the spike right out of the wall. He hooked the loose chain around Bramly's neck and pulled him back just before he reached Shelby.

Flames leaped up Bramly's jacket, threatening to burn Ian's arm, but he didn't let go. He tightened the chain on Bramly's neck until the man stopped struggling. Only then did he release him and try to beat out the flames. Ian rolled Bramly on the cold, stone floor and the fire was quickly doused.

◈

"Is he dead?" Shelby knelt on the floor beside Ian as he rummaged through Bramly's coat pockets.

"No." Ian found the key he was searching for and released her from the manacles encircling her wrists, then removed his own. He clasped them around his uncle's wrists and tugged the chain connecting them to make sure they were secure. That done, he immediately started putting out candles and turning out the lamps. Soon, only the torches that lined the walls lighted the room.

Shelby remained where she was, kneeling beside Bramly's prone body, shaking too hard to stand.

"Let's get out of here." Ian offered her his hand. "I'll send some men down to deal with him."

Grabbing his hand, she followed him on unsteady legs through the labyrinthine basement to a set of stairs that led outside.

"What will become of him?" she asked as they helped each other down the drive to the Dower House.

"Hanged, I would imagine. Or confined to a madhouse." Ian paused and his arm tightened around her. "I didn't want to believe how dangerous he was. Even after he beat you near to death, when I should have known, I couldn't see it. He was my uncle."

"And I was just a prostitute who probably brought the beating upon myself," she said quietly, not meaning it as a rebuke, just as a statement of fact.

"I may have thought that, yes. I'm sorry."

"You said yourself, Ian. People see what they expect to see. Believe what they want to believe. You saw a woman who sold her body for money. It's a dangerous occupation. Beatings are commonplace among the women of the night. You also saw a man who was born to privilege, who had been given all he could ever want. How could you suspect that it would not be enough for him? That he would covet the one thing he could never have, the earldom itself."

"There were so many times growing up when I actually envied Bramly. He didn't need to worry about taking on the mantle of responsibility that being Lord Chester implied. I freed him of that. I never saw how much he resented me for it. Or resented my father for being the first born. My God, he murdered them! Tried to murder me. For what? For a title? For position?"

"For money," she said.

"I still cannot fathom it."

And that was why she loved him. Because he could not fathom that such evil existed in the world. While she had not been surprised in the least by Bramly's confession.

෯

They arrived at the Dower House to a scene of excited activity. The servants had been finishing their evening meal when Mr. Atkins brought the news that Mr. Bramly had been spotted in the neighborhood.

Ian sank into a chair in the kitchen where Atkins and the servants were gathered, the remnants of their meal still on the table, and pulled Shelby onto his lap. He held her as he relayed to Atkins what had transpired in the dungeon room. Atkins and two of the outriders went up to the Hall to fetch Bramly, while the remaining two former soldiers went to the village, one to find the constable and the other to get a physician. Symmington brought a bottle of brandy to the table. Setting it down, he poured two healthy doses and handed one to Ian and one to Shelby. Bitsy started preparing baths for the two of them, personally heating water on the still-warm stove.

"Are you hurt?" Ian asked Shelby as the servants bustled around them, clearing the table, filling and carrying buckets of water to fill the tubs in their rooms.

"No worse than you," she replied, fingering the charred sleeve of his shirt, making sure the fire hadn't licked his unmarred right arm. "I imagine we will both suffer headaches for many days to come."

Atkins returned with Bramly trussed like a Christmas goose between the two outriders who had gone to the Hall with him.

"Where do you want him, m'lord," one of the men asked.

Ian pointed to the chair on the opposite side of the table. The two men stood guard over his uncle as they all waited for the constable to arrive. No one spoke. Shelby rested her head on his shoulder, and he lightly stroked her back while he stared at the monster sitting across from him.

It was not a long wait. Within the hour the constable was shown in. As soon as he entered the kitchen, Bramly started spouting his poison.

"He tried to kill me!" Bramly said to the constable before Ian could even begin to explain the situation. "And that harlot he married helped him. He's not right in the head since the fire, you know that. You know he set it even though you couldn't prove it."

The constable waited for Bramly to wind down before turning respectfully to Ian.

"Do you want him confined, my lord?" the constable asked.

"He murdered the fifth Earl and Countess of Chester. My parents. He admitted to setting the fire that killed them. He intended for me to die in the fire as well."

"He's lying." Bramly struggled against his restraints to no avail, the chain connecting the manacles clanking with the effort. "He's the one that benefited from their deaths, not me. I've done nothing but try to help the boy. And she's nothing but a cheap whore what seduced the addle-brained lad into marrying her. He's mad, I tell you, gone insane."

"You had better remove him from my presence before I do him harm," Ian said to the constable. He kept his voice soft, but it was taking effort for him not to rage at his uncle. He longed to wrap his hands around Bramly's throat and squeeze. At the same time, his heart hurt. This was his uncle, his family. How could he have treated his own blood so cruelly? Ian hoped it was madness because he could not accept that his uncle was purely evil.

The constable quickly acceded to Ian's wishes and with the help of the two outriders, took Bramly out.

❧

As soon as the constable left, Bitsy whisked Shelby away to her bedroom where a warm hip bath awaited her. She assumed Symmington had similarly taken charge of Ian.

"Oh, my lady," Bitsy exclaimed when she undressed Shelby. Until that moment, Shelby hadn't even realized the extent of her injuries. The fall down the stairs had left her black and blue. The manacles had scraped her wrists. Her hair was matted from the blood of her head wound.

"Why, it's almost as bad as when you were first brought to Chester House," Bitsy exclaimed as she helped Shelby into the bath.

That gave Shelby pause.

"Whatever do you mean, Bitsy?"

"I'm sorry, ma'am. I know we're not supposed to know about that."

Shelby's stomach did a complete flip. Afraid to ask, but unable to stop herself, she continued the conversation.

"You're not supposed to know about what, Bitsy?"

Shelby held her breath until Bitsy answered. Bitsy lowered her voice and practically whispered her response.

"Don't worry, my lady. None of us from Chester House will ever let on that you was once Chartreuse LaRue."

"Chartreuse LaRue is dead," Shelby told her.

"Yes, ma'am," Bitsy agreed. "And good riddance to her, I say. Her life was nothing but troubled. Ye're much better off now, my lady."

Shelby closed her eyes and let the steam from the bath surround her. She breathed it in deeply, trying to cleanse her lungs from the stench of Bramly's burning clothes. It had all been too much. The overwhelming fear of the past hours, seeing Ian terrorized, now her past coming back again to haunt her.

She hadn't fooled Bitsy or any of Ian's servants. They knew who and what she was.

And yet, they treated her with the respect the Countess of Chester deserved. They hadn't come forward even when Ian was accused of murdering Chartreuse LaRue, whom they knew to be alive and well and impersonating a Countess.

Shelby started to laugh. The absurdity of the situation struck her as exceedingly hilarious of a sudden.

"Bitsy, you would have come forward if his lordship was going to be hanged for murdering her…me, wouldn't you?"

"Well of course, my lady. But we knew you'd come forth before it came to that. We knew you'd do what was right."

Tears streamed from Shelby's eyes. She didn't know if they were from laughing or crying, since she was doing an odd combination of both.

Bitsy calmly tended to her as if she wasn't having an emotional breakdown before her very eyes. Finally, she calmed down enough to speak.

"Thank you, Bitsy. You have proven yourself to be a true friend."

Bitsy fairly beamed as she held out a towel and wrapped Shelby in it.

"It's a bit like a fairy tale, isn't it, my lady?"

"Very much like a fairy tale, Bitsy."

There was only one more dragon for her knight to slay for her.

Chapter 22

The invitation arrived a month later. They'd remained in the Dower House though the repairs of the west wing were nearly complete, and the Hall was quite habitable even without it. Somehow, they'd never made the decision to move up there, preferring the cozy intimacy of the Dower House to the cold expansiveness of the Hall. Perhaps in the spring, when they could move into the newly constructed west wing, they would set up residency there.

Shelby sipped her tea while Ian read the invitation that Dickie brought in on a silver salver.

"Your Aunt Lucia invites us to spend Christmas with the family," Ian said.

"In London?" she asked. "We will need to remove there after Christmas anyway so we can attend Bramly's trial."

After his hearing with the local magistrate, Bramly was sent to London to await trial in the Old Bailey.

Ian shook his head.

"Dorset," he said.

The eggs she'd just eaten congealed in her stomach. She rested her fork on her plate and put her hands in her lap so Ian wouldn't see them shaking.

"Who will be there?" her throat threatened to close, and the words sounded choked.

"She doesn't say specifically. Just 'the family.' It could be only the three of them."

Shelby knew it would not be. As a child, she'd spent every Christmas at the family seat with her parents, Phoebe, Aunt Lucia, and Uncle Phillip, as well as a slew of other, more distant cousins. Even after her father died, she and her mother attended.

And after her mother remarried, Mr. Granger attended, too.

"We don't have to go," Ian said, reaching over to stroke her arm. She hadn't been able to hide her distress from him, after all. "We can spend Christmas here or go to Acton Park if you'd prefer. You don't have to see them ever again if you don't want to, Shelby. I'll see to it."

She knew he was right, knew he would protect her from her past. He already had in so many ways. But just as Ian had to come back to face Chester Hall, she had to go back and face her stepfather. She didn't want him to have power over her any longer.

It was time, Shelby decided, for her to face her demons.

She reached up and touched Ian's hand.

"No," she said. "I want to go. I will write to Aunt Lucia today and accept. But I want to visit the farm first. I don't want the first time I see them to be in front of others. Knowing Aunt Lucia, she is planning a public reconciliation. She was most unhappy when I refused to invite Helen to the wedding." She had taken to calling her mother by her first name rather than the sobriquet 'Mother.' Her mother did not deserve the honor of being called one. Nell Ryan, for all her flaws, had acted more like a mother to her than her own had. Nell, at least, had believed her when she told her about being abused by her stepfather. Her own mother never had.

❧

It should have looked different, but the Dorset countryside was largely unchanged from when she'd last seen it.
The fields were at rest after the fall harvest. The village of
Hapshom on Green was tidy as always with freshly painted
doors and stoops recently swept.

A few of the villagers stepped out to watch the carriage
bearing the coat of arms of the Earl of Chester rumble
through.

The gate of Canby Farm was open, so their coachman
made the turn into the drive without stopping. There was
no time for Shelby to change her mind and cry halt. Before
she knew it, they were stopped in the yard that fronted the
modest farmhouse she'd called home for her first fourteen
years.

She was shaking. Ian, who had said nothing for the past
half hour of their journey, leaving her to her thoughts and
memories, pulled her close.

"You don't have to do this," he said again.

She felt faint, her hands clammy inside her muff.

"I do have to," she said, but it was barely above a whisper. She wasn't sure he heard.

The coachman opened the door and put the step down.
Ian got out first and reached up to help her down. As soon
as her feet touched the ground, the door to the house
opened and her mother stepped out.

She looked old and drawn, as though the weariness of
the past six years weighed her down. For a moment, Shelby
had the urge to run to her, gather her in her arms, and
soothe the lines from her face.

"Shelby?" Mother spoke tentatively from the doorway.

Shelby hadn't written to tell them she was coming. She
didn't want to warn Mr. Granger and give him a chance to
be away from home, to avoid seeing her.

Recognition struck, and her mother's face lit with a smile

that transformed her; the years fell away, and she resembled the woman Shelby had known. And loved.

"Welcome; please, come in." Mother moved aside so Shelby, followed closely by Ian, could enter the house.

Memories assailed her, warm ones of her father along with sordid ones of Mr. Granger. They went into the drawing room where a fire glowed in the hearth. It had always been her favorite room as a child, until the day Mr. Granger had defiled her in it.

Shelby stood in front of the fire, but it could not take away the chill that went to her very core.

"I've ordered refreshments," Mother prattled when she joined them. Shelby knew she had to introduce Ian to her mother but found herself unable to utter a word. She hadn't expected to feel so vulnerable. She had pushed the memories away for so many years, allowed herself to remain numb. Now, all the emotions she'd ignored were storming inside her.

Ian gently guided her to the sofa where she could sit before her shaking legs gave out on her. He stood next to her. His nearness helped her gain control.

"May I present Ian, Lord Chester, my husband." Nodding to her mother, she continued. "My mother, Mrs. Helen Endicott Granger."

Her mother stared wide-eyed at Ian a moment before collecting herself and remembering her manners.

"I'm so pleased to meet you at last, my lord." she curtsied respectfully to Ian, though her greeting implied a slight reprimand to her daughter. And to him, Shelby supposed. It was a breach of etiquette for him to have married her without at least meeting her mother first. But their situation hardly demanded that the normal rules of etiquette be followed. Mother had given up all rights to govern her life when she'd allowed her husband to molest her daughter.

Ian was her protector now. Shelby knew he would not

allow anyone to harm her. She reached up and grasped his hand. He gave her a gentle, comforting squeeze.

She felt him before she saw him. As soon as he entered the room, she shrank farther into herself, trying to disappear. Ian gave her another reassuring squeeze, then reached down to touch her elbow and encourage her to stand. Her legs were trembling so much, he had to circle his arm around her waist to hold her up. Her stomach revolted; she felt as if she might be sick.

She shouldn't have come. There was no need for this, no reason for her to confront the man who had so brutalized her. She should have declined Aunt Lucia's invitation so she would not have to encounter them at Christmas. She was about to ask Ian to escort her back to the carriage when Helen introduced Mr. Granger to him. Mr. Granger held his hand out to Ian, but he looked at it distastefully and refused to shake it. In a moment, Mr. Granger reluctantly returned it to his side. Shelby took courage from Ian's support. He was not going to pretend to the niceties. She didn't have to, either.

She straightened her posture and lifted her chin and looked directly at Mr. Granger where he stood next to her mother. She readied herself to do battle, prepared herself to confront the demon who had plagued her for years. She moved slightly forward. Ian dropped his arm from around her, allowing her to stand on her own.

The four of them stood in an awkward tableau, Mother smiling hopefully while wringing her hands, Mr. Granger fuming at Ian's rejection, Ian glowering at Mr. Granger looking ready to challenge him to a duel, and she unable to find a single word to utter into the uncomfortable silence.

The spell broke when a maid brought in the tea service. There was a flurry of activity as Mother arranged the cart and directed the participants in this one-act farce to their places.

Seated again, teacups in hand, the awkward silence again filled the room.

"Aunt Lucia wrote me about your wedding," Mother forayed. "How I wish I could have been there."

Shelby could only glare daggers at her . What could she say? *You weren't there because I didn't want you there.*

"Have you nothing to say for yourself, young lady?" Mr. Granger said. Shelby felt Ian bristle and feared he was ready to haul the man outside to beat him senseless. She put a calming hand on his arm.

It was time to do what she'd come here to do. Time to look her demon in the eye. She directed her gaze to Mr. Granger. And felt, not the fear she'd expected, but anger. Anger for the defenseless child she'd been when he broke her so thoroughly.

"You wouldn't want to hear anything I have to say to you."

"Why'd you come here then?" Mr. Granger said, getting belligerent.

"Why, I came to thank you, dear stepfather. If you hadn't raped me when I was fourteen, I would not have fled to a London brothel, which, odd as it may seem, felt like a safe haven to me. At least there, I got paid for doing what you made me do with no compensation in the least except fear, guilt, and threats of bodily harm. Had I not been at Nell Ryan's brothel, thanks to you, I would not have met Lord Chester. So, truly, sir, I have you to thank for all the good fortune in my life."

Mother paled.

"How dare you?" Mr. Granger stood. "Get out of my house."

"Your house, stepfather?" Shelby stood, also, and took a step forward, coming face to face with the man who had caused her so much pain. "This is my father's house. You are nothing but an interloper."

Mr. Granger raised his hand as if to strike her.

"I wouldn't, if I were you," Ian quietly threatened. He'd come to her side. Mr. Granger backed down.

"I don't know what lies she's told you," he said to Ian, "but she's nothing but a harlot. Always was and always will be."

"I believe, sir, that you just insulted my wife, the Countess of Chester."

"You heard her. She just admitted to working in a brothel. What kind of woman would do that?" Mr. Granger was warming to his subject. "She run off with a bun in the oven, she did. I can see that a man like you wouldn't have many options for wife-taking, but don't get angry at me when I speak nothing but the truth."

"Now you have insulted me. I don't think you would know the truth if you saw it." Ian held out his elbow to her. "Come, my dear, let us leave before I cause the man bodily injury."

Just as she placed her hand on Ian's arm, the door to the parlor opened and in burst a bundle of energy.

"Mamma, mamma, we have company!" the little girl, who could have seen no more than five summers, shouted joyfully.

Mr. Granger smiled indulgently at her, his entire demeanor softening as he gently pulled her to his side and ruffled her hair with his large hand.

"Make your curtsy to your sister and her husband, Emily," he instructed. Emily made a hurried, though creditable, curtsy.

"The child I was carrying when you left," Mother explained.

"She's beautiful," Shelby admitted. Tears welled in her eyes as she looked at Mr. Granger. "Please don't hurt her."

"I would never hurt her," Mr. Granger said. "She's my blood."

"Still," Ian said, "It may be best if she goes away to school when she's older, or perhaps comes to live with her sister. We wouldn't want you to be led into temptation, now would we?"

"Please leave." Mother commanded, having recovered from her earlier shock at Shelby's frank and crude discussion. "I will not stand here and allow my husband to be insulted in his own home. It is his home, Shelby, whether you like it or not. I had hoped that you were ready to make amends for your waywardness, but I see now that you are not. I think it best if you do not visit us again."

Shelby's heart sank as disappointment coursed through her. Nothing had changed. Her mother still refused to see what Mr. Granger had done to her. Once again, she took Mr. Granger's side.

It was easier for her mother to believe that her own daughter was an immoral trollop than to admit that her husband had committed indecent acts upon her. Shelby let go of the hope she'd been harboring since the night she'd run away, the hope that her mother might someday come to believe her.

There was no longer any reason to stay. She'd confronted Mr. Granger and survived. He could not hurt her anymore, not because she had Ian to protect her, but because he could no longer intimidate her. He'd lost his power over her. Her mother was lost to her as long as she took Mr. Granger's side. There was only one person she could help now.

Shelby knelt in front of Emily, who was clinging shyly to her father's leg. She took off the locket that her father had given her and placed it around Emily's neck.

"You keep this safe for me, Emily, and know that if you ever need me, I will come for you."

She stood and faced Mr. and Mrs. Granger.

"We will know if any harm comes to her," she vowed.

"And we will come for her."

"She is in no danger. I would never hurt a child of my own." Shelby realized that was the nearest to an admission from Mr. Granger that she was likely to receive.

They went out to the yard where the coach awaited them, the horses still in their traces. Ian had anticipated that it would be a short visit.

"We won't be seeing you at Uncle Phillip's for Christmas," Shelby said by way of leave-taking. "We'll be spending Christmas at home. I would ask one boon of you though, Mrs. Granger." She pointedly used her mother's married name, though she longed to call her Mama like she had as a child. Losing her mother hurt more than anything Mr. Granger had ever done to her. "I would like to take Pegasus with me."

Mrs. Granger looked to Mr. Granger for permission before granting her request. "He is yours, after all, as your father gave him to you."

Mr. Granger led Ian and a groomsman to the stable to retrieve the gelding.

"He is a good man, Mr. Granger is," his wife said to Shelby when they were left alone. "Though he may have had a weakness that you brought to light, I'll never stop believing in his basic goodness." She looked Shelby directly in the eye. "I'll send Emily to you if the weakness returns."

Though the blame was still squarely placed on her shoulders, at least the woman acknowledged that something had happened between Shelby and Mr. Granger. That, at least, was progress.

Pegasus trotted out at the end of his lead looking as handsome and spirited as she remembered. She greeted her old friend with a scratch and a stroke. She felt the broken pieces of her heart start to heal.

Shelby took one last look around and realized that leaving was easy this time. This was not her home any longer.

Her home was with Ian, wherever they chose to make it.

"What happened to your hand?" she asked when she and Ian were settled in the carriage and driving away from the farm. He'd been opening and closing it, and now she could see bruises forming across the knuckles.

"My fist may have accidentally come into contact with Mr. Granger's chin," he said, sounding rather sheepish.

"You hit him? Oh, Ian, I hope you didn't cause yourself any harm."

He rubbed his shoulder.

"May have pulled something," he said. "But it was worth it. Felt damned good."

"Didn't he fight back?"

Ian shook his head.

"Turns out the man has a glass jaw. Went down like a brick."

Shelby threw her arms around him and kissed him soundly on the mouth.

"I love you, Lord Chester," she said.

"And I you, Lady Chester. Let us get home so I can show you how much."

❧

They spent Christmas at Acton Park. The weather was mild, allowing them to ride every one of the twelve days, Shelby on Pegasus and Ian on Demon. On the morning of Little Christmas, they rode to the Roman ruins, where Shelby gave Ian the special gift she'd been saving for him.

"I believe I am with child," she said when they'd dismounted and stood in the shelter of the stone wall. "It's early days, so I can't be certain. I am almost afraid to hope that it's so because I never thought I would be able to conceive another child, but I haven't had my courses since our wedding night."

Ian lifted her up and twirled her around, and, setting her

gently back on the ground, kissed her soundly.

"And here I thought it was Cook's meals that were causing your waist to thicken," he laughed. "You have made me the happiest of men."

She smiled. "And you have made me the happiest of women."

Ian insisted on carrying her in front of him on Demon on the way back to the manse, with Pegasus following behind them. He said it was so she would not risk a fall, but she suspected it was so he could keep his arm securely planted against her stomach, with new life growing there. Whatever his reasons, she didn't care. Nestled in Ian's arms, she felt warm and safe and loved, as the squire's daughter and the monster earl made their way home.

A Runaway Bride

Jenny Carlisle's indiscretion leads to an arranged marriage with a man she cannot abide. Defying her father she refuses to go through with the ceremony. Fleeing to the safety of her aunt in Bath, she finds herself stranded alone at an inn.

A Returning War Hero

Wounded on the Peninsula, Captain Richard Mortimer is making his way home when a storm waylays him. He knows as soon as he sees the young, unaccompanied woman in the taproom that she's no strumpet selling her wares, but a lady who needs to be rescued.

A Marriage of Convenience

Jenny needs the security of Mortimer's name and protection. Mortimer wants the family Jenny can provide. Their arrangement appears to be a match made in heaven until a tragic accident changes everything. Mortimer releases Jenny from their agreement but Jenny refuses to be cast aside. Inconvenient or not, she will remain the captain's lady.

About the Author

Terri Kennedy is the author of the Regency-set historical romance novels *The Captain's Lady* and *The Squire's Daughter*. She lives and writes on Cape Cod in a cottage by the sea that she and her husband share with a black lab mix who's afraid of the water. After a career in high tech, she became a librarian where she could indulge her love affair with books. A martial artist, Terri at various times trained in tae kwan do, kensho ryu, and aikido and currently practices tai chi. Please contact her through her web site www.terrikennedy.-com.